Dear Reader,

History is such a strange, strange creature. I am constantly amazed by the things my research unearths, especially when it comes to sexual history. For those of you interested in what I uncover (and what doesn't end up in my books…) check out my blog, A Bit O'Muslin, at www. DelilahMarvelle.blogspot.com. It will give you an idea as to how much *real* history gets overlooked. When it comes to historical romance, in particular, people have a skewed vision of what Regency should be because of all the books they have read, without ever really digging into the historical facts. The modern reader has a tendency to forget that people back then were still people. They loved. They hated. They ate. They drank. And yes, they had sex. Lots of it. London's exploding population proved that.

The idea of *Prelude to a Scandal* was pieced together to reflect both history and hot-button topics that are still being passionately debated today.

Now as for all of those rakes running around London debauching themselves and whatever women they could get their hands on, I started wondering how many of these men were sex addicts. I mean, honestly. At least *one* of them had to be! And though they didn't have a clinical name for sexual addiction back in the 1820s, you had better believe it was there. So what would a sex addict's life be like back in the days when there were no clinics to provide assistance and understanding? I imagine it would have been a personal hell. One worth writing about.

It is my hope you will set aside what you think 1829 is and grace me to give you my version of 1829.

Cheers and much love,

Delilah Marvelle

Don't miss the rest of the Scandal series!

DELILAH MARVELLE

Prelude to a Scandal

HQN™

Recycling programs
for this product may
not exist in your area.

ISBN-13: 978-0-373-77537-8

PRELUDE TO A SCANDAL

Copyright © 2011 by Delilah Marvelle

This edition published by arrangement with Harlequin Books S.A.

For questions and comments about the quality of this book
please contact us at Customer_eCare@Harlequin.ca.

® and TM are trademarks of the publisher. Trademarks indicated with
® are registered in the United States Patent and Trademark Office, the
Canadian Trade Marks Office and in other countries.

www.HQNBooks.com

Printed in U.S.A.

ACKNOWLEDGMENTS

This book would have never made it to print if not for the incredible support of my friends, family and industry professionals who encouraged me in ways that go beyond any words I could write.

Thank you to my super sexy and incredible husband, Marc, who is the love of my life, my everything and the reason why I write romance. Thank you, Marc, for being my sugar daddy who oversees the bills and everything under the moon so I can continue to do what I love most. Thank you to my two amazing children, Zoe and Clark, who are so loving and so, so, so giving and patient in knowing mommy is almost always writing. I love you both.

Thank you to the fabulous Maire Creegan, who has been one of my greatest inspirations, my longtime critique partner, my tutor and my best friend and twinsie. Thank you to the Novelistas: Susan Lyons, Christina Crooks and Lacy Danes whose amazing attention to detail and creative skills push me forward and onward as a writer.

Thank you to my agent Donald Maass, whose wisdom and guidance remind me of my purpose and why I write. I am in constant awe of your ability, Don, to dig into my stories and pull out every thread and point out its worth. You encourage me to not only step out of the box but to try to smash it. Thank you to all of HQN and its staff, and to my editor Tracy Farrell, whose incredible enthusiasm toward my stories has sparked a blazing new sense of worth within me.

Thank you to Deb Werksman from Sourcebooks, who saw a diamond in the rough and made this writer believe she could jump off a cliff and fly.

Thank you to everyone, both readers and my fellow writers alike, who supported me during my transition between publishers. You all kept me going and I love you all.

This book is dedicated to every person in this vast world who suffers from any form of addiction. Believe that you can and will overcome all of the battles that lie ahead.

Prelude
to a
Scandal

An old Spanish proverb would dare claim—A great dowry can only bring a bed full of brambles. So what, pray tell, would a small dowry bring? Nothing, I suppose, but dirty linen in shambles. No matter the size of your dowry, ladies, understand that finding a worthy suitor will always be a gamble.

How to Avoid a Scandal, Author Unknown

London, England
Late April, 1829

LADY JUSTINE FEDORA PALMER knew all too well that her dear, dear father, the sixth Earl of Marwood, had always been an intelligent and upstanding, moral citizen. He would have never dared to provoke a political or social stampede amongst any of the tribes he'd befriended throughout his years as an African naturalist. Especially the most notorious and savage of all human tribes—the British *ton*.

But whenever it came to the subject of zoological breeding, her father became a soul of too many words with absolutely no sense of restraint. Which was why the poor man was now sitting in prison.

His newly published observations on innate buggery amongst South African mammals—which he argued God allowed in *His* Natural Kingdom and therefore His Royal Majesty should allow in *ours*—had ruffled far too many feathers to count. Including that of His Royal Majesty.

Though her father had been found innocent of conspiring to promote buggery and moral corruption, he was still caged in Marshalsea Debtors Prison due to an array of exorbitant fines he simply could not pay. Unlike most ladies, who might have long languished beneath such scandal mongering, Justine had never been one for wilting. Her unusual upbringing had made her worldly enough to understand that every female, no matter her genus and species, had the ability to physically coerce a male into full cooperation.

And yes, she knew just the male to coerce. A male she'd wanted to coerce ever since she first came to London two years ago at the age of eighteen: her father's sole academic patron, the notorious Duke of Bradford. Better known to the herds of London as *The* Rake Extraordinaire, whose appreciation for women knew no bounds and whose pockets and generosity were as deep as the sky is wide.

Despite his libertine facade, which boasted a slow, saucy grin and smoky dark eyes that invited every woman to play, there was so much more to him than his appearance. He had a genuine intelligence and depth outside of the wild antics he always used to garner attention. She remembered one evening in particular when her adoration for the man had fully bloomed into a yearning that made her toes curl within her silk stockings.

While her parents and the duke still played five card loo with a group of ladies and gents after a dinner party, she'd opted to sit in a chair on the other side of the room and read so she wouldn't have to be teased anymore by her overly competitive father. Promptly after her aloof departure from the card table, the duke had tossed his own cards and formally announced no lady ought to be disrespected for her lack of card skills. With an impressive sweep, he then hoisted his chair up over his head and swaggered with it across the room like an acrobat. He even pretended to stumble beneath its weight in an effort to make her giggle.

With a well satisfied breath, he'd settled his chair and himself across from her, insisting she set aside her book and tell him more about the fascinating life she'd led in Africa. Though his gaze had a tendency to wander flirtatiously to inappropriate places—which she rather enjoyed—he still listened very intently to everything she had to say as if every word that escaped her lips mattered, as if *she* mattered.

Tragic as it was, the man had never been the marrying sort, and no one knew that more than her parents, who'd repeatedly warned her to keep her virtue as far away from the man as possible. Despite all of their tiring lectures on the matter and despite having read *How To Avoid A Scandal* many, many times, Justine knew a lady couldn't *always* avoid scandal. Especially when one's father was being persecuted for demanding rights for sodomites using the animal kingdom as his platform.

After dotting a piece of parchment with rosewater she'd borrowed from a neighbor, Justine daintily scribed a missive to the duke, similar to the countless weekly missives she'd sent to him ever since first meeting him. The duke had never once responded, which her mother was thankful for, but Justine continued to scribe him weekly letters all the same.

In this particular letter, however, she offered Bradford a bit more than the usual gossip about herself and her family. She offered him several nights in exchange for her father's release. Having no dowry and no suitor, she wasn't too worried about harvesting her virginity to a man who offered no wedding prospect. She only hoped her mother and father would understand.

Though it had been many months since she'd last seen the duke, and there were muddled whispers about him being disfigured due to his involvement with a less than reputable woman, not a single drop of the story intimidated her. She felt that her father's comfort, safety and sanity trumped any of her own womanly misgivings.

To her astonishment, not even three days after her letter had been delivered to the duke, his footman appeared at their door and presented the following letter:

Lady Justine,
I can only apologize for ever leading you to believe I was capable of ruining anyone in their most desperate hour, let alone a lady of esteemed quality such as yourself. Although I cannot and will not be able to accept your offer, I would like to propose something else. At three and thirty, I have come to the profound realization that I am not getting any younger. Or prettier. It is time I take a wife. I have received and immensely enjoyed every letter you have sent and fondly remember every time we have met. Therefore, I foresee no complications in asking for your hand

in marriage. Whilst I am certain there are various rumors surrounding my current physical state, I can assure you, I am in excellent health. Though I did sustain one sizable scar it is nothing to fret over. Should you and your father agree to our marriage, a license will be applied for and the wedding will be set to take place in six weeks' time. In turn, I would be delighted to pay all debts imposed upon your father so as to ensure his prompt release from Marshalsea.

I await your response,

Bradford

And all along she had thought he'd never ask…

London be damned for treating her father with such horrid disdain. She was finally going to earn some respect for herself and her family. She was going to be the Duchess of Bradford, and she had every intention of demanding respect from everyone, at every turn, from this day forth.

SCANDAL ONE

Without a good chaperone, one might as well be dead. Remember, a chaperone is supposed to be another thinking head.

How to Avoid a Scandal, Author Unknown

Five weeks later, evening

WITH THE ASSISTANCE of her driver, Mr. Kern, Justine stepped out of the coach and swept down onto the pavement of the square. She eyed the shadowed, four-story alabaster home, noting that most of the windows were as dark as the night around her. Sparse golden light shone through only a few glass panes on the far side of the home.

An ominous feeling crawled through her. Despite countless letters to the duke, pleading for at least one audience before the actual wedding, he had responded to each and every letter with a firm, "No. Not until the appointed time of the wedding." Calling upon him repeatedly had not yielded much more. He simply would not see her. Which worried her to no end. Was he in fact more disfigured than he'd originally let on?

As if that weren't distressing enough, there appeared to be complications surrounding her father's release, even though her wedding was only a short week away. And whilst the duke's solicitor had repeatedly assured her everything would be resolved, Justine needed more than mere verbal assurance.

Mr. Kern lingered beside her and cleared his throat, awaiting payment for his many weeks of service. He eyed her reticule. "Milady." He pointed. "I thought this was tah be a friendly social call."

Justine glanced down at the ribbon-drawn reticule slung around her wrist. The rosewood handle of her father's pistol stuck straight out, like a gopher's head from a mound.

She feigned an apologetic laugh. "It *is* a friendly social call, Mr. Kern. This is simply to intimidate the servants. Which reminds me—" She yanked out the ivory flask of gunpowder from her reticule.

Mr. Kern paused. Then squinted at her.

After several failed attempts to uncork the flask, Justine huffed out a breath and dug her fingertips beneath the rim, giving it one last solid tug. Her straining arms jumped and the cork popped off.

Mr. Kern scrambled back as a huge plume of gunpowder blanketed her face, cloak, gown and the street, filling her nostrils with a gritty, sulfur-penetrating residue. She gagged as the flask slipped and clattered to the pavement, and frantically brushed the soot from her face and bosom. Of all the blasted—

She paused, glimpsing the flask on its side in the shadows. Oh, no. Plucking it up, she tapped at what little remained in the vessel and groaned. How quickly she'd become like the rest of the women in London. Completely useless. Unable to even prime a pistol. Her father would have been horrified at her incompetence.

Exasperated, she shoved the expensive flask into Mr. Kern's waiting hands. "Here you are, Mr. Kern. Pure ivory and worth well more than I owe you. This will officially bring your service to an end. I thank you."

"Much obliged." He tipped his wool cap, then made his way back to the hackney, inspecting his newly acquired trinket.

If only the wardens at Marshalsea were as easy to please and get along with.

Justine sighed, and eyed the pistol in her hand. She supposed she could bluff her way in. That way, when the authorities *did* arrive, no one could argue it was loaded. Cocking it, she tucked the pistol back into her reticule and marched with full intent toward the dimly lit house, past the wrought-iron gate which had conveniently been left open.

She hurried up the wide, shadowed steps and halted at the entrance. Swiping away whatever gunpowder she could still feel on her face, she drew in a calming breath and used the knocker. Then the bell.

Footfalls echoed from the interior. The bolts were eventually unfastened and the door to the house fanned open, filtering soft golden light across the wide steps.

A massive, blond-haired gentleman appeared. One she hadn't seen throughout all her earlier attempts to get in. His wide chin jutted over his tight collar, whilst his round belly threatened to pop every button off the embroidered waistcoat protruding from his dark livery. He stepped toward her, his hefty frame towering a good two heads over her own.

Her heart raced as she stepped back. What, by gad, had his mother been feeding him? Clearly, not the usual English fare.

She counterfeited a quick smile and hoped that, despite his imposing stature, this particular new servant was going to be more cooperative than the rest. "Forgive the hour, sir, and my overall appearance, but I was hoping for an audience with

His Grace. Would you please inform him that his fiancée, and future duchess, is here and that it is most urgent?" She hesitated, then repeated, "*Most* urgent."

The man's beady blue eyes raked the length of her. "Have you been sweeping chimneys, my lady? I hope all is well."

He was about as amusing as her situation. "I shall be in much better spirits once I speak to His Grace." She tried not to sound too agitated, or he wouldn't let her in.

He sighed. "As the previous butler may have already informed you, my lady, His Grace will not see you or anyone else until the appointed time of the wedding. He does, however, wish to assure you all is well." He bowed, stepped back and slammed the door shut.

Justine gasped with indignation. "All is not well, sir! I demand you open this door. *Sir!*" She paused and blinked at the door, which so rudely remained closed. Was this any way to treat a future duchess?

She huffed out a breath and glanced back toward the shadows of manmade iron fences and stone buildings that rose above the trees beyond. Though she'd always suppressed her true feelings of not belonging to this strange London world, it was time to admit that the men in England really weren't as refined and civilized as they claimed to be. If they were, they would not be caging an old man for having an opinion contrary to societal norms, and they most certainly would not be leaving a young woman on a doorstep, in the dark, alone. Whilst assuring her all was well.

The cowardly side of her wanted to dash straight into the night and disappear onto the next ship to Cape Town to avoid this entire mess.

But her heart and soul knew what needed to be done. Her father needed her, and she was not about to wait until the day of the wedding to discover her father was set to languish in Marshalsea for the rest of his days.

She needed reassurance. And she was going to get it. Setting her chin, Justine whirled back to the door and rattled the knob, only to discover it had already been bolted. Narrowing her gaze, she grabbed hold of the knocker and repeatedly pounded the brass ring against the block, hoping everyone's head inside the house was pounding right along with it. She was not going home and didn't give a ripe fig if all of London talked about it for ten full years.

The door eventually reopened.

Justine drew back her hand and announced in

her sternest tone, "Name your price, sir, or I shall
be forced to name mine."

The butler smirked, clearly amused, and adjusted
his snug livery. "I can assure you, my lady, I am
not one to be bought."

"Whilst I can assure you, sir, I am *not* one to
be turned away." Justine pulled out the pistol from
her reticule and pointed it straight at his chest. Her
forefinger played with the trigger as she boldly
stepped toward him, wishing it really was loaded.
"I recommend you step aside." If need be, she'd
thwack him on the head with the butt of her pistol
and dash right in.

The man froze and wrinkled his pudgy nose as
if realizing the residue dusting her entire frame was
gunpowder. He scrambled backward and silently
extended his thick, gloved hand toward the hall
behind.

"Your cooperation is greatly appreciated."
She entered the large hall, still keeping the pistol
pointed at him. Her heeled slippers clicked across
the Italian marble floors as the delicate, sweet
aroma of cigars teased her nostrils. She sniffed.
Since when did Bradford smoke cigars?

A rapid, bristling sound caused Justine to snap
the pistol toward the candlelit receiving room on
the left. She paused and blinked in astonishment.

For there, on all fours, was a young male servant in full livery wearing a ruffled, white apron. And of all things, he was scrubbing the floor as though he were a housemaid!

The young servant paused, clearly sensing she was watching him. He heaved out a long breath, as if his mother had died, then dipped the horsehair brush into a pail of soapy water and resumed his rapid scrubbing.

The butler shut the door and nervously glanced back at her as he fastened each bolt. "I hope you do not mind waiting whilst I inform His Grace of your arrival."

Justine swiveled the pistol back to the butler. "So His Grace can altogether escape through a back door? I think not." She readjusted her grip on the pistol, trying to exude deadly confidence, and purposefully stared him down. "You'd best take me to him."

She stepped farther back toward the curving mahogany stairwell and eyed the gray silk lampas walls decorated with gold framed mirrors and oversized family portraits.

Nothing had changed. What is more, it reminded her of the first night she'd stepped into this house. That enchanted night when she and her parents had privately dined with the duke in honor of their return from Africa.

She'd been so impressed. But what had impressed her far, far more than the massive, ornate home that night—and thereafter—was the Duke of Bradford himself. A more dashing, charming and intelligent man she'd never met. Of course, her parents had argued that anything would have been impressive to an eighteen-year-old who'd been residing in canvas tents and grass huts since the age of seven.

The butler blew out an exhausted breath and stalked past. He gestured toward the stairwell. "If you please, my lady. The duke's bedchamber is this way."

Justine's heart skipped as she gawked up after the butler, who was already mounting the stairs. Circumstances aside, was it crass to admit to herself that she'd always wondered what the duke's bedchamber looked like?

The butler paused midway up the winding staircase and glanced down at her.

She cleared her throat and lifted the hem of her gown from around her feet, trying to remain calm. She was not going to melt into a puddle. After all, a woman had to retain some amount of pride and dignity, no matter how scandalized she was.

Still keeping the pistol leveled at the man, she moved up the stairs. When she alighted onto the landing, she bustled straight down the wide corridor, trying to catch up with the butler who had left her far behind, moving with the grace of an elephant at full speed.

The silence grew more pronounced. Glancing toward a passing row of portraits, Justine slowed her pace and paused before a rather stunning portrait of a young woman dressed in a flowing, white brocaded gown. Her large gray-blue eyes stared at Justine with a wrenching beauty that managed to be both provocative and shy.

The candles set within the wall sconces emitted just enough light to cast a perfect, warm glow upon the woman's face, whilst shadowing the rest of the painting. Her pale skin was smooth, and gathered blond curls framed her face. A playful little smile lingered on her lips.

Justine lowered the pistol and blinked. Who was this beautiful woman to Bradford? A sister or a cousin she did not know of? Or was it—*heaven forbid*—his mistress? He was indeed always known to surround himself with less than reputable ladies, which sadly, if she believed the rumors, had brought him to his current physical state.

"You demand to see His Grace, yet you show

no urgency?" the butler tossed back at her from up ahead.

Justine cringed and hurried down the passage-way.

The butler opened a paneled door at the far end of the walkway and disappeared inside. Justine followed, entering a bedchamber that was about the size of a field.

She froze as the butler strode past an enormous four-poster bed draped with heavy, velvet burgundy curtains. The pillows, linens and coverlets were all in disarray.

The butler halted before a closed door on the other side of the room that adjoined another chamber. He cleared his throat and knocked. "Your Grace. Forgive the intrusion, but Lady Palmer is here. She insists upon a private audience and ardently awaits your attention within the confines of your bedchamber."

Justine gestured with the pistol in complete exasperation. Why, the man made her sound like a wanton! As if she did this sort of thing all the time.

There was a movement, followed by a rather loud splash of water against porcelain.

Blessed be her soul, was the duke bathing?

A deep voice suddenly boomed from the other

side, "Do my orders mean nothing? You've barely worked here a Goddamn week! I replaced the last butler for less."

The butler winced and adjusted his livery, shifting from boot to boot. "Yes. I realize as much, Your Grace. But I should probably point out that aside from the pistol she is toting, and the threats she is spitting, given the time of night, I was rather concerned about turning her away. Her overall appearance is rather...*disturbing*."

Justine cringed and glanced down at her daffodil gown, which was smeared with enough gunpowder to warrant an arrest in the name of public safety. And to think, she *had* worn her finest.

There was muttering from behind the door, followed by an aggressive splash of water within the tub. "Leave us. I will ring when it is time for you to escort her home. Which you will, Jefferson. As punishment. I also intend to temporarily suspend your wages."

"Uh...yes, Your Grace." The butler turned, set his thick chin a tad higher above his collar and strode toward her, never once meeting her gaze.

Justine sighed and couldn't help but feel remorse. Shoving the pistol into her reticule, she held it out. "Take this, Jefferson, along with my sincere apologies. Rest assured, it was never primed or loaded. I shall see to it His Grace does not hold you accountable."

The butler paused and lifted a thick brow, silently acknowledging her apology. He plucked the weighty reticule from her hand and strode out, shutting the door behind him.

One less soul to worry about. Justine blew out a shaky breath and turned to the closed paneled door leading to the bath chamber. If only she weren't so worried about Bradford. That dark, overly agitated voice sounded nothing like him.

After all, once upon a time, the whole of London could be burning and the man would have still retained that playful lilt in his voice and that devious twinkle in his eye. He'd never been one to easily ruffle and knew how to make everyone, right down to a tinplate worker, feel as though they were all equal peers. Libertine though he was, yes, a more genuine and kind soul she'd never met.

Her pulse throbbed against her ears as she eyed the faint light peering through the crevices of the door. "Bradford?" He'd always preferred being addressed as such.

"Do you have any idea what time it is?" he demanded. "Do you not realize you have a responsibility toward yourself and toward my name?"

Her brows rose. Since when did Radcliff Edwin

Morton, the fourth Duke of Bradford, ever touch upon the hour or respectability?

Justine edged toward the direction of the bath chamber, curious as to what she would find on the other side of the door. Realizing she was almost an arm's reach away, she halted. What on earth was she doing? The man was bathing, for pity's sake. And unlike the African Bushmen and Hottentots, who kept their genitals bound in straps of leather even whilst bathing, she doubted *he* did. She wet her lips, trying not to imagine what was below his waist, lest she forget her reason for calling on him.

She fidgeted, knowing she should try to be civil. She *was* interrupting his bath. "It's been quite some time since we've last seen each other," she managed. Exactly two hundred and fifty-seven days. "Are you well?"

He rumbled out a laugh. "Do you mean to tell me you infiltrated my home, armed, in the dead of night merely to ask how I am?"

She wrinkled her nose. Point well made. "Uh… no. Of course not. You see…I've been rather concerned about you and our…*arrangement*. Aside from not wanting to see your own fiancée until the day of the wedding, which even my own mother admits to being odd—*and she finds very few things odd*—your solicitor still hasn't fully explained the complications surrounding my father's release. I don't understand what is taking so long. It's been five weeks."

"My dear, dear Justine." His husky tone made the wonderful endearments sound insincere. "Much like His Royal Majesty and Lord Winfield, who first brought your father's observations to His Majesty's attention, I myself am still very livid with your father. Though for very different reasons. Fetch me up as daft, but what possessed him to go against the advice of his own patron—me—and publish not one but *three hundred* copies of observations most people would categorize as bestiality? But of course His Majesty was going to make an example of him. Hell, *I* wanted to make an example of him when I discovered every one of those bloody observations had been dedicated to me. *Me*. Thanking me for *years* of funding. Do you have any idea the amount of letters I had to write to His Majesty, apologizing for my financial involvement?"

Justine winced. Yes, she could understand him being upset. But what he failed to realize was that the dedication had been bestowed with the deepest of respect and gratitude. After all, if it weren't for his generous funding—funding no other peer in London had been willing to offer—her father's studies in South Africa would have never been possible. For although her father was an earl, he'd always been a man of humble means who barely afforded a townhouse in a respectable square.

Justine stared down at the ornate brass knob before her and willed herself to remain optimistic, even as her eyes pricked with stupid, stupid tears. "Please assure me this has not affected your decision to assist him. He is tired, Bradford. And weak. And refuses to eat. I've never seen him look so frail."

Bradford sighed. Loud enough for even her to hear. "I am not the one impeding his release."

Her eyes veered back up from the knob. "Whatever do you mean?"

There was a moment of silence, followed by the soft rustle of water. "As you already know, my solicitor has been diligently negotiating this case. What you do not know is that Lord Winfield, upon discovering my intentions to assist, once again brought it to the attention of His Majesty, who then insisted the bench increase all fines by another two thousand pounds. No sooner had my solicitor met those demands, when the fines were blatantly increased again. And again. And again."

Justine's eyes widened as she huffed out, "What does Lord Winfield have against my father to continue to persecute him like this? They used to be friends!"

"Emphasis on the *used to be*. Lord Winfield despises sodomites, Justine. Rumor has it his own son was brutally sodomized against his will many, many years ago at the age of sixteen."

Oh, dear God. No wonder the man hated her father. Justine sighed and shook her head. "I didn't realize that. And apparently, neither did my father."

"It would not be something a man would openly discuss."

"No, I suppose not." Justine was quiet for a moment. "So what have the fines been set to?"

"Fifty thousand pounds. Which is why your father is still at Marshalsea. Because I do not have fifty thousand in loose coins. Most of my money is shackled to land and investments I cannot touch. And His Majesty knows it."

Justine sucked in an astonished breath and kept herself from staggering by grabbing hold of the door frame. "*Fifty thousand pounds?* Oh, dear God. Why didn't you tell me?"

"I didn't want you to worry."

"*You didn't want me to worry?*" she cried. "I have a right to worry when it involves my father. I don't understand how any of this can be legal. His Majesty cannot up and—"

"Yes, he can, Justine. And he will," he said in a curt tone that forbade another word. "I have already arranged to have more comfortable furnishings brought in for your father, along with better food and wine. I am doing everything I can, and if all goes well, this will not go beyond another eight weeks. Now, be a good girl and yank on the servant bell there by the bed. Jefferson will escort you home. Despite your blatant refusal to respect my privacy before the wedding, know that I still genuinely look forward to seeing you at the altar next week. I bid you farewell and wish you a very good night."

Justine glared at the door. "Marriage and better furnishings be damned! The worst of what my father has to endure, aside from being confined to a maze of rooms and dreary brick walls, has to do with the public itself. Did you know Marshalsea allows anyone to visit those being kept? *Anyone?*"

She fisted her hands at the very thought of it. "Random men and women of all ages from every part of London stroll in during open-gate hours, to call on him, merely to offer mocking questions about buggery and animal copulation. Eight more weeks is going to be the death of him. I refuse to have him stagnate in that abyss for another day, let alone another eight weeks."

The duke cleared his throat. Twice. "And what exactly would you have me do? *Storm the Bastille?* Dust off the *guillotine* and set His Majesty's coiffed head beneath it?"

At her silence, he continued, "Justine. Even if I could raise the funds, your father's situation has nothing to do with money. His observations ultimately called for the rights of sodomites. Do you not know that the buggery laws in England were all recently strengthened? Had your father not been an earl, he most likely would have hanged, and His Majesty, not to mention Lord Winfield, simply wish to make a point of it."

Tears burned her eyes. How did one oppose the King's wrath? One didn't. "Then…then perhaps you ought to take your brother's lead. Carlton was gracious enough to call upon me yesterday morn. He offered to personally petition His Majesty for a full pardon. Can you not do the same? Will it not mean more coming from you?"

The duke paused. "I don't care if Carlton damn well promised you world domination. I forbid you to have any further association with him. He is not the same man you once knew and has lost the last of his rational mind. Much like your father, I suppose."

Her eyes widened. Oh, now *that* was simply too far below the vines to compare her father to Carlton. "I've had enough of this, Bradford. I demand you cease tossing insults, don your clothes and give me my due audience. I've yet to see you, and I refuse to be turned away until I do."

"Justine," he growled out. "I am bathing, and as such, I am not readily available to entertain. Now ring for Jefferson."

As if she could be intimidated by a growl and a few measly words. "Since you clearly have no intention of showing yourself," she icily warned, placing her hand on the brass doorknob, "you leave me no choice but to open this door. Whatever you look like, Bradford, I doubt it will even make me blink. I have seen far hairier and bigger things than you."

When he did not reply, Justine huffed out an agitated breath. Although she could easily give up her right to civil conversations, romantic picnics and carriage rides—niceties he'd never once offered during their brief engagement—she had no intention of waiting until the day of the wedding to see him. Setting aside her father's dire predicament, she was going to put an end to this hiding. And the best part? She wasn't going to have to wait until her wedding night to see the duke in all his glory.

SCANDAL TWO

Clothing is the one and only thing that separates us from the animals, Which is why it is absolutely imperative to keep clothes on at all times.

How to Avoid a Scandal, Author Unknown

RADCLIFF EDWIN MORTON, the fourth Duke of Bradford, sat up, sending a swirling wave of warm water against the porcelain tub around him. He raked his drenched, dark hair out of his eyes with a few agitated sweeps and seethed out a breath, trying to will away his throbbing erection. An erection brought on by knowing Justine was finally within reach.

Damn her for putting him in this situation. He refused to be in her presence until they were man and wife. For even after eight long months of confinement, it was more than obvious he couldn't trust his body to cooperate.

Radcliff stood, water streaming down the length of his frame. Gritting his teeth, he grabbed hold of the towel from the brass stand beside the tub and rubbed the water from his hair.

He stepped out onto the blue-and-white Italian tile, quickly dried the rest of himself and tossed the wet towel aside. Shaking his head, he swiped up his trousers from the floor, thankful his valet had dropped them on the way out or he would have had nothing to cover his lower half aside from a towel.

The door banged open, hitting the wall hard.

Still bent forward with his trousers dangling out before him, Radcliff froze in astonishment.

The acrid smell of gunpowder filled the air as a female gasp resounded within the confines of the bath chamber. No doubt in response to his full erection on display. Though probably also in response to his injury.

Radcliff slapped his trousers against his stiff cock, and snapped his spine straight, doubting she'd seen *everything* in the wild. His pulse thundered, dreading her reaction to the long jagged scar which dominated the one side of his face.

Justine's hazel eyes raked the length of his nude body, before darting up to his face. Her lips thinned as her soot-covered cheeks flushed, acknowledging not only his scar, but his lack of clothing and the erection he hid against his trousers.

Radcliff's brows came together as he eyed her. Jefferson had been spot on. She looked like a cinder girl. Her pale yellow gown, which was partly hidden beneath her dark cloak, was smeared with soot. The acrid stench of it clearly hinted at gunpowder. Even her chestnut hair, which had been gathered in pretty curls, was heartily dusted. And though the woman was still attractive, the soot was anything but.

Trying to appear nonchalant—for what else was he to do?—he let out a low whistle that had nothing to do with admiration. "I see you've been priming pistols for England's entire infantry unit."

The flickering light from the oil lamps within the bath chamber shifted across her features, which visibly softened. "I…oh, Bradford. 'Tis unfathomable. What happened? What happened to your face?"

Not wanting to discuss why it was sliced open, and most certainly not whilst naked, he shrugged. "'Twas a mere scuffle. 'Twas nothing." Certainly nothing compared to the torture and humiliation Matilda Thurlow had endured at the hands of six men.

"A mere scuffle?" she echoed. "You call *that* a mere scuffle? If I didn't know any better, I'd say someone maliciously took a blade to the entire side of your face."

As if he wanted to put into words what was done to him and to Matilda. "What is done is done. There is no need to linger on a matter that cannot be altered."

She stared at him. "Will you cease being so indifferent? I've been worried about you. You've been in seclusion for almost eight months. What man does that?"

Radcliff struggled not to let her words agitate him. "The reasoning behind my seclusion had nothing to do with my face. They are reasons I will discuss with you at length at another, more appropriate time. Now, I am asking you to leave. You've already seen far more than I would consider to be respectable, and we are not husband and wife just yet."

She set her hands on her hips and glared at him. "I am not about to leave or marry you, Bradford, whilst you continue to elude my questions and allow my father to be persecuted for reasons that go beyond justice. Isn't there anything more you can do for him? Anything at all?"

Hadn't he helped her father and his studies enough? Studies Radcliff had financially supported for many, many years because he'd always believed in providing humanity an understanding of what he knew they all were—*animals*. He simply hadn't been prepared for what had been discovered.

In chronicling the breeding habits of over a hundred South African mammals, the earl had consistently found correlations between animal and human courtships, providing proof that relationships did exist beyond that of a mere man and a woman, that a physical bond could also exist between a man and a man, or a woman and a woman, as it did in nature.

The work was fascinating, but far too dangerous and liberal for England. Which is why Radcliff had pried a promise from the earl not to publish any of those observations until all the buggery laws had been changed.

A year later, Radcliff was left with half a face and a brother who would forever hate him, but one thing had remained a constant in his life. Justine's endearing weekly letters. Though he had refused to respond to any of them, lest he encourage her or his obsession, she had continued to write, keeping him sane during those months of seclusion.

Then the damn earl had published his observations and forced his own daughter to make an offer that had crushed the last of Radcliff's will to stay away. For if her letters could offer him sanity in his darkest of hours, he could only imagine what she could offer him as a wife.

Justine icily stared him down. "You aren't even listening to me, are you? Nor do you seem to care."

He shrugged. "I care."

She dropped her hands to her sides and went on talking as if he were fully clothed. "Even your own brother has graciously offered to call upon His Majesty about this injustice. Can you not do the same?"

Radcliff narrowed his gaze. His brother knew nothing about graciousness or compassion. He didn't know what Carlton's reasoning was for getting involved in Justine's plight, but Radcliff was certain it had nothing to do with common decency. To be sure, there was only going to be one captain sailing this ship, and it most certainly wasn't going to be Carlton.

Not giving a damn if Justine altogether fainted, Radcliff whipped the trousers away from his lower half, sending them rustling toward her, and spread his arms wide. "Perhaps I ought to call upon His Majesty at this very moment. *As I am.* Naked and fully aroused by your presence! Would that by any means please you?"

A gasp escaped her lips as her gaze flicked

over his erection. Her face instantly bloomed with as much color as a British flag. She popped up a sooty hand, shielding her eyes, and further turned her head to the side, as if the hand simply wasn't enough. "For heaven's sake, I am attempting to have a civilized conversation with you."

He snorted and waved a hand toward her. "You haven't even been in London long enough to know the meaning of being civilized. Hell, your father seems to think he can publish books that insult our ways, our laws and our King without consequence, whilst *you* seem to think you can storm into my home, uninvited, and intimidate me with African tribal airs. Let me assure you, I am not a man who can be intimidated. There was a reason I did not want to see you before the wedding. If it isn't already obvious to you, I have a lack of self-control."

"So be it." Still hiding behind a hand, she frantically kicked his trousers away from her feet, sending them flying back toward him. "Regardless, I cannot take this conversation seriously with your member fully exposed."

Radcliff snatched up his trousers and violently yanked them on. Buttoning the front flap into place, he adjusted his erection, then gestured toward the tub. "I suggest you wash your face before you leave. You look like a native with all that gunpowder."

"Hah. I doubt you even know what a native looks like." Nonetheless, she set her chin and marched straight for the tub. Glancing back toward him every now and then, as if to ensure he kept his distance, she dipped her sooty hands into the water and scrubbed at her face. The backside of her skirts and her bum hidden beneath wagged enticingly at him.

Radcliff swallowed, trying not to envision what those buttocks and legs looked like beneath the fabric of her gown. Or what they would feel like against his roaming hands. He folded his arms shakily over his bare chest.

"There." Justine patted the sides of her dampened curls, sighed and turned back toward him. Lightly freckled, her smooth skin now glistened freshly. The powder had vanished, exposing a delicate nose, arched brows and the striking hazel eyes he'd never been immune to.

By God. She was even more alluring than he remembered. To wait a whole week was going to be merciless torture. Because what he really wanted to do was—

Radcliff clenched his jaw and dug his fingers deep into his rigid biceps. He knew better.

Lingering on his need would only allow his hedonistic side to fester. He had to prove to himself before he wed that he'd mastered his obsession.

Tightening his crossed arms against his bare chest, he tried to set whatever physical barrier he could between them. "I cannot have you here. I cannot have you in my presence until we are husband and wife."

She folded her arms over her full breasts, scattering a fair dusting of gunpowder, and continued to stand there before the tub. Clearly unwilling to cooperate.

He had to get rid of her before he ended up between her thighs. Radcliff strode toward her, closing the distance between them. "You leave me no choice."

Her self-assured stance grew more uncertain as her eyes warily watched him approach. "I am not done with this conversation."

"Yes, you are." He grabbed hold of her corseted waist and yanked her up. Hard.

A shriek escaped her as she turned and fumbled to get away from his grasp. "I am not a carpet bag!"

Shoving his head beneath her flailing arms and cloak, he crushed her warm softness against him and scooped her up onto his bare shoulder, his fingers digging into her curved thighs hidden beneath.

He froze, his bare fingers lingering on her warmth and the soft feel of her gown. This was a mistake. A horrid mistake. In a torrent of solid blows, she hit his backside, making him even more aware of her body and his own. His hands gripped her more firmly, pressing her against his hard chest, even as she flailed. His cock pulsed against the wool of his trousers, taunting him to indulge. Taunting him to break his fast.

He sucked in a breath. No. He wasn't ready for any of this. Yanking her off and down his shoulder, he dumped her slippered feet onto the floor and scrambled back.

Her eyes widened as her arms flailed for balance against the ledge of the tub.

Radcliff lunged to grab on to her, but she toppled backward, cloak, skirts, stockings, slippers and all, with a huge scream, and disappeared with a splash, causing the water to rise up from within the oval tub.

"Oh, damn. Justine—" He laughed, despite his own discomfort, and scrambled to yank her out of the tub by grabbing hold of her arms.

She sat up, pushing his arms away. "Do not touch me!"

He jumped back, shaking the water from his bare arms, his chest heaving and his heart pounding.

"Pfffff!" Strands of wet, long hair were unraveling from their pins and streaming around her face and shoulders. Well defined, full breasts rose and fell, the drenched, clinging material of her gown displaying each labored breath she took. "Why... you practically tossed me in!"

A shapely, pale limb, visible up to her rounded knee taunted him as she shifted, and her wet gown bunched up in the water, bubbling around her waist. Feeling his trousers clinging to a still solid cock, he hissed out a breath and desperately fought his need to spill seed.

He had to leave. Now.

Radcliff jogged straight into the bedchamber and slammed the door behind him, leaning his back against it. After a few heavy, almost-gasping breaths, he pushed himself away from the door.

Dear God. He was still the same man, unable to control his own lewd thoughts and urges. Thoughts and urges he was certain he'd mastered whilst in seclusion. He didn't realize his transition into making Justine a permanent part of his life was going to be this bloody difficult.

Shakily grabbing up whatever shirt he could find, he yanked it on, leaving the ends hanging out over the front of his trousers to better hide whatever displays of arousal he could not control. Noting his hands were smeared with wet gunpowder, he shook his head and swiped them against the front of his white linen shirt. So much for his bath. And everything else he'd bloody worked for. Hell, he had about as much control over his cock as a dog over its master.

The violent splashing of water coming from the bath chamber made him pause. "I merely needed to clothe myself. I promise to be right in!"

The splashing ceased. "I prefer you remain right where you are, Bradford. You've done enough. I'll pull myself out."

"I…" She didn't sound all too pleased. Not that he blamed her. He eyed the door and wondered if he should go in all the same. "Are you certain I can't—"

"I am more than certain. Stay right where you are."

He headed toward the bed and sagged onto the mattress with a breath. So much for making a good impression on his soon-to-be wife.

There was a huge splash, as if she'd jumped out of the water in one swoop. "Oh!"

There was a thud.

Radcliff winced. Most likely, she was on the floor. He jumped to his feet. "Justine?"

There were a few huffing breaths. "Never you mind. 'Tis my gown is all. The water is making it rather...*difficult*...for me to even...move my... *legs*."

Her legs? Radcliff lifted an inquisitive brow and eyed the closed door behind him, already envisioning them together. Her soaked gown, delectably clinging to every inch of her shapely, stockinged legs. Him ripping the wet material from her body, her gasping breaths mingling with his own. A thrill raced through his gut imagining his fingers gliding up the length of her thighs and spreading them. Her panting and the smell of her arousal drifting up between—

Radcliff scrambled to unbutton the flap on his wool trousers. He could hardly breathe or think or—

He instantly snapped both hands up. He stood there for a long, agonizing moment and focused on steadying his breath as his chest ached and heaved from the effort.

You have more control than this. You have already proven it to yourself. Radcliff stood absolutely still as his dewed skin and throbbing cock cooled from the memory of his lewd thoughts.

Lowering his hands, he rebuttoned the open flap of his trousers, doing his best not to graze his wanting erection.

He was such a bastard. He ought to be helping Justine off the floor. Not— "Perhaps we ought to remove your gown," he quickly offered, heading toward the closed door. "It will be easier for you to—" He cringed. Removing her gown was probably *not* such a good idea. Aside from the obvious, he had more respect for Justine than that.

There was a moment of awkward silence. "Stay right where you are, Bradford. I'll manage on my own."

Radcliff huffed out a ragged breath and veered back to the bed, sagging against the mattress. Fortunately, his erection had subsided.

There was a quick clicking of heels against the tile. The door banged open and out she sailed. Her gown alone must have dragged out half the bleeding tub. Water rapidly pooled and spread its wet fingers across the floor, streams and streams leaking from the hem of her gown and the edges of her now-flat sleeves. She glared at him, her smooth cheeks ablaze.

His breath hitched as he looked away, trying not to focus on the outline of her body or her face. He could still remember all too fondly when she'd first arrived from Africa two years ago at a lush eighteen and as sweet as Tokay. Her hair had borne brilliant streaks of spun gold and her skin had been so beautifully tinted from the sun, unlike the pasty faces London was notorious for. Though her skin had long paled, leaving behind a faint trail of freckles, and the golden streaks in her hair had faded into what was now a subdued, chestnut hue, she was still absolutely stunning. And that was just her face.

Justine set her chin and marched past his four-poster, trailing a glistening stream of water. "I require more respect than this. The marriage is off. Good night, good riddance and goodbye."

Radcliff winced, knowing she probably meant it, and jumped off the bed. He refused to be left alone with his thoughts anymore. He needed this. He needed her. A wife who would hold him responsible for who and what he was on a daily basis.

Jogging toward her, he grabbed hold of her soaked sleeve. "Justine, I didn't—"

"Do not touch me!" She moved back and away, teetering for a moment against the weight of her gown. "Does the devil reside within your soul? I can think of no other reason why a grown man would throw his own fiancée into a tub of water

and then up and blatantly shut the door, leaving her to pull herself out."

The devil *did* reside within his soul. And no one knew that more than he. But he'd come to believe these past eight months that he was stronger than the devil. And he was going to prove it. To her. To himself. To everyone.

"Forgive me. I—" He paused. Noting his hand was wet from touching her, he swiped it against his trousers. He eyed the wooden floor beneath his bare feet, which was steadily acquiring more water from her gown. "You're flooding the entire room."

She snorted. "But of course I'm flooding the entire room. Do you have any idea how much material goes into a gown? I have no doubt whatsoever that I soaked up most, if not *all,* of your filthy bath water."

Hell, he needed to get her back into the bath chamber and get his servants to clean this mess up. He gestured toward the adjoining room. "Go. Remove your gown. I'll…fetch something for you to wear." Though he didn't know what, seeing he'd dismissed every female servant from the house eight months ago.

"You want me to remove my gown?" Justine gurgled out a laugh and flung water in his direction as she waved her hand about. "If I did not know any better, I would say you were intent on bedding me before the actual wedding. And whilst I'm rather flattered, you haven't exactly earned it, have you?"

This coming from a woman who had originally offered herself without marriage. He leveled his gaze at her. "I did not mean it that way."

"I may be a virgin, Bradford, but that does not make me stupid."

He was not about to have her categorize him. Because he was not that man anymore, even though he still fought those same urges.

Radcliff pointed rigidly at her. "Now you listen here. I have spent these last eight months of my life reforming myself. I am not the same gormless man you once knew. I am a new man. A man capable of far more self-control than you dare mock me with."

"Oh?" she challenged, lifting both brows.

"Yes. *Oh.*" He purposefully stepped closer, waving a hand up and down the length of her body. "Why, I could easily strip you naked here and now and walk away without even deigning your body another glance. Do you wish me to prove it? Come. I'll prove it. To you *and* myself."

The force of his own conviction in that moment

was so strong and empowering, he almost wished she would put him to the test.

She scrambled frantically back, flinging droplets of water whilst trailing more streams across the wood floor. "Is crudely taunting me your way of showing love and affection? Because I do not approve of it!"

He couldn't help but snort. "Love and…hell, Justine, I thought you, of all women, born and bred unto a scientific, rational man, would have realized by now that love and affection have no place in the real world."

Her lips parted in astonishment as she shoved several wet, dripping sections of her hair from the sides of her face. "What world are you living in? Despite my scientific upbringing, I happen to believe in love and affection. Why? Because it requires sentiment and spirit and emotion and the desire and passion to genuinely display one's soul ardently to another."

He rolled his eyes at her rich, honeyed words. Similar words his own mother had often spoken to his father whilst making a cuckold out of him. "Someone hand me a dagger and spare me from listening to any more of this."

She narrowed her gaze. "'Tis obvious you have no respect for me or what I believe."

"Respect does not mean people need always agree, Justine." Radcliff strode past her to the dresser, and flung its wood-lacquered door open. Yanking out a nightshirt, he offered it to her. "Here. Don this."

She lowered her gaze and looked away, shaking her head.

He eyed her, sensing she was genuinely upset. Damn women and their ability to make him soft in the head and hard in the cock.

He blew out an exasperated breath. "Give me five days. If your father isn't released from Marshalsea in that time, the wedding is off and you owe me nothing. And rest assured, even then, I will continue to barter for his release. How is that for respect?"

Her gaze darted back toward him. In astonishment.

Her astonishment reflected his own. For if those five days produced nothing, he'd be without a bride. And though, yes, there were plenty of other women who'd be more than willing to play duchess despite his scar and his reputation, none of them were nearly as intelligent or as unyielding as Justine. He needed more than a beautiful face for a wife. He needed a soul made of iron. A soul capable of handling anything.

Radcliff shook the nightshirt at her. "Take it," he muttered. "Any gentleman would agree you should not remain in wet clothing."

Her full lips spread into a stunning smile that magically brightened not only her face but her beautiful eyes. "Will it really take only five days?"

"There is one highly placed man I've yet to contact. He is known to have the king's ear and happens to be Lord Winfield's rival. My solicitor mentioned him to me just yesterday. Perhaps it will end with him. Now go. Put this on."

She stumbled toward him. Grabbing hold of his shirt, she marched toward the bath chamber, still boasting a smile.

A smile that made it all worth his while.

She halted in the doorway and announced over her shoulder, "I always knew you had a heart, Bradford. Always." With that, she slammed the door behind herself.

He blinked, realizing that despite Justine's unusual upbringing, she still very much believed in all things female. Romance and words of love.

He was going to be a sore disappointment to her. But then again, that was all he ever seemed to be these days: a disappointment to everyone, including himself.

SCANDAL THREE

Allowing a man to kiss or touch you, at any time during your courtship, even before a set wedding, is allowing too much. After all, it is a lady's duty to give a man a genuine reason to run down that altar aisle. It is a lady's duty to give a man a genuine reason as to why, on his own wedding day, he should smile.

How to Avoid a Scandal, Author Unknown

JUSTINE SMOOTHED OUT Radcliff's white cotton nightshirt and hurriedly rolled up the large, loose sleeves. She glanced down at the gaping open front of his shirt which provocatively exposed her damp lilac corset and chemise. She cringed and clutched the front together, holding it shut. At least they were engaged.

"Are you clothed?"

She jumped at the sound of Radcliff's deep voice from the other side of the closed door. "I doubt you can call it that," she yelled back.

"You needn't fret. We'll throw a cloak or two over you and dash you home. Though I have a feeling your mother will hold me accountable for your absence and lack of clothing. Send along my apologies, will you?"

Justine smirked. "I really wouldn't worry about my mother. She doesn't even know I'm here. She overstayed past calling hours whilst visiting Father at Marshalsea and therefore won't be allowed back out until the gates reopen in the morning." She tiptoed with cold, bare feet across the bath chamber, avoiding puddles on the tile, then opened the door and edged out.

Bradford sat on the four-poster, one trouser-clad knee propped up, his bare foot rumpling the white satin linens. His shaven jaw tightened as his dark eyes trailed the length of her body.

Her heart fluttered in response. The way it always fluttered foolishly in his presence. She tried to shove away the erotic image of his large muscled body and that sizable erection, but it was no use. It had been seared into her thoughts and would remain there until she was given the pleasure of seeing him naked again.

Despite Bradford's long, puckered scar, he was still very dashing. His white linen shirt continued to hang open, exposing a strong neck and a sprinkle of soft-looking black curls. With or without clothes, the man had a commanding presence that was raw, overwhelming and beyond exciting. Why was it she had the strangest desire to consummate their marriage right now?

He lowered his trouser-clad leg to the floor and kept staring at her. As if he'd never seen a woman before.

The piercing silence lingering between them seemed to further emphasize how alone they really were. And how they were breaking every single rule set out by respectable society, what with her lack of clothing and his bed barely a few feet away. Given his reputation, she was quite certain this wasn't new to him. Not as it was for her.

Wanting to prove to him, and herself, that she wasn't in the least bit intimidated, and that she could rival any woman he'd ever had, she drifted in his direction and paused, lingering only a few feet away. "You're staring, Bradford," she teased.

He cleared his throat and looked away, sending damp strands of dark hair cascading into his eyes and toward his scar. "I…forgive me."

He cleared his throat again and rose to his full, imposing height of six feet. "We should cover you up a bit more. Your legs…they…they're showing."

How utterly charming. The Duke of Bradford, and soon to be *her* Duke of Bradford, *The* Rake

Extraordinaire, was actually stumbling and mumbling and apologizing for being a man. And was even telling her to further cover up!

This certainly deserved a bit more study and observation. Seeing she was going to be his fiancée for at least another five days, she had a right to know what a man of his years, upbringing and experience did or did not find attractive. Never mind if what she was about to ask would cause half of London to faint.

"What do you think of them?" she drawled.

He eyed her. "What do I think of what?"

"*My legs.* Seeing that you had mentioned them."

He stared at her. "What about your legs?"

"Well…ever since I can remember, I've always wondered what the preoccupation was all about. Did you know that the native women in Africa don't cover their legs and ankles the same way women do here? Now why is that, do you suppose? Does a leg mean more to us than it does to them? And if so, why? They're only legs, after all, taking us from one place to the next. You don't see male giraffes gawking at the legs of their mates, even though they're certainly long enough to warrant such a thing."

Justine shot out her right leg, her damp,

transparent chemise tightening against the extension, and pointed her bare toes in his direction. She tilted her head to one side, observing her own limbs in a scientific sort of way. "I'm afraid they're a bit bowed, and for that I can only apologize, but aside from that, what do you think? From a British male perspective? Are they at all attractive? Surely, you've seen more than enough to provide an objective opinion."

He continued to stare at her, abashed.

She returned his stare and quickly dropped her foot back onto the wooden floor. So much for the British male perspective. Apparently, she was being too crass for even a homo sapien libertine. "I suppose I should apologize. I didn't realize—"

"There is no need for you to apologize, Justine," he said in a low tone. "In answer to your question, they are not bowed. In fact, they are very shapely. Might I also point out, if we *were* giraffes, I would probably be gawking and whistling and making all the other giraffes feel very, very uncomfortable."

Her eyes widened as she gurgled out a laugh. Oh, now they were both being very naughty. And what was worse, she loved it. It reminded her of the wild and funny Bradford she'd shamelessly preened over. The Bradford who had always made everything so exciting in an otherwise very orchestrated and boring London world.

Though her entire face burned, she decided to offer her fiancée a tad bit more. She'd already tossed every etiquette book out the window and had every intention of showing how grateful she was he hadn't taken her up on her rash proposal of a few measly nights.

Offering him a shy smile, she gathered her wet chemise and slid it up to where his shirt ended to give him a better view of everything below the knees. In case her wet chemise wasn't transparent enough.

Bradford hissed out a breath—as if something were terribly wrong with her legs—and closed what little space was left between them. He grabbed hold of her chin, yanking it up toward his own face. "Drop it," he demanded, his fingers now digging into her skin, causing it to burn. "Drop it before I do it for you."

Justine instantly dropped her chemise and stared up at him in astonishment, realizing it wasn't male lust that had riled him. What was more, his marred face was hauntingly close. She swallowed, feeling as though she were looking at one side of his face through broken glass.

Instead of breaking her chin free of his pinching

grasp, she searched his eyes. "Why are you angry? I thought you would have enjoyed that."

His dark brows came together as he loosened his grip. The rough pads of his fingers slowly slid back and forth, as if trying to soothe her skin. "You don't know what you are doing, innocent Justine. Forgive me," he murmured. "I should not have taken that tone with you."

Justine blinked up at him, still unable to move. To be sure, this was not the same Bradford she'd once known. He was so morbidly tense, reserved and too serious for her own liking.

What on earth had changed his playful, adventurous soul into...*this?* She was certain his scar held the answer to her question. "What happened to you? What happened since we last met? You are not the same man. You once loved to engage in flirtations."

He dropped his hand from her chin, his dark brows softening, but continued to linger before her. "I don't want to be the man you once knew. He had no self-control or self-respect."

She sucked in a breath. "Libertine aside, he was everything I could ever want. He was generous and charming and playful and witty. He knew how to make me laugh and blush and always preferred to sit on the floor as opposed to a chair. I adored him. I...still do." She bit her lip, realizing she was practically flinging herself at him. As always.

His dark eyes took on an intense, blazing look as he suddenly grabbed her waist and yanked her hips toward his own, grinding her against the length of his large body.

She gasped as his hands molded her closer, pressing her more firmly against every inch of him. As if forcing her to feel the pulsing heat of his skin, the beating of his heart, and the rigid bulge in his trousers which dug into her damp, corseted stomach.

Her heart thumped and her stomach flipped. Having never had any physical relations with a man, and having never been held by one so close, either, the contact was shocking. Not to mention downright arousing.

"If you really knew who he was," he said in a low, clipped tone, "I doubt you'd feel adoration."

The tension in his muscles gave her a sense of the powerful force barely being restrained.

Justine's pulse thundered as she was torn between pulling away and melting against the firm, crushing embrace of those taut muscles. Endless sensations overwhelmed her body, which was probably why she couldn't make any sense of him or his words. "Bradford, what—"

He released her and stepped back, setting a notable distance between them. His broad chest rose and fell beneath his open shirt as if he struggled to breathe. He readjusted the erection within his trousers and swiped at his face with shaky hands, unable to look at her.

She swallowed, knowing his blatant rejection had nothing to do with her. Something was tormenting him. But what? Her throat ached at the thought of him suffering this much.

He turned away, blowing out a heavy breath, and purposefully kept his broad back to her. As if ashamed by his arousal, by his need. As if he truly hated himself.

Justine fidgeted with her hands, not knowing what to make of him. Perhaps it was best she leave. "I should go. But before I do...I...I would like to thank you."

"For what?"

"For everything." She paused. "Well. Aside from throwing me into the tub, that is." She feigned a laugh, but seeing he still hadn't turned or appeared amused by her little quip, she sighed.

She wished he would turn so she could look into his eyes and assure him how much he'd always meant to her. "Ever since I've known you, Bradford, you've always been very generous and supportive of my father. Even whilst all of London chose to mock him. You've always believed in the value of his work and treated him with respect. And for that reason alone, I would marry you. Without question."

He was quiet for a very long moment. He swung back toward her. Hissing out a breath, he shifted his weight from one bare foot to the other. "If we do marry, I wish to buy you a wedding gift. What is it that you want?"

"Pardon?"

He waved a hand toward her. "*What is it that you want?* Aside from your father's freedom, that is. What would make you happy knowing you are settling for a man with half a face and half a heart? Do you want jewelry? Clothing? Name it and it is yours. I genuinely wish to make you happy."

Abashed, Justine stepped back. Where on earth was this coming from, and what did he mean he only had half a heart? "Happiness isn't something that can be readily bought. Unlike most women, I've never been overly fond of trinkets. I prefer more nostalgic things."

His hand fell to his side as black eyes captured hers. "Assure me you aren't about to demand sentimental rubbish I cannot give. I am not that sort of man."

Ah. But she had faith he would eventually be that sort of man. Until then, there was only one other thing, aside from courtship, romance and love, that she, as a woman, would ever want from him. "All I am asking for is your respect, Bradford. The sort of respect London has never given me, my father or my mother. I don't want any more of this throwing-me-into-the-tub nonsense or you treating me with agitated disdain I do not deserve. I also humbly ask that your respect not be limited to public display, but to our own personal lives, which hopefully will include you having no other woman in your bed but me. In the wild, it may very well be acceptable to be promiscuous or polygamous, but I have witnessed first-hand how badly that can end if *any* of those partners feel threatened."

He stared at her and then belted out a hearty laugh that crinkled the edges of his eyes and shifted the mangled skin on the side of his face.

Oh, for heaven's sake. He really was hopeless.

"You speak with *such* conviction," he guffawed. "It's marvelous. Absolutely marvelous."

She supposed this was what happened when a monogamous female tried to pair up with a full-blooded libertine. "I suggest you set up a harem in the east wing of the house," she tossed out in complete disgust. "At least then I'll know where all the women are coming from and where to find you should I require attention."

His laughter and grin slowly faded as his features settled back into a tight, grim mask. "Forgoing associations with women will require no effort on my part. I am rather concerned, however, about the obligation that would fall upon you as a result of it."

She rolled her eyes. "Don't mock me, Bradford. It's beneath even you. I know full well what those obligations are, and I can assure you, I am more than capable, not to mention *willing,* to meet them."

He lowered his chin, challenging her with a hard, burning look. "I don't doubt your capability. Or your willingness. I do, however, doubt your stamina."

Her…stamina? What on earth was that supposed to mean? "What are you saying? That it takes a full eight hours of copulation for you to reach completion?"

He choked and raked both hands through his damp hair. "Your father bloody exposed you to his observations a bit too much. No. For God's sake, I…" He dropped his hands to his side. But said nothing more.

She blinked. "What, then?"

He shook his dark head but still said nothing.

She stepped toward him, oddly compelled, not to mention genuinely concerned. "I should hope that if there is something that will affect our marriage, you would find the decency to tell me now. Before we marry."

"I…yes. You are right in that. You deserve to know beforehand." He nodded, as if struggling to comprehend his own thoughts. Taking in a deep breath, he let it out and blurted, "Forgive my own tongue for even saying it, but I am obsessed with sex. I think about it all the time."

Justine pulled in her chin, startled by the admission, and laughed. "Forgive me, Bradford—and my father would agree with me on this—but what male of any species isn't obsessed with it?"

"Justine—" He squeezed his eyes shut, as if wanting her to understand something he simply could not put into words, then eventually reopened them and said in a cool, low tone, "Allow me to better explain this. If I gave in to every lewd thought and every lewd urge that ever possessed me—the way I used to before I ended up with this face—in time you would only learn to despise me and my advances. And I don't want that. I genuinely wish to lead a normal life by controlling all physical interactions to the best of my abilities."

Her brows shot up. Why…he appeared to be forthright.

He swiped a hand over his face. "If you haven't noticed, I have no female servants. It was necessary to eliminate any temptation that would have caused me to stray from the self-governed control I've adhered to these past eight months. As such, you will have no lady's maid. I've already enlisted an excellent French man for you, who is trained in all matters of female dress and hair. I can assure you, Henri is far more female than any lady's maid you'll ever have. My hope is that despite him being male, he will exceed your expectations."

Oh. Dear. God. Her lady's maid was going to be a…man? Whilst she was to be the only female in the entire house? Were Bradford's urges that uncontrollable?

Though, yes, she was looking forward to bedding him, she was somewhat concerned about what his definition of stamina really meant. Daily advances she could easily take on. But what if he meant hourly advances for the rest of her life?

Justine swallowed, trying to fend off the burning heat consuming her face. "Did you plan on disclosing any of this to me?"

"Yes. On our wedding night."

"Lovely. Why do I not feel comforted by that admission?"

He stared her down. "Rest assured, Justine, I have never forced myself upon a woman and I would never force myself upon you. Your submission would be entirely voluntary." He continued to intently hold her gaze. "Do you have any further concerns? Because now would be the time to name them."

Justine wet her lips and wondered what under heaven and above hell she was about to agree to. But then again...the man was a rake. That was what rakes did. Obsess about copulation and women. Everyone in London knew that. And no one, not even all the upper prudes, seemed all that concerned, aside from the moral aspect of it.

She eyed him. "I suppose I wouldn't be so concerned if I knew you weren't going to demand hourly performances for the rest of my life. Or involve other women."

"It is my duty and honor to alleviate those concerns." He held up his right hand beside his head and set his left on his chest. "I solemnly swear to never demand hourly performances or involve other women in our lives." He dropped his hands back into place. "There you are. You have no further concerns."

Justine couldn't help but stare at him. "Do you find yourself amusing?"

He pointed to himself. "Do I look amused? I am being quite serious. Now. I recommend we get you home."

Without sparing her another glance, he strode over to the braided bell pull and yanked on it a number of times as if he were worried Jefferson wouldn't respond. "If all goes well with your father's release, as I am hoping it will, I expect to see you in church next week at the appointed time. I will see to it all of your wet clothes are laundered and returned before then. Jefferson will fetch those cloaks for you and personally see to it you arrive home. Good night." He offered a curt nod, departed into the adjoining room and quietly closed the door, leaving her to wait for Jefferson alone.

She blinked. If only she wasn't so hopelessly smitten with Bradford. If only she wasn't smitten with Bradford *at all*. Oh, how she prayed and hoped to whatever God there was above he would keep all of the promises he had made to her tonight.

SCANDAL FOUR

A lady should always refrain from discussing vulgar topics. Not because it is crass, though indeed it is, but because once vulgarity is allowed, *everything* is allowed.

How to Avoid a Scandal, Author Unknown

SIX DAYS LATER, evening, and only twelve hours left before the wedding, which had been set after the surprisingly prompt release of her father from Marshalsea.

Justine found it rather annoying that her own mother, who was usually very calm and very poised in nature, was rudely pacing back and forth. Lady Marwood's graying brown tresses quivered atop her head with every frantic step, turn and swish of her flower-patterned skirts. All the while, she gripped Justine's red etiquette book *How To Avoid A Scandal* before her with both hands as if she were praying to it. Which her mother most likely was.

"Mother." Justine patted the space beside her on the bed. "Sit. There is no need for you to be more nervous than the little lamb who is about to be slaughtered."

Lady Marwood came to an abrupt halt and pointed the book at her with one hand. "I am not nervous. And you are hardly a lamb. I was merely thinking about how I should go about conducting this particular conversation."

Regally lowering her arm and the book down to her side, Lady Marwood focused her hazel eyes on Justine from across the short distance separating them. "Bedding a man isn't any more complicated than what you've witnessed in the wild."

Justine couldn't help but snort as she drew her robed knees up to her chin and wrapped her arms around her exposed ankles. "That doesn't sound all that promising, Mother. Some mates maul each other during mating."

Lady Marwood shook her head. "Bless your misguided heart, you always come up with something no one else ever thinks of." She sighed. "Do you have any specific questions you wish for me to answer?"

Justine eyed her. "I only have one question. Would you say daily advances from one's husband are to be expected?"

"Men are very, very lusty creatures. Especially in the beginning of marriage."

Well. Thank goodness for that. Bradford had made himself sound so abnormal. "Will it be enjoyable? At all? Please tell me it will be. I cannot imagine—"

"Not the first few times, dear. After all, your body will require time to ease into it. He will be forcing a rather large part of himself into a very small space. Once your body is accustomed, then yes, it will be pleasurable." Her mother paused. "If properly conducted, that is."

Justine shifted uncomfortably on the bed and yanked her nightdress and robe down around her feet. "So it will hurt."

Lady Marwood sighed. "Depending on how large his penis is, yes. It will."

Justine crinkled her nose, remembering all too well what she'd seen on Bradford in its erect state. She only hoped her body eased into it quickly, because she preferred getting to the enjoyable part right away.

"Speaking of size," Lady Marwood went on, "I should probably point out that it will double in length during every encounter. And though odd, it is in fact quite normal."

"Yes, yes. I know. I've seen it in the wild." And on Bradford. But she wasn't going to tell her mother *that*.

"Now, your grandmother, heaven rest her soul, gave me this solid advice on the eve of my wedding, which I am now gifting you. Never allow for more than two encounters per week. Feign headaches, if need be. That always works. For although a husband will try to convince his wife otherwise, twice a week is more than sufficient to produce children and still allow for pleasure."

Justine's brows went up. "Is that a suggestion or a rule?"

"It's a suggestion, dear. Limiting contact is simply best for your health. You don't want to end up with fifteen children."

Justine paused, then genuinely grinned, imagining the entire house overrun with beautiful, happy little boys and girls. And though yes, she knew there was far more to being a mother than holding soft, pudgy hands and sharing stories about fairies and bogies, she couldn't help but linger on all the fun she'd have along the way.

Justine shrugged. "The amount of children doesn't concern me. At least I'll be marrying a man who can afford them. Unlike father, who could barely afford me."

Lady Marwood set her hands on her hips and glared at her. "Justine!"

"I meant it lovingly."

Lady Marwood rolled her eyes. "My advice is that you bite your tongue whenever possible during the first year of marriage. At least until he grows fond enough of you and doesn't feel the need to kill you."

Justine smirked. "Yes, Mother."

Lady Marwood sighed, approached her and held out the etiquette book. "I know you've already read this many, many times. But I suggest you read it again and allow the words to govern your new life. Our family hasn't always catered to society's conventions. But you will be a duchess, and London society doesn't hand anyone respect. It must be earned."

Justine dropped her legs back over the side of the bed and leaned forward, slipping the red, leather-bound book from her mother's hand. Patting the book enthusiastically, Justine set it on the bed beside her. "I promise to earn full respect not only for myself and my husband, but also for you and father."

"I have no doubt you will." Lady Marwood leaned toward her, bringing with her the scent of lilacs, and kissed her cheek lovingly. "Sleep. You have a long day ahead."

Her mother caught her hand and smiled, causing the aging lines around her hazel eyes and full mouth to deepen. "By tomorrow, you will be a duchess. As you well deserve to be." Her mother released her hand, still smiling, then turned and swept out of the room, apparently quite pleased with the thought.

Justine smoothed the coverlet on the bed around her and muttered, "God save the King and all of his subjects I am about to unknowingly torment in the name of respect."

There was a quick knock.

Heaven forbid her mother forgot to mention something critical. "Yes?"

The door edged open, and her father, Lord Marwood, whose lanky frame was still encased in full evening attire, hurried in. The deep, aging lines surrounding his blue eyes crinkled all the more as he grinned and held up a sizable, leather-bound book. "It took me half the night to find it amongst all the crates, but here it is."

Justine sat up, surprised he hadn't already retired. It was well past his usual hour of sleep and he still hadn't entirely recovered from his long stay at Marshalsea. Their brief walk through Hyde Park earlier in the day had completely exhausted him. But at least he was eating again.

She smiled, more than pleased to see him. "Restless?"

He nodded his graying head. "Yes. Though in a good way. It isn't every day my daughter becomes a duchess."

She quirked a brow at the book he still held up. "And what is that? My very last bedtime story?"

He chuckled. "No, no, no." Striding the length of the room, he set the book beside her on the bed, atop the book her mother had just given her, and patted it enthusiastically. "'Tis one of my earlier compilations. Before my days in South Africa. This here is what ultimately convinced the duke to become my patron. The man was only one and twenty at the time, you know, but even then he had an eye for a good thing." He dragged a hand through thick, silvery hair and then dropped it to his side. "You should read it before going to bed. It should assist you in matters of the bedchamber."

Justine bit back a laugh. It was obvious her mother and father had two entirely different opinions as to how she should conduct herself as duchess. Though she knew her mother's advice was more in keeping with what London would want, she was nonetheless curious to see the book that had convinced Bradford to support her father all these years.

Justine smiled and glanced down at the book he'd placed beside her. She turned the large gold lettering right side up and blinked. "Principles of Animal Husbandry?" Gad almighty. "How…lovely. Thank you."

How *humiliating* was more the word. She'd officially been categorized by her own father with all the sheep, cattle and horses. As opposed to all the far more interesting mammals he'd studied throughout the years. And what on earth did this say about Bradford's tastes in copulation?

Her father cleared his throat. "The illustrations are quite good. Not to mention detailed. With the duke's reputation, I'm more than certain you'll make good use of it. Only this isn't yours to keep, seeing it's the only copy I have. Be sure to read it tonight and return it to me in the morning."

Any insight on Bradford and his tastes would certainly be appreciated, as she had no intention of disappointing him *or* herself on their wedding night.

She bit her lip and glanced up. "Uh…Father? Might I ask a more involved question? About copulation?"

He tugged on the lapels of his jacket and grinned, proud to be of assistance. "Why, this is rather unexpected. You haven't asked me an involved question since you were twelve."

She let out a laugh. "That is because you're

notorious for answering questions before they're even asked."

He nodded. "So true. What is your question?"

Her grin faded, and she cleared her throat. "Do, uh...certain men have...well...how shall I say this...*abnormal* copulation habits? As in obsessive habits that may be a cause of concern for a woman?"

Both his bushy gray brows went up as his hold on his lapels tightened, causing his knuckles to go white. "Why do you ask?"

She shrugged, not wanting to betray what Bradford had confided to her. She had a feeling it wasn't something he wanted everyone, especially her father, to know. "Curiosity is all."

Lord Marwood released the tight hold on his coat, then scratched at his shaven chin for a moment. "In my opinion, a man who does in fact have any sort of abnormal copulation habits is most likely never to discuss it unless forced. Which makes it rather difficult for anyone to assess. But, as in nature itself, I would imagine there's always some form of abnormality to be found within a species." He pointed at her. "For example. You remember that one male Equus Burchelli whose mate had unexpectedly died? And how he kept returning to her body to mount it even though there was very little left of it for him to mount?"

Justine wrinkled her nose, remembering that all too well. Heaven forbid that was the sort of abnormality Bradford was referring to. It would certainly give a whole new meaning to the term *until death did them part...* "I wasn't referring to that sort of abnormality. I was referring to a man's urge to pleasure himself more than what would be considered necessary."

"Oh. I see." He exhaled through his nostrils and shrugged. "Unlike animals, humans have an annoying tendency to censor their behaviors, which doesn't allow for anyone to come to any real conclusions. So sadly, I must profess complete ignorance to this particular subject."

That was helpful.

Lord Marwood sighed and drew closer. Leaning toward her, he fumbled awkwardly with her hand, gathering it with his long fingers. Tired blue eyes searched her face. "I sense you're worried about your obligations toward Bradford. You needn't be. The man has always been wildly enamored with you. Always."

"He has?"

He nodded. "Before he got himself into whatever stupid mess he did, he actually tried calling on you several times here at the house. I repeatedly turned him away knowing his intentions weren't in the least bit civil."

"He...called on me?" she asked softly. "Why did you never tell me about this?"

He grunted. "Smitten as you already were with the man? I think not. He wasn't prepared to offer matrimony at the time, but I am pleased to know that has all changed and here we are, well past any worry. I have known the man long enough to say he will treat you very well. He may be misguided at times, and randy, but that heart of his beats true. Be patient with him and guide him and I promise all will be well."

Justine smiled and squeezed his warm hand. "You are right. I suppose I'm a bit nervous, is all. I've always been quite the outcast in London, and now that I am about to become a duchess, and observed closely by all, I worry I'll only end up disappointing you and everyone else."

"You could never disappoint me, Justine. It is I who have disappointed you." He withdrew his hand from hers and looked away, drawing his gray brows together. "There are many things I cannot change. Aside from the mess I created foolishly thinking I lived in a free society, you should have been allowed a proper upbringing here in London.

Like the rest of the girls. I failed you in that way, and can only apologize."

Justine's throat clenched. "I'll not have you regretting the wonderful and amazing life you have given me. Africa will always be home to me. Always. 'Tis a glorious place of endless beauty London could never rival. I know without any doubt I'll be toting Bradford and my own children there from time to time to escape the London fog, smog and coal smoke."

She nodded at the very thought, then paused and teasingly emphasized with a lopsided grin, "Actually, I'll have no choice in the matter but to take my children to Africa. By then, I know their grandparents will be permanently living in Cape Town."

He looked away. "My days in Africa are over."

Her stomach squeezed at the thought. "Why would you say something like that? You and I both know where you belong. And it isn't here amongst all these snobs who don't appreciate the countless years of dedication you've given to your observations."

He sighed and eyed her. "Even if I had the means to return, it wouldn't be the same without you. You, my girl, have chronicled some of my best works and kept me company whenever your mother suffered from a headache. Which was quite often."

Justine bit back a smile, knowing her mother always feigned headaches whenever she was trying to avoid something. She reached out and gently nudged his forearm. "Perhaps I can convince Bradford to take us all to Cape Town for holiday? Wouldn't that be lovely?"

"Now, now. We mustn't financially burden the duke any more than we already have. Even the deepest of wells can run dry."

Justine fingered both books beside her. "It appears I have some studying to do before I go to bed."

Lord Marwood grinned. "That you do. Good night." He patted his book, then hastily leaned in and kissed her cheek. "You have always brought pride to my name, and as duchess, I know you will continue to do so." He straightened, nodded, then strode across the room, quietly closing the door behind him.

Justine sighed and prayed her father was right. For the Marwood name had already endured more than enough scandal.

Twelve hours later

THE SOFT FLOATING FRAGRANCE of fresh flowers mingled with the heady scent of melted beeswax.

It tinged the sultry air of the quiet church and every breath Justine took as she walked the length of the aisle toward Bradford.

Every wooden pew and marble pillar she passed had been meticulously decorated with boughs of white blossoms, pink roses, and forget-me-nots. The bright morning sun sparkled through the rows of stained-glass windows high above, highlighting portions of the marble altar with a rainbow of muted colors. And there, at the altar, past all the vacant pews, stood Bradford.

Her Bradford. A wonderful, even if flawed, man who had nobly rescued her father and was about to become her husband.

Her heart fluttered as she paused beside him and glanced toward the bishop and the only witnesses who stood at the altar dressed in their finest—her mother and father.

She smiled at them.

Their aging faces beamed with genuine warmth and pride. There was no greater joy than seeing the happy faces of those she loved whilst knowing she was marrying a man she genuinely adored. A man she hoped she would quickly come to love.

Justine spun back toward Bradford, bumping into him in clumsy haste. His large hands steadied her as the expanse of his gray satin waistcoat and its row of silver-and-diamond-encrusted buttons overtook her entire view. She stepped back, a nervous laugh bubbling from her lips, and shyly glanced up at him.

Bradford's dark hair had been smoothly brushed back from his forehead, displaying his entire rugged profile, including the jagged scar dominating the one side of his face.

A sense of pride filled her. For despite that scar, he was still unbelievably dashing. He looked like a seasoned pirate who had decided to become an aristocrat for a day. A smile overtook her lips at the very thought. She met his gaze.

Bradford's dark eyes observed her, his expression suggesting he was too troubled to smile. He looked away and focused on the bishop before them.

Justine's smile faded and her chest tightened. What if he'd never genuinely wanted to marry her? She'd not truly considered that until now. She'd been so focused on overseeing her father's freedom, she had not considered how Bradford even felt about their wedding.

She swallowed as the bishop's calm voice floated around her. An unexpected sense of dread overwhelmed her. The weight of her pearl-encrusted, lilac gown seemed to pull her down toward the marble slab at her feet. She wanted to give in to its weight and crumple to the floor but somehow managed to remain standing.

The bishop glanced at each of them, his gray brows rising toward his gold-threaded dome cap. "I require and charge you both, as you will answer at the dreadful day of judgment when the secrets of all hearts shall be disclosed, that if either of you know any impediment why you may not be lawfully joined together in matrimony, you do now confess it. For be you well assured, that so many as are coupled together otherwise than God's word doth allow are not joined together by God; neither is their matrimony lawful. If any man do allege and declare any impediment, why they may not be coupled together in matrimony, by God's law, or the laws of this realm; may he prove his allegation now."

Justine glanced over at Bradford, half expecting him to say something. Yet no opposition fell from his lips. His jaw merely tightened.

The bishop went on, tonelessly reciting more words. Words she could no longer make sense of. Her thoughts blurred into a panic. After all, this was supposed to be the happiest day of her life. Why didn't it feel like it?

Bradford suddenly leaned toward her and reached out. His warm fingers gently grasped her wrist. She stiffened, realizing his hand was visibly trembling as he lifted her own hand and held it up high between them.

Could it be possible he was as nervous as she was?

He retrieved the lone ring from the leather-bound surface of the bible the bishop held up and momentarily met her gaze. Her heart raced and her cheeks blazed as he slowly and sensually touched the slim ruby ring to the tip of each and every one of her fingers, making his way toward what was to be her wedded finger.

Lowering his gaze, he recited his devotion, "With this ring I thee wed, with my body I thee worship, and with all my worldly goods I thee endow. In the name of the Father, and the Son, and of the Holy Ghost. Amen."

He then placed the glinting ring upon the third finger from her thumb. The cool metal grazed her moist skin as his large fingers adjusted the ring into place.

Never once did he meet her gaze or hint at any form of emotion. Justine swallowed against the aching dryness overtaking her throat and couldn't help but wonder what he was thinking or feeling. She only hoped it wasn't regret.

Together they knelt before the bishop, Bradford's

large hand still holding hers. More words echoed around them but all she could think about was his hand. And how her hand was now his hand. Forever.

Their hands fell away. They stood and the ceremony ended, formally announcing it was time to sign the parish registrar in the side room off the altar. She didn't even remember leaving the altar or walking into the room as she blankly watched Bradford sign the registrar with a few sweeping strokes.

He turned and held out the quill toward her.

Justine gently took the feather and approached the small oak table. Dipping the tip into the inkwell beside the registrar, she carefully and neatly scribed her full birth name beside his, fighting the trembling in her hand.

Sliding the quill back into the inkwell, she released a shaky breath as the old bishop gathered up the large book and congratulated them with a blessing. It was over. And no matter what Bradford's true intentions were in marrying her, it was done.

A firm gloved hand touched the side of her arm. She jumped and whirled toward Bradford, who lingered behind her.

He leaned in, bringing with him the alluring

scent of sweet cigars and heated sandalwood. "You look very pretty." His gaze swept toward her lips before trailing back up and meeting her eyes again. "Give me your lips."

She sucked in a breath. He wanted to kiss her? *Now?* Before the bishop? That simply wasn't done. Even she knew that. "I prefer you ravage me later." She paused. Then cringed. For she hardly wanted to say the word *ravage* in church, let alone before the bishop.

Bradford straightened and stared down at her with penetrating dark eyes, as if he weren't in any way pleased she had opposed his request.

Her pulse surged, realizing she had not only challenged her own husband, but had done so before the bishop, who was still in the room listening.

Bradford stepped back and readjusted the sleeves of his coat. "As you wish," he replied tersely. "I should probably inform you I did not make any arrangements for a wedding breakfast. I simply don't want to entertain and seek to spend as much time with you as possible. I will be waiting outside by the carriage to take you home." He gave her and the bishop a curt nod, turned and strode out of the small side room.

The bishop rounded the table he'd been loitering behind and eyed her, his full, round face visibly flushed to the tips of his ears touching his dome cap. Setting his wobbling chin high, he wordlessly breezed out of the room, his robes rustling as he tucked the registrar beneath his arm.

Justine released the breath she'd been holding and steadied her shaky limbs by gripping the oak table behind her. Bradford was already taking her home. For heaven's sake, even in the Lord's house, it seemed all her new husband could think about was, as he had so crudely put it, sex.

May the Lord have mercy upon more than her soul, for she had a bizarre inkling that being married to him was going to be like keeping a rhinoceros for a pet. A rhinoceros in heat, that was.

SCANDAL FIVE

Refrain from ever questioning a man's intentions toward you or any other lady, because most of the time, the poor dear doesn't even understand what those intentions are himself.

How to Avoid a Scandal, Author Unknown

The Bradford House. That evening

JUSTINE STOOD STIFFLY, lingering beside the hip bath she'd just emerged from, whilst her lady's maid, *Henri,* patted her naked limbs dry with soft towels. With pursed lips, the man turned and plucked up an ivory chemise, then turned back and pulled it over her head and down the length of her body.

Although Henri was young, very pleasant, and moved and spoke like a refined lady in male clothing, she confessed it was still rather awkward having him for a lady's maid. Her mother, not to mention all of England, would have been appalled knowing a man who wasn't her husband was tending to her naked body.

Henri shoved the curling ends of his blond hair away from his large blue eyes and stepped back, scanning the length of her. "I suggest we not fuss, Your Grace. A chemise is elegant and will put less between you and His Grace. *Oui?*"

"Uh...*oui.*"

"Bien." Henri whisked toward the vanity in the far corner of her new bedchamber and enthusiastically patted the verdant cushioned seat before it. "Come. His Grace has asked that you be ready within the hour."

Justine let out a shaky breath and made her way over to the backless chair. She sat, and her eyes visibly widened at seeing her own reflection. Her chestnut hair was piled high onto her head, her round breasts and darkened nipples, along with everything else belonging to her nude body, were fully visible through the sheer mulsin chemise Henri had chosen. With some curiosity, she realized that she barely had the urge to cover said breasts with both hands in front of Henri. He projected a friendly, businesslike air, as if performing a great duty to humanity.

So Justine opted to bite her lip instead and purposefully stared up toward the ceiling as Henri pulled out the ivory pins from her hair one by one. Her hair slid and all tumbled down.

Henri moved behind her and swept up her silver-handled brush from the vanity before her. He gathered her hair in sections, brushing those sections one by one. "Might Henri confess something bold, Your Grace?" he asked between brush strokes. "Something I hope will not offend you."

Justine set her chin and continued to stare blankly toward the ceiling, hoping he wasn't going to point out how small her breasts were. "I don't easily offend, Henri. Feel free to say or ask me anything."

Henri released her hair and leaned toward her from behind. "Tell Lord Marwood Henri spits upon those who do not appreciate his genius."

Justine snapped her gaze down to the mirror and stared at the reflection of the slender man hovering behind her. "Pardon?"

Henri's sparkling blue eyes caught hers in the mirror. As if afraid someone might hear, he leaned in even closer and whispered, "His observations give hope. Perhaps one glorious day men will not be unjustly hanged for the desires they are born with. After all, if a female chimpanzee, created by God and unaffected by the sins of humans, feels no shame when it pleasures another female chimpanzee, then what shame should exist if two men or two women choose to pleasure each other in a consensual manner? *Oui?*"

Justine's breath hitched as she slowly turned to Henri. No one had ever professed to her they had actually read her father's observations, let alone confessed finding any value in his work.

Catching Henri's soft, large hand, she squeezed it lovingly. "So you have read his observations?"

Henri let out an impish laugh and leaned closer, his shaven, boyish face lingering. "*Mais, oui.* It was well worth every shilling of the ten. My respect knows no bounds."

Justine's chest tightened as she brought Henri's hand to her lips and kissed it. "I thank you for your kind words. As does my father who dedicated eleven years of his life to it. It means the world to me. To us."

Henri yanked his hand away from hers and tsked. "Tut. I should be kissing *your* hand." He made a circle above her head with a finger. "Turn. We must finish or His Grace will toss me and it is back to France for me."

Justine grinned and turned back to the mirror. "His Grace would never dare."

CLEAN AND COIFFED and more than ready for her husband, Justine nestled back against the verdant embroidered pillows set atop her massive mahogany bed. Though everything in Bradford's home was needlessly large, expensive and imposing, she was grateful for all the male servants who made her feel welcome and at home.

Knowing there wasn't much time left before Bradford visited, Justine snatched up her book, *How To Avoid A Scandal,* from beneath her pillow and hurriedly paged through it remembering there had been something pertaining to the subject of the bedchamber. Albeit brief.

She paused and stared blankly at what was indeed a disappointing single page. With no illustrations to assist, she prayed the author would mention something about the position in which the wife was to present herself. Because she really didn't want to do it bent over and rear out, like a waiting sheep or goat or horse or cattle as had been illustrated in her father's book over and over and over again. She knew what went where, and that it resulted in pleasure for both the male and female, but there had to be a better position than that.

Justine shifted beneath the coverlet and squinted at the lettering, determined to memorize whatever she possibly could.

As a new wife, various duties await. Especially duties involving the siring of children. By having no expectations, this author can assure you, those duties will lead to far less disappointment. Whilst some men do understand the needs of a woman, sadly, many do not. The likelihood is that your husband has the sensitivity of a brick. All you can do is encourage him to be gentle. I also recommend you only allow for him to lift what little of your night clothing is necessary. Nudity, after all, will only rile more aggression, which can be very tedious depending upon his stamina and level of experience. You will know when he is done, when he shows no further interest. Apply a cool, moistened cloth against the affected area as it will ensure less irritation and soreness and prepare you for the next encounter. Each encounter should become less tedious, although this author cannot readily promise that.

It was a good thing animals didn't know how to read, or extinction would have been imminent for all. She shook her head side to side. Useless was what this book was. Absolutely useless. She should have asked her father about more creative positions to assume when she'd had the chance.

Exasperated, Justine slapped the book shut and shoved it beneath her pillow. She yanked the thick coverlet further up her body, covering up more of her chemise, and shivered. Her skin was still moist from the rosewater bath Henri had earlier drawn.

Footsteps echoed from outside her door. She froze, knowing they were Bradford's.

Her heart pounded as she eyed the closed oak-paneled door. This was it. She was finally going to join the rest of the animal kingdom and glory in it.

There was a curt knock. "Might I enter?" he asked in a cool, civil tone.

At least he didn't pounce in like a famished jackal. Though that might have actually been more exciting.

"You may," she called back.

The door opened and the candles within the bedchamber wavered, shifting light and shadows across the length of the cream walls.

Bradford's large frame lingered in the doorway.

She wet her lips, realizing the man wore only a long, green brocaded robe and hadn't even bothered to place slippers on his bare feet. His chest, which was exposed by the open flap of the robe, displayed dark curling hairs.

He stared at her with a raw intensity that made her stomach flutter and squeeze in marvelous anticipation.

His dark eyes never left hers as he stepped into the room and banged the door shut behind him.

She jumped and bit back a nervous little giggle. It was as if the man were making it known to every servant in the house that they were about to consummate their marriage. She sank deeper against the bed, her fingers fidgeting against the satin fabric of the coverlet. No more dreaming, no more wondering.

Only doing.

He approached slowly, the floorboards protesting beneath the weight of every movement he made. His continued silence, given what they were about to do, unnerved her a tad as she had no idea what he was feeling. Or thinking. The only thing she did know was that he wanted to do this. Just as she wanted to do this.

He towered beside the bed. And lingered. "We don't have to do this tonight."

She blinked and sat up. Was he daft? "I've waited two whole years for you to marry me and I am not about to wait another night to collect what is rightfully owed me."

Knowing there was no sense in letting him take the lead in this, as he clearly was reluctant, she decided to assume the one position she did know would please him. For if there was any man closer to a wild animal, it most certainly was Bradford.

She lowered the coverlet down to her lap,

painfully aware that her breasts were visible through the sheer fabric of her chemise, and scooted out from beneath the coverlet toward him. She tried to ignore his heated stare as she crawled to the edge of the bed where he stood.

She turned, on all fours, and presented him promptly with her backside. She let out a shaky breath with a mix of anxiety and excitement. "Have at it."

There was a moment of complete silence.

She paused and glanced over her shoulder.

Bradford stood there quietly, his hands tightly fisted, and his eyes affixed to her backside. "Uh…" He winced as he cleared his throat. "I would prefer we not do it that way."

Embarrassed, she turned and plopped herself down onto her derrière. "I didn't realize my backside was that unattractive," she grumbled.

He let out a strained laugh, his face flushing. "Far from it. I am the luckiest bastard alive."

Her cheeks grew unbearably hot. "Well, then, what is it?"

His eyes captured hers. "With this being your first encounter, and my first in eight months, I recommend a different…position. I want this to be a pleasurable as well as memorable experience for both of us." He moved even closer to where she sat.

His eyes flicked over her breasts with blatant admiration as he gestured to the edge of the mattress before him, bidding her to come closer. "There is no need to be nervous. I can assure you, as of right now, I am far more nervous than you are. For this night will determine what we both can expect from here on out."

Oh, dear. She swallowed and hoped she didn't disappoint him. Covering her breasts, she slid herself toward him, her chemise twisting and bundling up her bare legs. She settled before him and quickly shoved her chemise back down onto her legs which dangled off the edge of the bed.

Ever so gently, as if she were made of rose petals, Bradford placed his large hands on each side of her thighs and leaned into her, the scent of crisp soap and mint hair tonic floating around her, drugging her into complete submission. His large hands were overly warm, almost hot as they seared straight through the thin muslin of her chemise and burned the skin hidden beneath.

Her heart pounded hard in a mixture of anxiety and arousal, which she was quite certain not only Bradford could hear, but all of London, as well.

He met her gaze. "Might I lift your chemise?"

How charming. The man planned on getting right to it. She smiled shyly and half nodded.

Lowering his gaze to where his hands were, he slid the material of her chemise up, causing the feathery movement to prickle her skin until her lower waist was completely exposed. Cool air lapped against her heated thighs.

He wet his lips, scanning everything he'd uncovered, then met her gaze. "Spread those beautiful limbs, and above all, relax."

The rustle of the cool linen against the movement of her spreading legs seemed to be the only thing she could hear aside from her own breath. The moisture between her thighs increased in anticipation. To finally have him like this was intoxicating.

With a grace that revealed more experience than she cared to acknowledge, he stepped into the space he'd created and slid his large hands toward her backside.

Firmly gripping her buttocks, he lifted her, then yanked her toward his body and up against his solid thighs, closing off whatever gap had been left between them.

He kissed her forehead, softly here and softly there, lingering with his lips, leaving a trail of velvet warmth against her skin. In that moment, she felt lighter than air. Nothing mattered. Nothing but him and nothing but this.

His warm hands slid firmly and purposefully beneath her chemise and rounded from her back up toward her breasts. He grazed them, circling her nipples with his thumbs, causing them to harden.

She shivered at the thrill of his touch and wondered how she had ever survived without it all this time.

He drew in a harsh breath, causing his chest to notably rise and expand before her, then pinched her breasts so hard, an astonished gasp tore from her lips.

Pain throbbed against her nipples as her eyes flew up to his. "What are you…*that hurt.*"

He shifted his tight jaw, his body and eyes fully dominating hers. Ever so tenderly, he massaged her nipples and breasts, drawing out the throbbing sting. "Forgive me. Some women like that."

She snorted. "Lest you forget, this is my first time and my tastes will most likely be different."

"I…won't do it again."

"Good." She smiled for him, hoping to demonstrate that her breasts were fine and that he could continue.

He smiled in turn and frilled his knuckles down the length of her stomach. His hands paused right at the curling hair between her thighs. She spread her legs further apart, wordlessly encouraging him to penetrate her. To make her his.

He leaned in and whispered into her ear, "Open your mouth to me."

Her breath hitched in her throat, and her mind blanked as he captured her mouth, forcing her lips open with a hot, wet, roaming tongue. Justine froze against him, her eyes stark wide at the realization she was actually being kissed by Bradford, and that his tongue was erotically circling against hers. It was their first kiss.

The room spun and fell over on its side as her heart thundered in her ears. Unable to focus on anything but his incredible kiss, her eyes fluttered closed. She moved her tongue more forcibly against his and gave in to her own rising need to take more and feel more of him.

His mouth pressed harder against hers as his hands roamed her backside and waist, demanding she give even more. His tongue slid alongside her inner cheek, glided against her teeth and the sides of her tongue.

Needing to touch every part of him, she blindly slid her hands beneath his robe, rounding his smooth broad shoulders, desperately wanting to feel him against her palms and confirm that this was in fact real. That she was kissing and touching him and that he was hers, all hers.

She slid her hands lower, down to his smooth, muscled stomach and boldly drifted toward his erection hidden in the soft folds of his robe.

His muscles tensed beneath her wandering touch. He groaned and yanked his mouth away from hers, leaving it cool and moist. "No. Enough. None of that."

Her eyes popped open, realizing their kiss had already ended. And not as she'd expected. She tried to catch her breath, even though her lips and her face burned like fire. "What is it?"

"It isn't you. I—" He heaved out a heavy breath and lowered his gaze to where his hands were on her thighs. His fingers spread the folds of her sex. Her entire body quivered as his finger slipped between them and entered her body.

"God. Justine." He leaned in once again and captured her lips, clearly unable to stay away. A guttural groan escaped him as he sucked her tongue savagely deep into his mouth, astonishing her. Her tongue was kept firmly locked within his wet mouth as he fully slid his finger deep into her. She moaned against him as he further penetrated her with his finger.

He released the aching suction he held on her

tongue and further pushed his finger against her virginal tightness, causing a slight pinch. She stiffened.

With his finger still buried deep within her, his thumb rubbed at the upper tip of her opening. Slow, firm and steady.

Heart-pounding sensations rose up through her stomach and drifted back down the length of her legs. She gasped, realizing he was pleasuring her in the manner she had secretly pleasured herself whenever thinking about him.

He watched her intently and increased the stroking of his thumb. His stroke quickened, causing her breath to quicken in turn. Her body stiffened from the soaring sensations overwhelming her.

"Have you ever done this to yourself?" he whispered, leaning in closer.

"Yes," she choked out. Her cheeks burned at the unexpected confession he had so easily pried from her lips.

"Who taught you?" he insisted, his finger quickening.

She panted, focusing on the delectable sensations overtaking her very breath. "I…taught myself. It wasn't all that…difficult to learn."

"Has anyone ever touched you this way?" he demanded.

"N-no." She grabbed hold of his arms, which were thick and muscled beneath the soft velvet of his robe, and squeezed them as she openly rode his hand, wanting more. She gasped, whimpered and panted as he rubbed and flicked, rubbed and flicked.

"Show me how much you enjoy my touch." His gaze dominated hers all the while, letting her know that he was very much aware of what he was doing.

She rode his hand faster, harder, trying to keep up, needing more of what he was boldly offering.

He leaned closer, burying his chin firmly into her hair, all the while rubbing faster.

She pressed her cheek against the smooth warmth of his tight, muscled chest and dug her fingers into his arms. All of her sensations suddenly expanded, and, though she bit her lip, trying to hold back an agonizing moan, she failed.

Her hips bucked against his hand, and she threw her head back and away from his chest as she arched her body. Her muscles clenched in rhythmic bursts as she rocked back and forth, not wanting the explosive sensation to ever stop.

He continued to hold her firmly in place, fingering her relentlessly until she could do nothing but cry out again and again and again.

Eventually the blinding moments of bliss subsided. As did the movement of his thumb. His finger, which was still deep within her, slowly slipped out. His now damp fingers dug into the sides of her exposed thighs and pressed against her skin with silent urgency.

With her chest still heaving, she leveled her head and stared up at him, more than ready for all of him.

He skimmed his large hands down the sides of her thighs toward her knees, all the while lingering. He rubbed her skin softly, in perfect sensual circles, intently watching his own hands move.

She spread her legs wider and leaned slightly back, meeting his gaze and tauntingly inviting him.

Tightening his jaw, he shoved her back hard, causing her to gasp as his solid weight climbed on top of her, crushing the breath out of her chest. She gasped again, unable to breathe, as his muscled body shifted and his thick erection brushed her leg.

He paused and met her wide gaze. He scrambled off her and the bed, his chest heaving. He adjusted his robe to cover himself. "I didn't mean to do that."

He stepped farther back, the protruding thick

line of his penis pressing against the robe draping his body. "Forgive me. I cannot do this. Not tonight. Good night."

He turned and strode toward the door.

She sat up in bewilderment, still breathing heavily in an effort to draw in the air he'd pushed out. "There is no need for you to go. I can forgive a little aggression, Bradford, especially if you're aware of it. I am not made of porcelain."

Bradford paused beside the door and glanced over his shoulder, presenting that mangled, scarred side. His dark hair slid into his eyes from the movement.

She could sense his reluctance to leave. The tension in his broad back and stiff stance more than alluded to it.

"No. I am not prepared to engage you." With that, he yanked open the door and stepped out, shutting it behind him. His steps retreated until they ceased to exist.

Justine blinked. When was a man not prepared to engage a woman? Drat him. He'd left her a virgin. On her own wedding night. So much for hourly performances! She'd be fortunate to get one with the way he reacted.

She crawled across the expanse of the large mattress, grabbed hold of the coverlet he had earlier thrown aside and pulled it over her body, burying herself beneath its comforting warmth.

She stared up at the red velvet canopy of the four-poster bed, listening to the humming silence. Silly as it was, she considered writing to the editors of *How to Avoid a Scandal* and insist they include a bit more accurate information pertaining to matters involving the bedchamber. For the book was seriously misleading every single woman in London. But then again, given the taste she'd just received, if every debutante realized just how wonderful copulation truly was, there wouldn't be a single virgin left in England.

SCANDAL SIX

Do not give in to the slightest of temptation,
unless, of course, you possess the mind and the
heart of a saint, which, we all know, you do not.
How to Avoid a Scandal, Author Unknown

HIS OBSESSION WAS going to be the death of him.

Radcliff slammed the door of his bedchamber
shut, the few candles around him flickering from
the action, and bolted it. He leaned against the door
for a moment, eyes closed, picturing Justine at the
height of ecstasy.

Sweat beaded his skin as he fought the trembling
within his body. He had to. This once. Otherwise
he'd never survive the night.

Hissing out a breath, he leaned against the oak-
paneled door, and reached beneath the folds of his
robe. Deliberately using the same hand that had
touched Justine, he repeatedly rubbed the soft head
of his cock, each rapid jerk of his hand causing his
core to tighten with the anticipation of release. A

release he hadn't allowed himself to experience in eight months.

His breath caught in his throat as Justine's whimpers and gasps echoed within his mind. The way her soft, perfect body had rocked back and forth against his hand slowly stripped the last of his thoughts.

He groaned, his own pleasure escaping his lips. Though he had mindlessly wanted to consummate their marriage, he knew by the way he had almost taken her by force, he wasn't physically prepared. As a virgin, she deserved tenderness and patience. Something he had yet to master, considering every time he engaged his obsession, his need and desire grew in demand. The less he engaged her, the better off they would both be.

Radcliff envisioned his cock slamming deep into Justine's sleek, tight, hot wetness, her full breasts bouncing with each solid plunge. He licked his lips, stroking faster. They would have to consummate their marriage, he knew. But he needed to learn more self-control before he allowed that to happen. And until then, pleasuring himself would have to do.

He groaned again and grew unbearably hard. He jerked harder, needing to release the guilt, the pleasure and the raw emotions buried deep within him.

His heart thundered, his body stiffened, and his heavy cock pulsed, spurting the wet warmth of his seed against his hand. He threw his head back as wave after wave rippled through him, giving him the mindless pleasure he'd denied himself all these months.

But the climax ebbed too soon. Knees weak, he sank against the door, pressing his forehead to the cool, hard wood. When? When would it ever be enough? For he already wanted to return to that moment of climax.

His shoulders slumped. He always did. It was what drove his obsession. He'd barely spent himself before the emptiness, the need, urged him to seek pleasure again.

Swiping his hand against his robe in a disgusted attempt to remove his seed, he slowly made his way toward his bed, exhausted, not wanting to think about anything.

Yet thoughts of Justine's beautiful naked body and the feel of her warm, wet quim against his fingers kept assaulting him. Over and over. The urge to storm back into her room and mount her by force from the backside as she had originally suggested steadily rose within his chest.

A knock came to the door.

He swung around. "Who is it?"

"Your Grace," the butler called from the other side.

Radcliff blew out a relieved breath, forcing his shoulders to relax. Thank bloody God it was only Jefferson. Adjusting his robe, he strode back toward the door, unbolted it and yanked it open. "What is it?" He blinked, glancing down at the sealed parchment being held out toward him.

"This was just delivered with the request that it be read and responded to at once." Jefferson, still in full livery, brought the glass lantern he held with his other hand to better display the letter. A red wax imprinted with his brother's crest glistened on the flap.

Radcliff stared at it in disbelief. It was the first time Carlton had ever contacted him since storming into his home and blaming him for what had happened to Matilda. And though Radcliff wanted to burn it and disregard any more pointless words, he knew his curiosity would not allow for it. He had to know what it said.

Slipping the letter from his butler's hand, Radcliff hesitated, then cracked the seal apart. He unfolded the parchment and leaned toward the lantern Jefferson held up. His brows rose. The letter hadn't been scribed by Carlton, but rather, Carlton's mistress…*Matilda*.

> Your Grace,
> There is not a single day that goes by that I do not think of you and the amount of suffering you have endured on my behalf. I must admit that since the night of my assault, Carlton has been very difficult to contend with. And now, more so than ever. Though I have stayed all these months, due to my delicate state, I simply cannot justify another night. I do not wish to evoke pity, but there is no one left for me to trust. No one. I require money and a place to stay until I can better situate myself. Please call upon me at 14 Craven Street, if you are able. God bless.
> Ever your dearest friend,
> Matilda Thurlow

How fated it was indeed that such a note would find him on his own wedding night. How he wished he could lock away the self-loathing that continued to rot within him. The self-loathing of knowing that he and he alone was responsible for the suffering Matilda had endured that night at the hands of six men. He swallowed. Although Matilda was the last person he wanted to see, he owed her what little she asked. For it had been his mindless pursuit of her that had ultimately led to not only his downfall, but hers.

Radcliff refolded the missive and shoved it at Jefferson. "Burn it. The moment you do, have a carriage waiting. If anytime during my absence my wife—" how bizarre to think he had one "—should inquire about my whereabouts, inform her that I do not wish to be disturbed until morning. Is that understood?"

"Yes, Your Grace." Jefferson bowed, turned and disappeared down the corridor.

Radcliff stalked into his room, stripping off his robe, and whipped it to the floor. Knowing what Carlton was capable of, he downright dreaded discovering the state Matilda was in.

He quickly dressed, adjusted and buttoned everything, and shoved his feet into his boots. Striding over to the large mirror set above the mahogany sideboard, he washed his hands and splashed cool water on his face from the basin, the lingering scent of Justine's pleasure mingling with his.

He paused and stared at his reflection as water dripped from his chin. Black eyes stared back at him, as if he were a stranger to himself. Which he was.

He once had a good, handsome face. A face that had only poisoned every aspect of his life and brought more women to his side than he ever knew what to do with. Now, it seemed he didn't even know what to do with himself anymore.

SCANDAL SEVEN

Only heathens call upon brothels. It is best to avoid such men at every turn, for once a heathen, always a heathen.

How to Avoid a Scandal, Author Unknown

14 Craven Street
Half past ten that night

RADCLIFF ADJUSTED HIS HOOD more securely around his head in an effort to not only draw away attention from his scarred appearance, but shield himself from the world he'd vowed never to be part of again. He silently walked past the row of closed doors and intently followed the plump, older woman who led him down a long passageway of unevenly papered tawny walls adorned with yellowing, nude prints.

The heavy, stagnant smell of sweat, sex and urine penetrated his nostrils, causing his throat to clench. Every moan and movement behind those closed doors reminded him all too well of the animal he'd once been. Of the animal he still in some ways was.

The madam leading him eventually paused at the end of the corridor, lingering before the last closed door, and gestured toward it. "In there."

Radcliff withdrew a gold sovereign from his pocket, held it up for her by the tips of his black-gloved fingers, then took hold of her hand and pressed it into her palm. "For your silence."

The woman closed her pale, veined hand around the sovereign without meeting his gaze, gave a curt nod and whisked past.

Radcliff hesitated, eyeing the closed door, and mentally prepared himself. The last time he'd seen Matilda had been that night. That night when his face and his life—not to mention hers—had forever changed. He drew in a deep breath and let it back out. He could do this. Opening the door, he stepped inside, closing it behind himself.

The glow from an oil lamp set on a small side table was more than enough light for him to make out ivory-and-burgundy-flowered wallpaper. And there, in a large oak bed set against the right side of the wall, tucked beneath linen, sat his brother's mistress. Matilda Thurlow herself.

Radcliff closed the distance, his boots echoing within the emptiness of the room, and paused beside the bed. He stared down at her in complete disbelief.

Dark blue-and-yellow flesh bloomed around sections of Matilda's jaw as she stared up at him with astonished gray-azure eyes. Thick, tangled blond hair clung to the sides of her face.

His gaze dropped to her hands which rested protectively upon the rounded top of a large, pregnant belly. He'd heard the rumors, whilst in seclusion, that Matilda was carrying his brother's child, but for her sake, had hoped they were not true.

What was as disturbing as her appearance was her taking refuge in the same brothel she'd once serviced before Carlton had decided he wanted her for his mistress. Did she have no other place to go? And no one else to turn to?

Matilda shifted into a better sitting position and stared at him in both horror and pity. She'd never seen the full extent of what had happened to him. He'd never wanted her to feel any more guilt than Carlton had already imposed upon her.

"Those savages," she whispered, still staring up at him. "They destroyed you. They destroyed your face."

As if he didn't know.

"I… Forgive me, Bradford. I am to blame for all

of this. I should have never followed you that night. I should have never sought to engage you."

"It wasn't your goddamn fault," he snapped, agitated she would even think to blame herself.

She scooted closer toward the wall, the frayed yellowing linen pooling down onto her lap, exposing more of her plain, beige gown. With shaky hands, she smoothed her hair around the sides of her pale, bruised face. "You and I make quite the pair."

Son of a bitch. There really was no mercy in this world, was there? He dropped onto the mattress beside her and shoved his hood back. "Why in God's name are you here, given your tender state? Have you no other place to go? I thought you had a sister. Why aren't you with her?"

She shrugged but said nothing.

Agitated by her silence, he waved a hand toward her face. "Who did this? Carlton?"

She drew in a harsh, shaky breath and then released a soft, heartbreaking sob as she pushed out a breath. Tears slowly streaked down the sides of her bruised face as she looked away. "Yes."

"Shit." He knew his brother to be a good many things, but this? "Has he done this to you before?"

Her lips trembled as more tears spilled down her

cheeks. "No. He hasn't. I...I cannot help but feel as if that night...when those men..." She squeezed her eyes shut, shaking her head, then reopened her eyes. "It affected Carlton. I grew tired of arguing with him about it, day after day. I grew tired of constantly defending myself against his accusations as to why I followed you that night. Even worse, he doesn't think the child is his. And in the end, he may be right. Because how would I know after what was done to me? For all those reasons and more, I informed him this past week that I didn't want to be his mistress anymore. And needless to say, he repaid me for it."

Radcliff fought the impulse to smash his fist into the side wall. As if Matilda hadn't already been through enough.

He stood, struggling to remain calm. "Carlton is under the delusional belief that he has the right to do whatever he pleases. But you needn't worry about him. All you need worry about is retaining your strength for the birth of your child. I'm going to leave for a small while, but I promise to return with a doctor I trust. The same man who saw to my face. All I ask is that you stay here. Once the doctor approves of moving you, I will see to it you are given money and returned to your sister. You'll be safe with her."

She shook her head, almost violently. "No. I can't involve her in this. I can't. She's respectable. Nothing like me. She is married and has two children. I could never...no. No." She kept shaking her head. "Carlton cannot be trusted not to come after me. If I stay away from my sister, she'll be better off. I know she will."

So *that* was why she was here. Because she preferred to expose herself to harm than bring harm to the doorstep of the only family she had. "Noble though it may be to consider your sister, you are needlessly endangering yourself and your unborn child by staying here. Go to her, Matilda, and surround yourself with good people. You needn't worry about Carlton. I will see to him. I promise."

She sobbed again, lips still trembling, and shook her head. "No. He will only make life more difficult for me. And for my family. Please. I...I barely escaped."

He hissed out a breath. No one deserved this. He settled beside her on the bed again and firmly met her gaze, hoping to give her some measure of assurance and comfort. "Carlton will not contact you again. I swear it."

She was quiet for a long moment. Shakily reaching out, she caught his gloved hand with both of hers and brought it to her lips. "You are not like your brother, are you?"

She repeatedly kissed the top of his knuckles, as if she never meant to stop, then slid his gloved hand down toward her full breasts. "I don't belong to him anymore."

Radcliff sucked in a savage breath and yanked his hand up and away from her. He leaned back and adjusted his cloak around his shoulders. "For God's sake, woman, I am not seeking payment. I am assisting you because it is the right thing to do."

She blinked in astonishment. "I...thank you. I meant to call on you in person months ago, to thank you for what you did, but Carlton wouldn't allow it. I understand why he hates me, but I don't understand why he hates you. Please know that despite what Carlton thinks, you are not to blame for any of it. You were merely one against six. There was nothing more you could have done."

"No," Radcliff growled out. "I could have done more." He'd simply been so disgustingly inebriated that every blow he threw had slid and every step he took had swayed.

Matilda searched his face, lingering momentarily upon his scar. "You've always been so kind to me. Please. Won't you consider taking me as your mistress? I know you once wanted me."

Radcliff swallowed, remembering that all too well. It was what he once did. It was what he once was. He had wanted every beautiful woman. Even if that woman belonged to another man. Even if that woman belonged to his own brother.

"I'll not deny you, Bradford. Not ever again. If you want me, you can have me." She leaned toward him, offering up her full lips.

Radcliff choked and stumbled onto his booted feet. He stepped back and away from the bed. "Please. I am a married man."

She stared up at him, earlier tears still streaking her battered face. "You're...*married?*" She blinked rapidly, as if unable to comprehend it. "Why didn't Carlton tell me? Who did you marry? Do I know of her?"

"The details of my life should not concern you any more than they should concern Carlton."

She pinched her lips together, half nodded and glanced down at her oversize belly. She rubbed it gently. Lovingly. "All I ever wanted were the very things Carlton was never willing to offer. He made so many promises. So many."

She looked up again and intently met his gaze. "I have nothing. Which means this child will have nothing. Radcliff, please. I cannot depend on Carlton for anything. I beg of you. Provide for me and this child. Provide for us and I will give you everything you could ever want. Married men take mistresses all the time."

"Some men don't seek payment for the things they do. I will see to it you and the child are taken care of. For God's sake, Matilda, why do you continue to put yourself in these damn situations? Here you are, about to give birth, and yet you choose to hide amongst savages who only care about spilling their seed?"

She looked away and shrugged. "In some morbid way I feel more at home here than anywhere else. There are no pretenses I need to adhere to. I can be who I really am in the eyes of society—*nothing*. I used to have pride, Bradford. I used to be the daughter of a merchant. Now look at me. I hide from myself."

Yes. He himself was guilty of that.

She shook her head, then veered her gaze back to his face, an odd hope dancing in her eyes. "You must love this aristocratic wife of yours to deny me. Tell me. Is she everything you ever wanted in a woman? Was it a romantic wedding? With lots of flowers?"

"There were flowers, but I was too bloody

nervous to notice anything else. A man like me doesn't marry for love, Matilda. It suited me, is all. She suited me. I needed a good wife and have always found her to be attractive."

Matilda stared at him for an abashed moment, then narrowed her gaze. Gritting her teeth, she kicked her slippered foot toward him. "Is that all a woman will ever be to you and Carlton? Attractive? It is a shame, Bradford, that a woman should mean so little to you, as it does your brother. A shame. I think it is time for you to leave. I have decided not to make use of your assistance."

Radcliff rigidly pointed at her and stepped farther back. "I am not about to leave you like this. I have a conscience, despite what you or anyone else thinks. And if you so much as wander from this room or this brothel in your current state before I return with the doctor, I vow you'll regret that decision. Do you hear me?"

A sob escaped her as fresh tears rolled down her flushed cheeks. "Why does Carlton continue to punish me whilst refusing to let me go? I don't understand."

Jesus Christ. This was a nightmare. "I… Matilda. He wasn't always like this. He had a soul once. And I have not been the best sort of brother, imposing upon what mattered most to him. Which was you." He cleared his throat. "It's late. I should fetch the doctor. Promise me you'll stay right where you are. Promise me you will not leave."

She nodded and whispered, "I will not."

"Good girl. I shall return shortly." He yanked the hood up and over his head, turned and stalked out.

Just past midnight, long after delivering Matilda to her sister

RADCLIFF WASN'T SURPRISED to find Carlton's lavish abode filled to the ceiling with people the *ton* always avoided.

Pushing back the hood of his cloak, he strode by pompous, overdressed men and women smothered with perfumed oils that had lost their scents over the course of a long night spent dancing and drinking. Scents that were now giving way to the raw stench of sweat, heat and wine.

Radcliff paused within the gold-and-ivory-accented ballroom and scanned his candlelit surroundings, trying to find Carlton amongst the masses.

A few strides away, an older but very pretty dark-haired woman dressed in a stunning alabaster gown watched him with marked curiosity from behind her fluttering ostrich fan. Her sable eyes drifted across the length of him in a predatory manner before boldly meeting his gaze again. She smiled.

He smirked, amused she even thought him worthy. Perhaps his scar provided greater appeal to some women.

Her fan stilled. She lowered it and erotically ran the feathered tips of the fan across the rounded edges of her breasts. Her pink tongue darted out and disappeared back into her mouth as she wet her lips.

Radcliff's smirk faded and his chest tightened. He stepped back and away, her flirtation infringing upon his ability to breathe.

The sparkle in those dark eyes invited him to play as she slowly made her way toward him, her fan still tracing her breasts.

Radcliff drew in a shaky breath and let it out as he continued to move backward. He had no doubt he could whisk her into a corner somewhere in the back of the house and hitch up her skirts. For he knew that devious look all too well.

He seethed out a breath through his teeth and quickly turned. He pushed his way through the crowd, toward the direction of the dance floor, moving as fast as he could without startling those around him.

Sweat coated his skin as he kept moving and pushing forward, trying to ensure that the woman did not engage him. He knew once his obsession took hold, there was very little he could do. Fortunately, she did not follow.

He blew out an exhausted breath and focused on his surroundings. He was not here to bloody hunt for women.

He searched the crowded dance floor before him. Carlton's tall, muscled frame came in and out of view before him. The side of that rugged profile appeared and disappeared as his brother danced and moved among those around him. A young, attractive redhead draped in a mauve evening gown danced seamlessly alongside Carlton, pairing up with him whenever she could.

Radcliff tugged on the cuffs of his sleeves beneath his cloak and coat. It had been quite some time since he'd last seen the man. Almost eight months.

Watching Carlton engage in jovial festivities whilst Matilda suffered disgusted him. All he could do was quietly wait for the dance to end. The last thing he wanted was to cause an uproar on his own wedding night. A night which should have been spent in Justine's bed.

As he waited, watching the growing flirtation between Carlton and this red-haired beauty, he angrily flexed his gloved hands, opening and closing them. God save him from killing his own brother.

The orchestra finally ceased playing the set.

Carlton bent his dark head toward his coquette. She offered him a radiant curtsy with a saucy smile, then turned and sashayed toward a group of randy men who all broke out into competing raptures.

Carlton stared after the woman, then turned and strode closer, until their gazes locked.

Radcliff stiffened, the tension in his body coiling. Despite the mounting strain of anger within him, he managed to incline his head in a polite form of salutation.

His brother came to an abrupt halt and stared with piercing blue eyes no one in the Bradford family had ever borne. It was the only physical characteristic that separated their otherwise similar appearance. Aside from his scar, of course.

Carlton inclined his dark head.

Radcliff swept a gloved hand toward the direction of the doors leading out into the garden, but otherwise said nothing. His brother nodded, turned and set off in the direction he'd indicated.

Radcliff wove through the people around him, following Carlton to the other side of the room. He ignored the passing faces of those who openly gawked at him in response to not only his inappropriate attire but his scar, which had not been introduced to London until tonight. It was but the beginning of what he could expect for the rest of his days.

Carlton disappeared through the doors leading out onto the darkened terrace, and within moments, Radcliff joined him.

The light breeze of the summer night cooled his heated skin as he stepped out. Carlton walked farther into the garden, disappearing down the stone path into the darkness, away from the festivities.

Radcliff moved down the narrow, stone terrace stairs and strode across the garden path after him. He paused when a tall shadow appeared before him barely a few feet away.

Radcliff steadied his breathing, readying himself for the confrontation he'd been waiting for all night, and closed the distance between them in three swift strides.

Despite the darkness, he managed to grab hold of the lapels of Carlton's evening coat and yanked his brother's broad frame violently toward himself. "Have you seen Matilda? Have you seen what you bloody did to her?"

Carlton stiffened but otherwise did not attempt to move. "Has that whore run to you again?" he replied in an overly composed tone.

Radcliff released Carlton's clothing and seized his throat with a hand, digging every single tip of his gloved fingers deep into that windpipe. He willed himself not to squeeze and suffocate his own brother. "You could have killed her. And the child."

Carlton lifted his chin to expand his throat but otherwise did not struggle. "You are overreacting. She is fine."

Radcliff leaned in closer. "She is *not* fine. And rest assured, I haven't even reacted, you fucking bastard."

Carlton grabbed hold of Radcliff's hand, which still held his throat, and ripped it away in a solid forceful sweep. Carlton rigidly pointed at him and seethed out in a low, predatory tone, "Don't call me that. Don't ever call me that."

Ah, yes. It appeared, seventeen years after the truth had been revealed to both of them, Carlton still struggled to contend with who he really was.

A bastard.

They used to get along. Before their mother had pulled them out of Eton one winter day, merely to inform them that Carlton was a bastard and that she could not bear the guilt of knowing that their father, who had trusted and loved her so much, had died never knowing it.

Radcliff could only helplessly watch as their mother had suffered from a complete shattering of nerves brought on by guilt and loneliness. She had died shortly afterward, and their lives had been a mess ever since. A mess Radcliff had tried to assist his brother through, only to be pushed away every single time.

Carlton stared him down. "Aren't you supposed to be home shagging Justine?"

Radcliff narrowed his gaze and focused on the hazy outline of Carlton's shadowed face, trying hard to keep his fist from smashing straight through the man's skull. "She is officially Duchess to you, ingrate. You'd best remember to show her due respect and stay the hell away from her. Because I don't need another mess."

Carlton held up both gloved hands and gurgled out a laugh. "Do not insult what little remains between us. Unlike you, I'd never fuck the same hole my brother has. Frankly, the very thought of us crossing swords shrivels me. If only it shriveled you."

Radcliff hissed out a breath. "Nothing happened between Matilda and myself. Nothing. I refuse to apologize for something I did not do."

"Matilda would have never followed you that night if you hadn't insinuated interest," Carlton seethed through clenched teeth. "For the first time in my life I felt as if I finally had something you did not. But you had to rip away what little was mine and reduce me to what we both know I am—*nothing*. I suppose I really must be nothing if I can't even retain a mistress."

"What little you know. She was tired of your vile, empty promises. She was bound to move on whether it was with me or someone else." Radcliff shook his head, wishing he could somehow rid himself of all this lingering remorse. "I don't want to discuss this with you ever again. The only reason I even came here tonight was to ensure Matilda's safety. She has already been through enough. There is no need for you to further punish her."

Carlton boldly stepped toward him, their boots almost tip to tip. "So you came here tonight, uninvited, into *my* home to inform me as to what I can or cannot do with my own mistress? Sod you, Bradford. Sod. You. I am merely ensuring she never strays again. Because you and I both know what she really wanted that night when she followed you to that slum of a party. But instead of your prick ending up in her, it happened to be six others. As far as I'm concerned, she deserved it. Just as you deserved having your face carved up like the belly of a goose at Christmas. Because I know what would have happened between you and Matilda if those men hadn't accosted her. And that is why I loathe you. That is why I will always loathe you. Because you are only worth the length of your prick, and that, I can assure you, isn't very much."

Silence hung between them, thick as the thickest fog. Radcliff fisted his hands hard, feeling his heartbeat throbbing within them. "I deserve your wrath, Carlton, because you are right. I most likely would have engaged Matilda that night if I had known she was there. Despite that, one thing gives me peace. That I, Radcliff Edwin Morton, the fourth Duke of Bradford, actually have a few redeemable qualities left within me. Unlike you. Because no woman, no matter her sin, deserves to be raped and beaten by six men, and then further beaten and degraded by the man who claims to be devoted to her. You know absolutely nothing about devotion. You are only devoted to yourself and yourself alone."

His brother said nothing, merely stood there with his chest heaving.

"Carlton?" a woman called out from somewhere behind them. Slippered feet shuffled down the darkened path, coming closer.

Radcliff glanced over his shoulder toward the sound of rustling skirts. Someone had followed them into the garden.

Carlton sucked in a harsh breath.

Radcliff smirked, then leaned toward his brother. "It seems I am not the only one whose worth is about to be measured by the length of his prick."

"I suggest you leave."

"Gladly. In the meantime, stay the fuck away from Matilda, but more importantly, stay away from my wife. Otherwise, you will wish to whatever bones you have left within you that our mother never brought you into existence."

Radcliff yanked his hood back onto his head, burying himself within it, and turned. He stalked down the path and said to the woman brushing past, "Be aware, Madam, that your safety is at risk if you choose to associate with Carlton."

She paused, yet despite his warning, hurried on.

Radcliff shook his head and walked away. He couldn't save them all.

SCANDAL EIGHT

A wife should dutifully submit to her husband. At least every once in a while. It will make her life considerably easier, more tolerable and worthwhile.

How to Avoid a Scandal, Author Unknown

The following afternoon

AFTER TAKING BREAKFAST alone in silence, as well as afternoon tea in the drawing room alone without any sign of Bradford, Justine opted to drift in and out of each lavishly decorated room, trying to make sense of the life she had chosen. The soft rustling of her pale blue muslin gown was the only sound drifting around her.

She didn't know why she felt so inclined to look at everything Bradford owned. The value of his belongings meant nothing to her. All she truly sought amongst his furnishing and portraits and vases was an understanding as to the sort of man he really was. Yet nothing whispered to her of any truth, mostly because they were all superficial heirlooms of generations past.

She used to know who he was, or at least she thought she did, but sensed there was more to him than he had ever let on. She only hoped there was a way to expose the man who hid beneath that scarred veneer because she couldn't help but feel haunted not knowing what had happened to him.

She paused when she came across a set of closed double doors and lingered. Except for the occasional echoing steps of servants in the far distance as they carried out their daily duties, silence hummed.

Justine glanced down the empty corridor, ensuring that no one was watching her, then reached out and turned the knobs, expecting them to be locked.

To her surprise, the knobs moved.

She hesitated, then fanned the doors open and entered a sunlit oak-paneled room with lofty ceilings. She purposefully left the doors behind her open in case anyone happened upon her. She didn't want the servants or Bradford thinking she was poking about.

Justine paused in the middle of the large study. The wall on the far end of the room was lined from floor to ceiling with shelves and shelves of old, leather-bound books. Before those shelves sat a large mahogany desk whose pristine gleaming surface held stacks of papers and several glass inkwells and quills.

Her gaze fell upon the only painting to grace the room: a portrait just above the marble mantelpiece. She blinked up at the standing figure of a rosy-cheeked, beautiful dark-haired woman whose gloved hand was propped against a garden wall. She was dressed in a flowing daffodil gown, which barely allowed the tips of her white slippers to peer out.

Though the woman did not smile, her dark eyes stared at her with a shining playfulness that made Justine look back in silent awe. Bradford's mother. The last Duchess. The one she'd never met, as she had died many, many years ago, when Bradford was seventeen. Oddly, Bradford rarely spoke of her. Nor did he speak of his father, whose dashing portrait was in the corridor.

Justine tore her gaze away from the woman and walked over to Bradford's writing desk. Her hand slid along the smooth, gleaming surface as she rounded it, wondering how often Bradford had sat at this particular desk.

A large leather chair had been pulled away from the desk, waiting for someone to be seated. She sat, compelled to be part of a life she knew nothing of and felt rather small against the towering sides of the chair. She eyed the neat stacks of correspondences and noted how tidy everything was. Her father's writing desk had never been this tidy.

She dragged the chair over so as to sit closer to the desk and smiled saucily, wondering if she should write a letter to her parents and sign it with her new name—the Duchess of Bradford. Her mother would probably chide her for putting on airs.

Justine daintily reached across the desk, making sure not to touch anything she shouldn't, and slid an inkwell closer. She plucked up a quill from its bronzed stand, then took up a piece of parchment from the stack on the desk and set it squarely before her.

She was about to dip the tip of the quill into the inkwell when the double doors leading into the study creaked closed. Her gaze flew up, and to her surprise, Bradford strode toward her.

He was dressed meticulously in a perfectly cut gray morning coat, a brocaded waistcoat with brass buttons, and dark wool trousers that clung to his muscled legs. All topped off with a polished pair of black leather boots. She couldn't help but stare as he approached, mesmerized not only by how dashing he looked, but by the smooth movements of his large frame.

When he reached the writing desk, the only thing separating them, he leaned forward and planted his hands on the surface of the desk. He eyed the blank parchment she had set before herself. "Good afternoon."

She shoved the quill back into its bronze stand and scrambled to her feet, pushing back the over-size chair behind her. "My afternoon is indeed good now that you are here." She smiled. "I was beginning to wonder if I'd ever see you again. How are you?"

He merely shrugged.

"I was going to write a letter to my parents," she quickly went on. "Mind you, I could easily visit them, and plan to, but I thought—"

"There is no need to explain. I am very pleased to see you are settling in so well. That said, I have a few matters to tend to with my secretary before the end of the day. So I won't be about." He huffed out a breath and eyed her. "I wanted to apologize for my behavior last night. I should have stayed with you. I should have consummated our marriage. If it is your wish, as it is mine, come to my bed at nine. I will be waiting." He nodded, then pushed himself away from the desk and walked back toward the closed doors.

She blinked, her cheeks flushing. Dear God. Was this to be her life? One of limited conversations and fleeting midnight visits to each other's bedchambers depending upon his mood? She realized it was a marriage of convenience, but did it really need to be that convenient?

Justine rounded the desk and quickly made her way toward him. "I cannot help but feel as though you have been avoiding me. What is it? Did I do something wrong?"

He paused, then rigidly turned back toward her.

She swallowed and waited for him to say something. For the briefest of moments, she thought he would. Yet for some odd reason, he appeared unable to.

She threw up her hands in exasperation and let them drop back down to her sides. "Even a simple conversation about the weather would be pleasantly tolerable. Anything aside from this silence. I loathe to say it, Bradford, but we've barely been married a day and I am already concerned about the direction of this marriage. What happened to the charming rogue who used to banter with me only months ago?"

His brows rose as if intrigued by her sentiment. He fully turned, then strode back toward her, closing the space between them until the tips of his polished leather boots touched the outer hem of her gown.

Though he still said nothing, in that moment, he didn't need to. For his black, penetrating eyes said it all. They held the same raw need she had witnessed the night before, when he had entered her bedchamber and relentlessly touched the softness between her thighs until she had melted beneath his hands into blazing oblivion.

She wet her lips. "I refuse to be neglected."

"Whilst I refuse to let you think you are being neglected. Come here." He reached out and effortlessly swept her up into his arms and carried her over to the desk.

Her heart flipped at the unexpected display of affection. She grabbed hold of the lapels on his coat and with a lopsided grin said, "My, aren't we dashing."

"I try." He smiled as his muscled arms crushed her even more against his broad, hard chest, forcing her to feel not only the heat of his body, but every contour of it.

Setting her atop the edge of the desk where her slippered feet dangled over the edge, he swiftly went around to all the windows. One by one, he yanked the curtains shut, until they were enclosed in low light.

Her eyes widened as she watched him stride back toward her. What on earth did he intend to do? That? Here? Now? Oh, dear. She wanted to, yes, but not…now. No. No, no, no. Not in the study. Not with all the servants running about.

He paused before her, lingering. "If I may be so bold, I think you look very beautiful today."

"I…do?"

"Yes. You do."

She offered up a nervous smile and repeatedly smoothed the front of her gown, not knowing how she should respond. She'd never had anyone tell her she was beautiful. Pretty, yes. But not beautiful.

He leaned closer, the crisp scent of mint from his hair tonic teasing her senses. "Might I ask where you got this particular dress?"

She blinked. Why, if she didn't know any better, she'd say her husband was trying to have a conversation. 'Twas a boring conversation, but it nonetheless qualified. "Well," she offered, "when I first came to London and had the fashion sense of a crocodile, someone recommended this fabulous shop on Regent Street. The Nightingale. Have you heard of it?"

He smirked. "No. I don't usually wear female clothing."

She laughed. "And there is no reason you should. You look very dashing as you are. The Nightingale is where I bought this gown last year. For my first season. I could only afford this one, seeing they are terribly expensive, and with my father's yearly annuity being what it is, I preferred a more inexpensive means of filling my wardrobe."

"Your days of settling are over, dearest. I suggest we purchase this shop's entire inventory. It is obvious they know what the hell they are doing."

She rolled her eyes. "I don't need their entire inventory."

"I say you do. I also say we should arrange it as quickly as possible so that I may benefit. We've yet to make an appearance in society as husband and wife, and what better way to do it than on Regent Street whilst shopping?"

She beamed. "You wish to make an appearance with me?"

His brows came together. "But of course I do. It is my intention to make every man in London heave with envy. In the meantime, I've decided to change my meeting and spend this afternoon with you. What do you say to that?"

He dropped his gaze to her lap, wet his lips and

slid his large hands down the sides of her muslin gown. He fisted the material, gathering up the layers of her gown, and slowly dragged it up the length of her dangling legs. The movement playfully caressed her stockinged legs and thighs.

Her senses pulsed in yearning.

The fabric of her gown slid higher, and his steamy gaze slowly lifted, scandalously caressing not just her skin but her soul. He leaned toward her and whispered, "I wish to ensure my wife never feels neglected. Not ever again."

He firmly pressed his lips to the side of her exposed neck. Her breath caught. His hot tongue flicked across her skin, then tauntingly traced the hollow of her neck.

The entire room swayed and she along with it. Even though she ached to give in to him, she didn't want to engage him in this way.

She gently pushed at his chest, causing his lips to break away from her heated skin. She raised a brow and held her hands against his chest, trying to hold him in place. "Later, you ruffian, you. Tonight. In your room."

He removed her hands from his chest, setting them back at her sides, and leaned in again. "Tonight? Why? You were just complaining about being neglected."

She let out a nervous laugh. "I wasn't complaining about that sort of neglect, Bradford. I was referring to the lack of words exchanged between us."

He leaned in and licked her lower lip. "Words mean nothing to me, Justine, and will only lead us astray. I prefer witnessing what your body has to say. Because that, I know, is real."

God save her, he was in some way right. But she also knew physicality would never fill the space of the words she sought. A duchess also had a duty not to look like a wanton in front of her servants, which would only carry itself outside of the house.

She leaned as far back against the desk as her corset and gown would allow. "Bradford, I prefer we—"

"Don't call me Bradford." His hands rubbed her exposed thighs. "You are my wife. Call me Radcliff."

"Uh…Radcliff?" she prodded, wishing he'd stop distracting her so much with his hands.

"Yes?" He closed the space she'd created, his hands sliding up and down the length of her legs, causing her skin to tingle.

She swallowed, trying to fight the urge to throw him onto the desk herself, but knew a duchess ought to have a little more self-control than that. "I prefer we wait until tonight. In the meantime,

I was hoping we could get to know one another better."

He leaned in and flicked his tongue across her earlobe. "I thought we already knew each other," he whispered. "Very well. Now cease this. Cease resisting me."

She swayed against his body, her hands gripping his shoulders. "I want this. I do, but—"

His hands jerked her skirts up higher, above her knees, causing her to jump. "Then fuck me," he growled. "Fuck me, or by God, I will take you by force."

Her heart skittered. She shoved his hands away, yanked her skirts back down and glared at him. "You most certainly won't be taking me by force or using that sort of language. I'm merely trying to get to know you, is all. Before we forget what is important."

"This *is* important." He leaned in again and slid his tongue down the length of her neck, toward her breasts and dipped it between the valley tucked beneath her neckline.

She gasped against the melting sensations and grabbed hold of his broad shoulders to steady herself. "You aren't being…fair. I am desperately trying to converse with you, Bradford."

"Radcliff. The name is Radcliff." He lowered his

head and nipped at the upper sleeve of her gown, as his warm hands circled in between her thighs. "I eagerly await our conversation, Duchess. All I ask is that you limit it to fifteen minutes."

She let out a nervous laugh. "That doesn't leave us much time."

His brows went up. "Then you had best make use of your time."

She wet her lips and grounded her thoughts, focusing on what it was she'd been longing to know all along. "Forgive me for being forward, but…you never answered me that night when I had asked about your scar. It haunts me knowing only muddled whispers. Won't you tell me what happened?"

His hands stilled. He lifted his dark head from her shoulder, but refused to look at her. The material of her gown, which he'd held up, slid from his grasp, and cascaded back down and over her legs with a quiet rustle.

After a prolonged moment of silence, he stepped back and said, "A blade met my face. What more do you wish to know?" Without sparing her another glance, he stalked toward the other side of the study, threw open the doors with a resounding bang and disappeared.

Her eyes widened. She realized it was probably

difficult for him to discuss but at the very least, she deserved some measure of respect.

Scrambling off the desk, Justine gathered up her skirts and dashed after him. When she eventually caught up to him at the end of the large hall, she grabbed hold of his arm and yanked him to a complete halt, forcing him to turn. "Don't insult what little we share by running off when I ask you a question."

He released an agitated breath through his nostrils. "I didn't run off."

"Yes, you did."

"Are we done with this conversation? I have an appointment with my secretary. The estate doesn't run itself, you know."

She glared at him, exasperated. It was like trying to reason with a warthog. "I suppose I didn't realize we were *having* a conversation. Perhaps I should offer you a better incentive to stay. The only incentive you seem receptive to." She grandly gestured toward the expanse of her neckline and breasts.

He smoothed the front of his waistcoat and looked away. "I made you full aware of my obsession."

"Yes, but you didn't mention you'd also be excluding all forms of conversation. I want to get to know you. I want us to genuinely engage each other, and I have no intention of relenting on this. I deserve to have more involved conversations with my husband."

He smirked and stepped menacingly close. "You want a more involved conversation with your husband, Duchess? I'll give you a more involved conversation. Tonight. In my bed."

She gasped. The man really did belong in the animal kingdom! She pointed at him, not at all caring that her behavior was equally rude. "I don't know the sort of women you're used to associating with, Your Grace, but until you begin treating me with the respect you promised, and the conversations I deserve, don't expect this marriage to be consummated anytime soon. Despite what you and the rest of London thinks, intimacy is a privilege. *Not* a right."

With that, she set her chin and swept past him, trying to prove that she was not just a duchess in name, but also a duchess at heart.

Early that evening

RADCLIFF STRODE DOWN the candlelit corridor, donning only a robe, more sexually frustrated than he had ever been in his entire life. He knew full well if he was going to survive this night, as well as all the other nights, he needed to formally apologize and offer Justine the intimacy she wanted. For he wasn't about to allow his stupid pride to get in the way of consummating this marriage.

Reaching her bedchamber door, he let out a soft breath and gripped the handle, turning it. Only it wouldn't budge. His brows came together as he rattled the raised grain knob in disbelief.

"Is there something you wanted, Bradford?" Justine called out from the other side, obviously knowing it was him.

He cleared his throat and dropped his hand away from the knob. "Yes. I came to apologize."

"Oh, no, you didn't. I know what you came for, and I suggest you wait until morning. You can apologize to me then."

His jaw tightened. She was truly something. Of all the women in London, he would end up taking a fancy to the one who could not only read his mind but who intended to unravel the last of him. "Justine, I want you to open the door."

"If you were me, Bradford, would *you* open the door?"

He narrowed his gaze. "I don't find your blatant defiance amusing."

"It isn't meant to amuse you. I suggest you retire. We'll discuss this in greater detail in the morning, once you've been given more time to think about how it is you intend to interact with me."

Perpetuating his own suffering was not what he'd had in mind when he'd put in his offer for her hand. She was supposed to be a distraction. Not a torture mechanism.

He ran a hand through his hair and reclenched his fist, his cock pulsing and in desperate need of release. "Whether or not I choose to offer you an apology and conversation takes no precedence over my legal rights as husband. Now open this door."

She snorted indelicately. "You are clearly delusional if you think I would open the door after *that* pathetic excuse for an apology."

"Justine." He pounded the door, sending thudding echoes throughout the corridor around him. "You owe me this much. You owe me after everything I've done for you and your father."

She feigned a laugh. "Is that what you think? Well. In case I didn't formally inform you of it, Your Grace, the sort of relationship I am seeking from my husband is going to include more than mere physicality. I want what goes on inside your head and inside your heart before these legs will ever part."

Bloody hell. What the blazes had he gotten himself into? "You are my wife and I have a right to bed you."

"I can only apologize, Your Grace, but I am not about to bed a man who has no respect for me. Whether he is my husband or not."

He gritted his teeth and kicked the door. Hard. She was his wife. He had every right to bed her.

"I only hope I don't have to listen to this all night," she snapped. "Because I am tired. *Good night.*" There was a movement, as if she settled into bed, and then all went quiet.

Radcliff pressed his eye against the thin crack of the door but could see nothing. He growled beneath his breath and hit the door with his fist one last time, shaking it on its hinges. He paced the corridor back and forth a few times, glancing toward the door, then swung around and veered back to his room, knowing he had no choice but to frig himself. He couldn't go to sleep with an erection that had been pestering him most of the day.

God damn it all!

It was obvious if he wanted to bed his own wife—without altogether taking her by force—he was going to have to come up with something. And hell if he knew what it was.

SCANDAL NINE

Never powder your face or anything else, for that matter, in public, for a lady should only be vain in the presence of a mirror set in her room.
How to Avoid a Scandal, Author Unknown

The following morning

JUSTINE ARRANGED HER napkin tidily upon her lap, plucked up the silver and commenced eating her breakfast, pretending that she was all alone at the table and having a jolly good time at it.

Which she was not.

Bradford sat across from her, intently and quietly staring her down the whole while, as if what he really wanted to eat was her.

Yes, well, she thought to herself, he could starve. He needed to learn a few lessons on self-control and respect.

When she had finally finished eating, she drew back her hands and allowed the servants to take her plate and setting. All that was left now was to enjoy her tea. And she certainly wasn't in any hurry to finish it. Not at all. She wanted to prove to him that she wasn't intimidated.

Bradford shifted in his seat and waved away the food he hadn't even touched. The servants hastily cleared his entire side of the table.

After a few moments of continued silence, he rumbled out, "I've arranged an outing. You and I will do the sort of things that a husband and wife should do."

She raised a brow over the porcelain rim of her teacup. "How very lovely. Thank you. Where are we going?"

"To the opera. I own a balcony and wish to make use of it before the season comes to an end."

She swallowed the earthy warmth of her tea and set her cup onto the small blue-and-ivory flower-patterned porcelain plate. She sighed. Sadly, she'd never cared for the opera. Every time her parents had taken her—when they had still been able to afford it, that was—she'd spent the evening depressed, listening to men and women sing to each other about how heartbreaking life was.

As if she needed to be reminded. "Can't we do something else? I've never cared for the opera. All they ever sing about is how miserable life is."

"I happen to like the opera. It portrays various

aspects of life other forms of entertainment here in London don't ever touch upon."

"Yes, I suppose, but can't we—"

"You are going, Justine. And herein ends this discussion. Is that understood?"

She glared at him. "You are being needlessly rude."

He glared back her. "*How?* By asking you to go to the opera? I think you are the one being rude for not wanting to go."

She narrowed her gaze. "Is that so? Perhaps I don't want to go because I feel being married to you is already depressing enough without having to set it to music."

He shifted his jaw and let out a single, agitated breath through his nostrils. He leaned back into his chair, his gaze never once leaving hers, and coolly drawled to the servants standing in the corners of the dining room, "My wife and I require privacy. Any servant found wandering about the house over the next two hours shall be terminated without references. Or pay."

Her eyes widened as she met his scalding gaze.

There was a pause. Then all the servants scrambled out of their corners and thundered straight into the corridor, completely disappearing from sight.

"Into quarters!" one of them hollered with full force. "Right quick! Anyone found wandering about the house over the next two hours will be terminated. Without references *or* pay!"

The echoing of male shouts and thudding and scrambling of boots within the halls eventually dissipated.

Everything was quiet. So quiet, Justine could not only hear herself breathing but if she listened hard enough, she could hear Bradford, as well.

She swallowed. Hard. And tried to keep from fidgeting within her chair. He was merely trying to intimidate her was all. As if he scared her. After all the animals she'd seen in her lifetime, he was naught more than an aardvark rounding an anthill in the distance.

Bradford stood, shaking the large table from the weight of his hands as he pushed up. Still staring her down, he rounded the table. His large frame, enrobed in a gray coat, matching waistcoat and full morning attire, advanced steadily.

Justine grabbed hold of her teacup with both hands and brought it up to her lips, trying to quell the trembling. She supposed she should have been more mentally prepared for the challenge she had set.

He paused and towered beside her chair.

Although she knew he had every right to bed her, she refused to acknowledge that right. What she deserved first and foremost was respect. Respect came before right.

"Ask me what it is I want," he said, spacing his words evenly. "Ask me why I continue to patiently stand here, waiting for my own wife to acknowledge me."

Her heart pounded, and for a moment she wondered if he would have the audacity to take his rights at the breakfast table. She shakily set the teacup back onto the small plate, making it clink, and turned herself and her gaze toward him. Trying to appear indifferent.

"All right," she obliged. "What is it that you want? Why do you insist on standing so needlessly close to my chair?"

He shifted toward her, cornering her in.

"Seeing my civil attempt to court you isn't to your liking, *Duchess,* I've decided to offer you a less civil alternative that won't require an outing at all. Choose whatever pleases you most. The opera. Or your innocence taken right here at the breakfast table. Either way, you have one minute to decide before I make the decision for you."

Oh, for heaven's sake!

She shifted in her seat and frantically waved her

hand toward his trousers. "All right, all right. I'll…
go to the opera. Now, step away! Gad. You really
ought to learn to control yourself more. This sort
of behavior is not acceptable."

He chuckled low and throaty, as if he found himself amusing, and retreated to his side of the table.
"I never thought it was. I simply didn't know how
else to get you to cooperate. We leave at six. Wear
something attractive, will you? Something that will
show off your breasts. Oh, and powder them while
you're at it. I like powdered breasts." He hesitated,
as if deciding against seating himself at the table
again, then turned and strode out.

Justine shifted in her seat, once, then twice, as
she waved her hand frantically before her hot face,
trying desperately to cool it. Shameless as it was,
she didn't know how much longer she could keep
resisting him. Though the lady residing within her
soul wanted to toss him out on his nose for not
giving her due respect, the animal clawing at her
soul wanted to lure the man straight into her own
bed and be done with it.

JUSTINE WRAPPED HER cashmere shawl tighter
around the verdant silk evening gown, which Bradford had not even commented on, and nervously
made her way through the crowds of people. Every

person she and Bradford passed seemed to pause and take note.

She realized all too painfully that this was the first time Bradford had willingly stepped out in public. And drat them, they were all staring, as if he were somehow more deformed than a leper.

Knowing it was anything but proper, Justine grabbed hold of Bradford's arm as they moved across the gilded domed entrance of the opera and tucked herself against him. She didn't know why, but she wanted to prove to each and every person watching that, despite his appearance and despite all their arguing, there was a united front. Little did they know that once she had enough time to properly tame him, he was going to make the rest of the men in London look like wildebeests.

Though she felt the muscles in Bradford's arm tighten in response to her blatant affection, it was brief. And what was more, he allowed her touch.

They climbed up the marble staircase leading to the viewing boxes upstairs. Bradford led her down a long wide hallway, past several numbered doors.

They paused when they came to the end of the corridor.

He released her arm, opened the door, then leaned toward her and drawled, "Powder those round tops of yours a bit more. I recommend you do it out here in the corridor as opposed to in the box where everyone will be watching." He winked, then yanked open the door, stepped inside and closed it behind himself, leaving her out in the corridor.

She blinked, not once, but twice, before glancing down at the top rounds of her breasts which were already shamelessly displayed by the low-cut evening gown. Why did she even want to please him? As if he deserved it.

She blew out a disgusted breath, pried open her reticule and hunted for her tin of powder past the opera glass, loose coins and a lace handkerchief. She yanked it out, along with a small feathered brush, then glanced down the long corridor behind her, at the couples entering their boxes.

How on earth was she to put it on with all these people around? She turned away, toward the silk-embroidered wall, pretending she was admiring one of the paintings on display, then did her best to apply the powder, without applying it all over her dress.

Feeling she was more than well-powdered, she shoved the tin back into her reticule, turned away from the wall and approached the door.

She took in a deep breath and touched her hand to the brass knob, letting herself in. She quietly closed the door. Turning toward the balcony, she paused. Thick red velvet curtains draped the open sides of the viewing box, making her feel encased in the folds of a luxurious gown. Two glass bulbs delicately etched with flowers hung from the low ceiling, providing flickering light from the candles within.

Bradford's black top hat had been set beside him. He sat in one of the plush mahogany chairs, his broad back to her, his large, white-gloved hands folded rather casually behind his dark head as he looked out onto the large open auditorium. He had even scandalously propped his long, muscled legs, which were draped in black formal trousers, atop the wooden ledge of the viewing box. His black shoes reflected the golden light from the hall, displaying how perfectly polished they were.

In that moment, he reminded her of the Bradford she sorely missed. The one who had always been at ease with himself and the world. Had that been merely a façade to a troubled soul?

Her cashmere shawl slipped from her shoulders and floated down onto the green-and-red-flowered carpet. She didn't even care, because in that moment, she was enjoying her chance to watch him without him knowing it.

His hands and feet suddenly dropped to the

floor as he turned, his scarred face now completely facing her. Black eyes boldly skimmed the length of her, causing her heart to skip.

A dizzying warmth overcame her even as she desperately tried to remain aloof.

"*Perfection* is the only word to define you." He rose to his full height, stepped around his seat and came back toward her. He bent and swept up the scarf that had slipped from her shoulders. Rising, he leaned toward her, gently wrapped it around her shoulders and lingered.

"Come." He took her hand and led her to their seats at the opening overlooking the ledge.

Justine couldn't help but breathe in this unexpected moment of what felt like a genuine attempt at courtship. She reveled in it, wanting to remember every detail. From the feel of his hand, to the beautiful carved gold ceilings above, to the stage draped with lush, red curtains bearing the royal emblem, right down to the enormous auditorium below, which seemed crowded with half of London.

Various overly coiffed women with large feathers in their hair, with emeralds and pearls and every stone imaginable on their gloved wrists and exposed necks, were already whispering busily amongst themselves, occasionally pointing with fans in their direction. The men weren't quite so bold or obvious. With creased brows, they all pretended to be regally admiring the architecture.

Justine thought she might faint from the reality that everyone in London was not only discussing her and Bradford, but watching them. She sat in her designated chair to steady her shaky legs. She clutched her shawl, wishing she could crawl beneath it.

"Don't deprive me of everything, Justine." Bradford leaned toward her, the tips of his gloved fingers grazing her exposed shoulders as he swept off the cashmere shawl.

A cool breeze caressed her as he lifted it off and away. Her shoulders were openly exposed by the dip and cut of her gown. She didn't know why, but she felt as if Bradford had officially put her on display.

He seated himself beside her and shifted in his seat. "Did you bring the opera glass I left out for you?"

She nodded and fumbled to remove it from her reticule. Her shaky fingers repeatedly tried to loosen the drawn cord, yet she had somehow lost control over her ability to make them function.

Bradford's large hand swept over her fumbling ones. He wedged his fingers past hers and effortlessly loosened the cord, opening the reticule for her.

"Thank you," she murmured.

"You are most welcome. Despite what you think, I can be quite useful from time to time outside the bedchamber." A muscle flickered in his tight, scarred jaw as he gazed beyond her and toward the stage.

It was obvious that the Duke of Bradford, whom she thought didn't give a drat about her opinion, was in fact trying to prove his worth. In the littlest of ways, mind you, but surely it would lead to more.

For if an insignificant hard granule of sand could be used by an oyster to create a beautiful, priceless pearl, then surely the Duke of Bradford would one day become the man of her dreams.

As THE DRUMS BEAT in time to the trumpets and the violins joined in on top of the voices that pitched higher and higher, Radcliff could only sit and watch Justine's glowing face. It had been quite some time since he'd been to the opera. He hadn't realized how much he had missed the music and the atmosphere until now.

Justine lifted her glass to look at the singers, a

smile flitting across her full lips. "Radcliff?" she whispered.

How he liked hearing his name on her lips. He leaned toward her, the soft scent of rose water and powder floating up toward him from the heat of her exposed, creamy shoulders. "Yes?"

"What is it they're actually singing about? I can only understand a few words here and there. I suppose I should have studied more Italian and less Swazi and Zulu, yes?"

He chuckled. Very few women admitted to what she just had. Of course, that was exactly what had always fascinated him about her. She never hid her thoughts the way other women were trained to do.

Radcliff listened for a long moment to the woman's piping voice, catching all the words. "She longs for her husband." Unable to resist, he leaned in closer, and added, "Her only chance of ever knowing true and lasting happiness is to allow him to bed her. Every morning and every night."

Justine tilted her face toward him and lifted a brow. "I thought her husband was dead."

He choked on an astonished laugh and cleared his throat. Twice. "Your Italian is better than you let on."

"Certainly better than yours." She grinned,

apparently pleased with herself, and turned back to the stage.

As the opera continued, so did his unexpected fascination with his own wife. Why did he never think to offer on her hand sooner? Could things have been different for him? Could all of those women have been nothing more than passing faces he could have resisted? Perhaps he would have still had a face to offer her. A face she could be proud of.

He lowered his chin, still watching her. For someone who claimed not to care for the opera, her eyes hadn't left the stage. She breathed in sharply whenever the powerful voices pierced the air. And naturally, every single time she caught her breath, it brought his attention back to those beautiful, perfectly powdered round breasts.

Indeed, he'd always had a weakness for powdered breasts at the opera. For it highlighted the softness of the skin and the curve of each breast every time a woman drew in a breath in reaction to the dramatic music and voices.

Throughout the rest of the night, there were many moments, whilst sitting next to her, that he wanted to reach out and caress the side of her smooth face and her long graceful neck with the back of his hand. Mostly whenever he thought of how she had publicly grabbed for his arm when they had first made their appearance that evening.

She had obviously sensed what he'd already known. That everyone was staring at his face. And though the gesture had been subtle, without a glance or a word, it was by far the most endearing thing a woman had ever done for him.

In some way, he'd known when he'd walked into his drawing room that one summer night, two years ago, that the ravishing debutante, who had stood so regally beside her parents, was going to do more than take his breath away. He'd known she was going to change his life.

That entire night, he'd spent the evening fascinated by the way she talked and walked and boldly met his gaze every time he spoke to her. She'd been so refreshingly different from all the other aristocratic young women he'd ever known. Most were taught to lower their gazes at the appropriate time and only speak in demure tones. He himself had always preferred a bit of fire. Which had, in fact, always been the problem. His obsession enjoyed challenges.

Indeed, the air around Justine had been so fresh that night, he could have sworn every time she breezed past, the fragrance of sun-burnt grasses had permeated the air around her. Sun-burnt grasses he'd wanted to roll around in. Grasses he'd *tried* to roll around in on a few occasions by calling on her, only to find that the earl had been on to him. The man had warned him that unless Radcliff had marriage in mind, he'd best stay the hell away. So he had. Only now he wished he hadn't.

Instead of giving in to the growing urge to caress her cheek before all of London—for that would have indeed been vulgar and disrespectful of him—he opted to place his gloved hand to the back of her chair, to keep it from straying.

"So what is it that they are saying now?" she whispered again, interrupting his thoughts.

He snapped his attention away from her and back to the stage where a dainty female, dressed in a silk moss costume, fluted her notes across the stage to a group of perfectly still and silent men and women.

He focused on the words, knowing he had better not stray in his Italian, lest she correct him. "She wonders why her life is destined for sorrow and does not understand why the fates have abandoned her. Regardless, she believes she is destined for happiness and intends to triumph over all adversity."

Justine drew in a long breath and slowly released it with a sigh, as if more romantic words she'd never heard spoken in her life.

She leaned slightly forward, toward the ledge before them, and eventually pointed at the group gathered to the left of the main singer. "And those people over there? Who are they?"

"They represent the village."

She crinkled her nose. "The village? What village? This is so embarrassing. Am I the only one unable to follow every word?"

Radcliff smirked at her genuine attempt to follow the path of the opera's story. Most people fell asleep. Or watched others through their opera glass. "I thought you didn't like the opera."

"I don't. But this one is surprisingly romantic in the way it's being presented." She paused and eyed him. "I suppose I should thank you for convincing me to come. Brute force aside, that is, I am actually enjoying myself." She smiled and returned her gaze to the stage.

He smiled and shook his head. Women certainly looked at everything so differently. He scanned the wide audience and paused, noticing Lord and Lady Winfield sitting in the box directly across from theirs. Radcliff's smile faded as he narrowed his gaze at the old Marquis responsible for bringing Justine's father before the bench and King.

Lady Winfield's silver head bent toward her husband as she whispered something urgently to him, her opera glass fixed in Justine's direction. The Marquis shifted in his seat, shook his tonic-brushed gray hair and whispered something in turn behind a white-gloved hand, looking rather agitated.

It was obvious they were discussing his wife.

Radcliff leaned toward Justine and whispered into the soft, chestnut curls that covered her ear, "I suggest we take our leave, dearest."

Justine stiffened and tilted her head toward him. "Why? Is something amiss?"

There was no sense in lying to her. "Lord Winfield and his wife are sitting directly across from us. I prefer we leave. Before I end up jumping into their box and making your father's scandal look like Sunday prayers."

Justine paused, her eyes darting over to the box across from them, where Lord Winfield sat with his wife. After a quiet moment, she set her chin toward the direction of the stage and lifted her opera glass. "We stay. I am not missing the end of this opera. If you genuinely feel the need to jump into their box, I most certainly won't object."

Radcliff grinned slowly, silently cheering his Justine on, as he removed his hand from the back of her seat. He never expected anything less of her.

Knowing Lady and Lord Winfield were still watching them, he eyed Justine's hand, and purposefully slipped his own down and across the lap of her evening gown. Gathering her gloved hand, he strategically brought it to his lips and kissed it ardently several times.

Kissing it again, he sensually rubbed the rounded tops of her gloved knuckle with his fingers. Justine's chest rose from a quick intake of air, but otherwise, she remained indifferent as she slowly lifted her opera glass to her eyes with her other hand. "What on earth are you doing, Bradford?" her lips asked from beneath the rounded brass. "You do realize all of London is watching and you are being very crass?"

"I am merely making the Winfields jealous," he drawled, continuing to rub her hand. "From what I hear, their marriage is so miserable, in comparison ours is meant for storybooks. We should revel in it."

Justine squeezed his hand. Hard. "Revel for us, then. But don't think you can hold or kiss anything else."

He bit back a laugh and pressed his lips to her hand again. No matter how long it took, he had every intention of wooing his own wife and claiming her one small inch at a time. He'd keep wooing and claiming and wooing and claiming, until she was finally his. In mind and in body.

The following afternoon

IT SHOULDN'T HAVE surprised Justine when a footman in full red livery arrived at the door bearing a letter from Lady Winfield. What surprised Justine was the fact that the footman refused to leave without a response.

So she was forced to read the letter without being able to share it with Bradford who, of all days, was out with his secretary.

The letter read:

To Her Grace the Duchess of Bradford,
It was most endearing to observe a happy couple of such quality at the opera. I confess I have not seen such genuine adoration between a man and his wife in some time. I wish you and your new husband continued happiness. Though my husband has been an adversary to your father these past few months, he was first and foremost always a friend. I humbly ask that Your Grace understand that my husband was merely seeking to protect the rights of His Majesty's people after an unspeakable incident involving our son devastated our lives many, many years ago. I believe Your Grace will have influence here in London throughout the coming years and that your benevolence is so great, I would even venture to ask for forgiveness in this matter and hope you and I might commence anew. I believe it would benefit us all.
Sincerely,
Lady Winfield

Justine snorted and wanted nothing more than to tear up the letter before the footman into dozens of dozens of pieces and send him along with the words, "Bugger off and may the Zulu *Tokoleshe* descend upon you." But a true duchess would not be that hasty, crass or insensitive. More so, she had her husband's name to uphold. And her parents', as well.

Being a duchess certainly presented annoying dilemmas. It required one to be a complete hypocrite.

Knowing the footman was waiting outside the study, Justine seated herself at Radcliff's desk and neatly scribed the following letter:

To The Most Noble Marchioness of Winfield,
I am humbled by your apology. As you know, my father has suffered greatly at the injustice brought against him due to his unconventional beliefs. My father's studies have consistently proven that preference is innate. God does not create misunderstandings, we as humans do. I understand that your son suffered greatly at the hands of a monstrous scoundrel, and for that, my heart bleeds. Your son should have never endured what he did. Please understand, however, that the pain you and your husband have endured is not completely dissimilar to the pain I have endured whilst witnessing my own father's life being stripped to a public form of nakedness

from which he may never recover. I suppose I
would be more willing to offer forgiveness in
this matter if I knew you to be genuine.
Sincerely,
The Duchess of Bradford

The footman scurried off and returned not even
an hour later with the following letter which the
footman wanted a reply to:

To Her Grace the Duchess of Bradford,
Our apologies are indeed genuine and we hope
to prove them in time. My husband has given
thought to the situation and has nobly decided
to reimburse any funds lost during your father's
tribulations in an effort to prove our intentions.
Although we will continue to disagree with his
convictions, in the end, we believe that respect
does not necessarily mean people need always
hold the same beliefs. We hope that you agree.
Sincerely,
Lady Winfield

Justine stared at the letter in complete astonishment. Curious, that. Bradford had once told her
the same thing about respect. As such, this Lady
Winfield had to have *some* amount of merit.

Though a part of Justine didn't entirely trust the
Winfields after what had been done to her father,
she knew one could not play with the other children
in the park without allowing the ball to actually

leave one's hands. Playing with naughty children known to steal balls was always a risk, but if all went well, which Justine hoped it would, playing often resulted in genuine fun meant to benefit all.

So Justine seated herself at Bradford's desk once again and daintily scribed what she hoped to be the last letter:

> To The Most Noble Marchioness of Winfield,
> I humbly agree with your sentiment of respect.
> As such, I know in time all will be forgotten.
> Sincerely,
> The Duchess of Bradford

Two days later, her father was reimbursed an astounding fifteen thousand pounds and she and Bradford were invited to attend the Winfield ball. Needless to say, Justine was beginning to believe that the name of duchess did earn one unprecedented respect in London. Though oddly enough, she was still trying to earn it from the one person she wanted it from the most: her husband.

SCANDAL TEN

Never allow a man to lure you into the darkness
of a quiet garden or any other quiet destination
where you might find yourself alone. For it will
lead to far more than mere ruin and scandal. It
will lead to far more than any woman is prepared
to handle.

How to Avoid a Scandal, Author Unknown

*Four parties, two theater outings, five car-
riage rides through Hyde Park, three visits to
his new in-laws, fourteen new gowns from The
Nightingale—along with matching slippers and
an expensive emerald necklace Radcliff had dug
out from his safe—and now a ball hosted by
none other than Lord Winfield, which Justine
had insisted on attending, later...*

RADCLIFF TIGHTENED HIS HOLD on Justine's slim
waist with one hand, his gloved fingers digging
into the lilac satin of her evening gown, and tightened his hold on her gloved hand which he held up

and out during their waltz. And here he thought he wasn't a saint, yet he'd somehow endured two whole weeks into their marriage without ever once knocking on her bedchamber door. Which he had to admit he was bloody proud of. The trouble was, his right hand had been keeping him company every night, several times a night. Something he could not refrain from, though he tried.

"You are holding me much too close," Justine whispered as they whirled across the dance floor, past other couples. The emerald necklace he'd given her glinted at him.

He smirked, amused how she kept her hazel eyes fixed on his waistcoat as if she'd never danced with a man so intimately before. "This is a waltz, Duchess. I'm supposed to be holding you scandalously close. Enjoy it. I know I am."

To emphasize his point, he yanked her even closer against his body and whisked them past a bunch of gawking old crones whose days were long past and who most likely would crumble like biscuits if they had attempted to move the way he and his wife were now.

Justine kept her steps in time with his, her hips brushing his as her thighs gracefully followed every move he made. By God, she knew how to dance.

Knowing that his own brother was somewhere

in the crowd and probably watching made Radcliff dance with even more pride and enthusiasm. For he had something not his brother nor anyone else would ever have: Justine.

The more time he spent with his wife, the more he realized what a lucky bastard he really was. And slowly, ever so slowly, he was mastering his own obsession in a way he never thought possible, knowing Justine had everything to do with it. She was firm with him when he needed her to be firm and gentle at the most unexpected times.

As the waltz finally ended, he set out his arm and led her off the dance floor. He leaned toward her and drawled, "Lord Winfield has informed me there is a new fountain in his garden which his wife brought in from Venice."

She paused just beyond the dance floor and slipped her gloved hand from his arm, quirking a brow. "Are you proposing what I think you are proposing?"

God, how he wished. Little did she know she'd won. She had finally broken his stubborn soul in half. For no one was more aware of it than he, that every glance she offered him, every smile, and every word, it all seemed to come back to one thing. Her wanting to have a genuine understanding of who and what he was. And he intended to share himself with her tonight, whilst his spirits were strong.

Radcliff leaned toward her again and whispered, "Find the fountain."

Without waiting for a response, he rounded her and moved through the crowd. He only hoped he was making the right decision by telling her the truth behind his scar.

THE IMPORTED ITALIAN FOUNTAIN, Justine realized, wasn't all that far from the festivities. Barely a few brisk steps. The area was even lit by light from the house and further illuminated by the half moon lingering above.

Whatever Radcliff's intentions, they couldn't have been all that amorous, unless he planned on scandalizing all of London. But then, it wouldn't be the first time for either of them, would it?

The cool night breeze skimmed across her bare shoulders and rustled her skirts, making her shiver. The water from the fountain gushed in constant rhythm, splashing every now and then beyond its allotted basin as music from inside the house played along with it.

Justine rubbed her arms as another strong breeze whirled around her.

"Are you cold?" a familiar deep voice asked.

Justine's pulse thundered and warmth frilled her body knowing Bradford was standing right behind her. These past two weeks had been divine. Ever since the night of the opera, the lilt in Bradford's voice had returned, reminding her of the man she had first swooned over. They spent every moment discussing everything. Everything but the one thing she wanted to know most—the story behind his scar. "I am a little cold," she quietly confessed.

"Here. Take this." He gallantly draped his warm evening coat, which held the faint scent of sandalwood and cigars, over her exposed shoulders. "Better?" he whispered from behind.

She inwardly melted and shivered again. "Much better. Thank you."

His gloved hands skimmed her shoulders, then dropped away as he rounded her and came into view. His exposed crisp, white shirt beneath his ivory-embroidered waistcoat glowed, reflecting whatever moonlight surrounded them.

"Brisk night for summer, isn't it?" he commented, looking around. As if the summer night was all that was on his mind.

Justine bit back a smile. How adorable. He was genuinely pining for more conversations. "Yes. It is."

He drew in a hefty breath, then just as heftily let it out. "Good air."

She struggled to remain serious. "For London."

He nodded, then drew his dark brows together as he glanced down at his gloved hands. Without saying anything more, he yanked loose the tips of his gloves from each and every single finger.

He smoothly tugged off his right glove, then the left, exposing his wide, powerful hands. He tucked his gloves into his trousers and cleared his throat.

She tightened her hold on his coat and couldn't help but stare at those hands. Hands which had never once strayed, not since their night at the opera. Her heart pounded, wondering if tonight was going to be the end of the gentlemanly guise she had been so ardently enjoying.

He eyed her. "It has taken me some time, but I am ready to share with you what happened to me the night my face was scarred. Do you still wish to know?"

Justine felt heat spreading up her neck and into her face as her breath quickened. This most certainly was not what she had expected. It was far more.

She glanced around them, toward the house, surprised he would choose this particular moment, when they were out in public. "Yes, of course. Perhaps we should discuss this in a more private setting?"

"No. I prefer this. It gives you an opportunity to step away if you don't care to listen to any more."

Justine swallowed. Why did this not sound all that promising? "I have no intention of stepping away."

"That is for you to decide." His sensual features tightened in the dim light that filtered out toward them from the French windows of the house. Eerily, his handsome side remained visible, whilst the marred half remained shadowed. "I suppose I should begin with a name. Matilda Thurlow. At the time of the incident, she was my brother's mistress."

Justine blinked. She'd heard about the involvement of a less than reputable woman, but never realized it was his brother's own mistress.

Looking away, he murmured, "Carlton was absolutely enamored with her, though he refrained from publicly flaunting her. Not because he was worried about his reputation, but because he was worried about me encroaching upon her. She was indeed that beautiful. I tried to respect that she was my own brother's mistress, but every time I saw Matilda, whether it was out riding in Hyde Park, or on Regent Street, I became all the more intrigued. In time, I started calling on her at night, trying to engage her. But she refused me each and every time. Which only riled me more."

Justine didn't know why jealousy bit into her, hearing how he had ardently pursued another woman before they were together. Perhaps because this adoration of hers was turning into something far more involved.

Bradford shrugged. "Needless to say, my brother was not blind to my attempts. He confronted me repeatedly about it. What is worse, he knew I had no self-control when it came to women and thought it was amusing. So much so, that one day, he delivered a life-size portrait of Matilda Thurlow to my door. I was livid, and yet I couldn't bring myself to get rid of it. So I put it up on my bedchamber wall and soon my obsession reached a fever pitch."

Justine sucked in an astonished breath. The portrait. The portrait of the beautiful blonde. Was that the one he was referring to?

She tried to keep her voice indifferent, even though inside she was anything but. "Is it the same portrait still in the corridor outside our bedchambers?"

He cleared his throat. "Yes."

After a moment of awkward silence, she forced herself to ask, "Is there a reason it is still there?"

He paused, then nodded. "When I went into

seclusion, I removed it from the wall many, many times, only to put it back up each and every time. I eventually moved it out of my bedchamber into the corridor. I would have tossed it, but I wanted to prove to myself that I could pass the damn thing without having it evoke a physical response within me. It took me a month, but I did it. Now, it is simply there as a reminder of what I once was. And what I still am."

Justine didn't know why his admission frightened her so much. Perhaps because it made her realize that even the best of men could have the most horrid of secrets.

Bradford awkwardly rubbed at his chin and looked away. "I was soon in dire need of engaging a real woman, as opposed to pleasuring myself before a portrait. So I decided to go to a champagne party being hosted near Covent Garden. I ended up not letting any of the women there touch me for fear of the pox and opted to simply drink and watch as others frigged." He shifted his jaw and eyed her. "Do you know what a champagne party is?"

She shook her head, her eyes never once leaving his face. "I gather it involves men and women and champagne."

"Champagne and laudanum, to be exact. That same night, Matilda bribed my footman to learn my whereabouts. Apparently, she was tired of Carlton making promises he would not keep and decided to pursue a relationship with another man. Me being that man, no doubt because of the interest I had displayed. Hoping to engage me, she arrived, but six toughs grabbed her, stripped her, bound her and mounted her one by one. No one did a goddamn thing, even though she screamed the entire time."

Justine brought a shaky hand to her mouth, covering it, as tears burned her eyes. "Oh, God."

Radcliff threw back his dark head and stared up into the night sky above them. "Through the haze of my own delirium, a woman dragged me through the quarters of the house, begging that I assist a woman in need. I wasn't prepared for what I saw."

He leveled his head, then spun away and violently swung a clenched fist through the air. He turned back toward the house, raking both hands through his hair before letting them drop. "There was Matilda, being held facedown as she screamed and sobbed. One of the men was carving his initials into the flesh of her backside with a blade. So she might remember him, he kept insisting. 'Twas a blur when I threw myself at them, and that same blade gouged my face full force from lip to temple. As inebriated as I was, I felt nothing."

Her throat burned in agony for what he and this poor Matilda Thurlow had lived through.

Bradford gritted his teeth and swung his fist through the air again, as if trying to release everything within him. He then seethed in a low tone that almost wasn't his, "Every time I pulled one off and cracked another upside the skull, another one climbed right on her. Even as my own blood poured everywhere. Eventually, decent men, realizing that my face was hanging open, assisted me in bringing it to an end. But Matilda had already endured the worst of it."

He swiped a shaky hand across his face and shook his head. "Witnessing that firsthand only emphasized what I already knew due to my own experience with my obsession. That your father's studies were important in better understanding ourselves. Because once the clothing is removed, men become animals."

Justine tried to choke back a strained sob, but couldn't keep it from escaping her lips.

"Barely three days after the incident," he quietly went on, "with thread still holding my face together, and all six men in custody awaiting trial, Carlton stormed into my home and blamed me. As if I had somehow encouraged what was done. In a way, his resentment made sense. I had been irresponsible with my obsession for far too long, indulging in a lifestyle that served no one, not even me. I sulked about it in seclusion for many, many months refusing to pleasure myself even once."

He captured her gaze. "But one thing kept me sane. Your weekly letters. The ones I burned the moment I read them. I did not want to respond for fear of encouraging you or myself. Then that mess with your father occurred, and shortly afterward, a letter arrived with your offer to bed me in exchange for his freedom. It tossed my ability to think. I didn't want a few measly nights. I wanted every night. Whether I was even worthy of you was not something I even bothered to ask myself. So I married you, thinking I could readily control my obsession, only to discover that it still controls me. There are many times I struggle with myself, and for it, I feel worthless, but you give me hope and guidance." He nodded and looked away, clearly unable to say more.

As if he needed to say anything more. If she had ever once doubted that Bradford had a heart and a soul, she could not doubt it anymore.

Justine swallowed against the dryness of her throat and rushed straight to him, unable to stay away. She threw her arms around his waist, pulling him to herself, and buried her face against the solid warmth of his broad chest, squeezing him as tightly as her strength would allow. "You are not worthless," she insisted against him. "Not to me. You never were."

He sucked in a harsh breath, but otherwise did not move or even attempt to embrace her.

Perhaps she had said far too much, far too soon.

She drew away, slipping her shaky arms back to her sides, and awkwardly lingered before him not knowing what else she could say or do. All she knew was that she wanted to help him in any way she could.

Radcliff brushed the side of her exposed neck with the back of his warm, bare hand. He trailed it down toward the hollow of her throat, his fingers grazing the weight of the emerald necklace he'd given her just a few days ago. It was a touch that bespoke a genuine longing to connect with her beyond the realm of lust.

Justine swallowed, unable to break his dark, haunting gaze, which revealed a silent form of suffering, a suffering he had tried to hide behind curt words and flippant airs.

He yanked his hand back and stepped away. "I am certain everyone has noticed our absence. We ought to return to the festivities."

Imagine. The Duke of Bradford was actually using propriety as an excuse to end this wonderfully tender moment between them. An excuse he had used these past two weeks. An excuse she had grown tired of.

"Hold me, Radcliff," she insisted, hoping to entice him to stay, hoping she could prolong this feeling of genuine intimacy between them.

He glanced toward the house behind them. "No."

"You are my husband." She moved closer. "Hold me."

He stared at her from across the distance he still kept. "I…no. Not now. I can't."

"I am not afraid of you, Bradford. And you should not be afraid of yourself, either. Now hold me."

He hesitated, then closed the distance between them. Towering before her for a moment, he fiercely seized her and yanked her so close and so tight against himself, his muscled arms and large solid body squeezed a huge, puffing breath straight out of her lungs.

"Perhaps not so tightly," she squeaked out.

He chuckled, loosened his hold, though barely, and slowly leaned forward, brushing his warm lips against the exposed skin of her neck. Lifting his dark head, he searched her eyes. The moon above faintly highlighted the vicious but noble scar upon his face. "I vow to protect you from everything, Justine," he whispered. "Even from myself, if need be."

The dark sky above her seemed to spin in response to her blooming emotions. She loved this man. She really did. Justine stared up at him in awe, her head helplessly spilled back, not wanting this moment between them to end. More than anything, she wanted to reach out and touch every part of that soul which he hid from her and the rest of the world.

"I have to kiss you." His tone was raw and simmering with restraint as he lowered his lips.

Her gloved hand jumped up to his lips and stopped him, her fingers resting hesitantly against his mouth. "No. Do it because you *want* to."

"I *want* to," he said against her fingertips. "My beautiful Justine, do you not realize you are everything I could ever want." He aggressively nudged her hand aside from his mouth and seized her lips, causing her heart to skip. His muscled arms surrounded her completely as his kiss deepened and his tongue ardently searched the corners of her mouth.

Her very soul melted in response to that kiss.

Her hands moved up the length of his chest toward his shoulders and found their way to his stiff collar and into his thick hair.

She tried matching his physical demands by imitating the same motions with her mouth. She pushed her tongue against his, hoping to demonstrate to him that she wanted him now more than ever and was genuinely thrilled to be his wife.

RADCLIFF GROANED AS he pressed Justine closer to his heated body. Her softness. Her warmth. His cock instantly thickened and pressed against his trousers. He wanted her. And it wasn't his cock that wanted her. It was *him*.

Her mouth moved more forcefully against his, and he found himself wanting more. His hands shook as he rubbed her hips with his hands, inching higher and higher. He wanted to explore more than her mouth. He wanted to explore everything that had been borne unto her, and he didn't care if all of London watched.

He pushed away the evening coat draping her, exposing the velvet softness of her creamy shoulders. His palms rounded her bare shoulders and moved toward her neck. A shiver escaped her.

Cool emeralds grazed his fingers, interrupting the sensual journey he intended to make. Emeralds that had once touched his mother's own neck. Emeralds that did not deserve Justine. He would buy her a new set of jewels. Jewels that had been untouched or tainted. Much like her.

He blindly undid the clasp, his lips still devouring hers without pause. He felt her stiffen as he slowly removed the heavy jewels.

To his disappointment, her gloved hands abandoned his nape and pushed at his chest, asking him to desist. He released her mouth, without really wanting to, and stared down at his new desire, this dream. He fisted his mother's emeralds in his right hand, the stone biting into his palm.

She hesitated, her hazel eyes searching his face. "I thought you said they were mine."

He smiled, knowing full well what she was thinking, and dangled the commodity with the hand he'd freed from her. "They belonged to my mother and they don't deserve you. I intend to buy you a new necklace. One worthy of you." With that, he tossed the emerald necklace up and over toward the fountain where it splashed out of sight.

"Bradford!" she exclaimed, losing the softness he was just getting to know. She whirled away and scrambled over to the fountain, frantically peering left and right, searching for wherever the jewels had landed in the bubbling water.

He chuckled and approached. If he didn't put an end to it, she'd most likely climb right in.

Radcliff grabbed hold of her waist again and spun her back toward him. "Let the damn fountain keep them. Come. I am not done with you."

Lowering his lips, he slowly slid his tongue down across the soft, graceful curve of her throat, further down toward the exposed upper rounds of her perfect, full breasts. "Take it as the greatest compliment I will ever bestow upon you. I never respected her. She betrayed my father for a moment of pleasure she could not even admit to until long after his death. A moment of pleasure which resulted in the birth of Carlton."

Her chest rose from a sharp intake of breath. "I...never knew."

"Now you do." He swallowed. "Allow me to touch you." His hands slid across the smooth silk of her gown and up toward those velvetlike voluptuous mounds. The soft fullness he needed to feel.

His cock throbbed, thickened and pressed against his trousers. Touching her wasn't going to be enough, and if he wasn't careful, he'd take her right there by the fountain.

A sound from the festivities broke through his fevered haze. Radcliff stepped back, putting up his hand, and cleared his throat. "I think it wise I refrain."

She was quiet for a moment, then whispered up at him, "Come to my bed tonight. There is no reason you should stay away. You have more than proven your respect for me."

His pulse thundered in disbelief that she was offering him the one thing he had refused to beg for these past two weeks. Out of pride, yes, but more so out of respect for her. "Do you wish it?" he whispered back.

She smiled. "With all my heart."

He was indeed the luckiest, luckiest bastard alive. "I...yes. I will come." He nodded and yanked his tucked gloves out from the side of his trousers and pulled them on each hand. Trying to distract himself from even thinking about their night ahead, he turned, strode over to where his evening coat still lay on the ground and grabbed it up. Shaking it out, he pulled it on and over his shoulders.

Radcliff turned back toward her, where she still lingered by the fountain, and held out his arm. "Come. We should join the others."

She jerked a gloved thumb toward the fountain behind her. "Not without my emeralds," she drawled. "I don't care what your relationship was with your mother. They are worth a sizable fortune."

He laughed and shook his head. Taking a few steps toward her, he grabbed hold of her hand and yanked her back toward the house. "I thought you didn't care for trinkets."

She resisted and pulled back against his grip. "I don't. But I can't have a necklace of such worth going to waste, either. If you don't want it, which clearly you don't, I'll give it to my father. He dreams of returning to Cape Town, and between the money he recently received from Lord Winfield and this, that may very well be a possibility."

Radcliff rolled his eyes and pulled her forward again. A bit harder. Toward himself. "Justine," he growled. "If your father dreams of moving to Cape Town, I'll see to it. But as of now, I am asking you to leave the emeralds alone. I don't want to see them. Not ever again. Is that understood?"

She huffed out an exasperated breath and muttered something before dutifully accompanying him back into the ballroom.

SCANDAL ELEVEN

Few husbands ever genuinely appreciate how much their wife does for them. Which is why it is a wife's duty to make her husband understand what it is he must appreciate.

How to Avoid a Scandal, Author Unknown

JUSTINE WAS QUITE certain that Radcliff had lost the last of his mind. How could anyone toss a perfectly good set of expensive emeralds into a fountain like that? Merely because he didn't get along with his mother! After all the financial woes she'd been through these past few months, no amount of hard feelings warranted *that*.

Justine entered the ballroom alongside him and paused, realizing something was very wrong. She froze in the doorway of the balcony alongside Radcliff.

The large ballroom, which had earlier echoed with unmeasured merriment, was eerily quiet. The seven-piece orchestra, set up in the far corner of the room, sat with their instruments clutched in their now unmoving hands.

Couples still stood on the polished dance floor, having clearly been interrupted by the silencing of the orchestra. Then chaos erupted as gentlemen in their finest scrambled about left and right like ostriches.

Justine tightened her hold on Radcliff's hand and stepped closer, glancing up toward him. He in turn tightened his hold, his brows coming together as she scanned the scramble.

"Radcliff," she said hoarsely, unable to say much more.

"No one seems to be shouting for doctors or yelling about a fire. So why else would everyone be scattering like rats and raving like lunatics?"

"Your Grace!" someone shouted. *"Your Grace!"*

"Speaking of raving lunatics." Bradford pointed toward the man heading straight at them. "Here comes one now. Wouldn't you agree?"

Justine choked on a laugh and smacked Radcliff's arm just as their host, Lord Winfield, dashed toward them, his brow visibly dampened with perspiration. The gentleman skidded to a halt, trying to prevent his lanky, awkward frame from smacking straight into them.

Lord Winfield gasped for air, snapping his

shoulders straight. "Please forgive the commotion. This is not how I envisioned the night unfolding."

Bradford stepped toward the man, still tightly holding Justine's hand. "What is it, my lord? Is it serious?"

Lord Winfield's lean, aged face flushed. "My wife's pendant seems to have disappeared. She was wearing it not that long ago, but no one claims to have seen it. I tell you, a man cannot trust a single soul these days in London. Not a single one."

"Lady Winfield's pendant is missing?" Justine echoed in disbelief. And here she thought someone had been murdered. "Is that all?"

Lord Winfield adjusted his evening coat about his chest as if trying to defend his course of action. "I do beg your pardon, Your Grace, but that pendant happens to be an heirloom worth five hundred pounds."

Radcliff let out a whistle. "I don't think anyone will be leaving anytime soon."

"'Tis baneful to whistle at a time like this," Lord Winfield chastised before altogether turning to Justine. "My sincerest apologies, Your Grace, but only women will be allowed to depart. If you would be so kind as to accompany me, I shall escort you to your carriage. Your husband will join you once we resolve this situation."

"What the devil are you suggesting?" Radcliff interjected, shoving his way between them. His large, muscled frame towered over Lord Winfield's. "My wife is *not* stepping out into the night without me."

Justine bit back a smile and set her chin, feeling rather pleased that she had someone like Radcliff to oversee her safety. "Quite right. I apologize, my lord, but I am not leaving without my husband."

Lord Winfield hesitated, then cleared his throat and leaned toward Bradford. "The men are going to be stripped and searched, Your Grace. It really wouldn't do to have a lady watch."

Justine bubbled out a laugh at the idea of Radcliff being stripped in public. He was going to make every man jealous. "I should probably leave. Heaven forbid I should be forced to see my husband naked."

Radcliff choked.

Lord Winfield's face grew bright red. He cleared his throat, then gestured toward the double doors on the other side of the ballroom. "Please join my wife in the receiving room, Your Grace. Heaven knows she is particularly fond of you. All I ask is that you be mindful. She has a rather delicate constitution."

"I completely understand, Lord Winfield."

Justine raised a brow at Bradford, who was struggling to compose himself, then gathered up her skirts and dutifully followed the crowd of women who were all being ushered out of the ballroom.

RADCLIFF BIT BACK THE ridiculous smile he hadn't been able to rid himself of. Justine was much wilder at heart than even he had realized.

"Will every gentleman please line the wall?" Lord Winfield called out. "I apologize for the inconvenience and appreciate everyone's cooperation, but the pendant has still not made an appearance."

Radcliff, along with all the other men around him, obediently lined the length of the east wall. Some men rolled their eyes. Others swore beneath their breath.

This is exactly why he always hated attending any Winfield gatherings. Although Lord Winfield and his wife were pleasant enough, they always overreacted to everything.

Radcliff leaned against the wall behind him and waited for further instructions, wanting it to be over so he could take his wife home and finish what he hadn't had the opportunity to complete in the garden.

When all the gentlemen present in the ballroom

finally stood in the orderly fashion the host had requested, the hunt began.

Lord Winfield looked at the long line of men, his mouth and brow wrinkling with distress.

"If you would all kindly remove your shoes and coats," Lord Winfield announced. He paused. "Your Grace?"

Radcliff met the man's gaze.

Lord Winfield leaned toward him, bringing up a gloved hand to cup the side of his mouth and whispered, "I have no intention of subjecting you to any of this. I know full well you were out in the garden enjoying the uh…fountain." He winked. "I told you it was something to see."

Radcliff smirked. "Nonsense. I should be treated like everyone else." With that, he joined in the rustle of taking off jackets as well as the shuffle of shoes being removed. "A five hundred pound pendant is well worth the cause."

"Thank you, Your Grace." Lord Winfield quickly leaned in again and whispered, "You will be in good hands. Your brother has graciously offered to assist."

The man's humor knew no bounds.

Radcliff leaned forward, glancing down at the end of the line in which he stood. Sure enough,

Carlton cockily strutted down the line toward him, as if newly appointed chief inspector.

He'd known he'd end up seeing Carlton sometime before the end of the night. Radcliff leaned back and waited.

His brother halted before him, those blue eyes of his sparkling with age-old mischief. "Well, well," Carlton drawled. "Who do we have here at the Winfield ball? Who would have thought such harmony could exist in the world that would cause a woman to forgive her father's own nemesis." He snorted. "You haven't seen that pendant, have you, Bradford? I hear it's worth a small fortune."

Radcliff narrowed his gaze. Most likely Carlton had arranged for Lady Winfield's pendant to disappear. Not for its worth, but rather as a nod to their youth and days gone by. Days when he and Carlton used to stupidly outdo one another by throwing unexpected chaos into each other's path, taking it to a ridiculous crescendo until one of them called it off and paid three guineas.

That was when they used to get along.

Radcliff held out his coat. "I've had a rather long night, Carlton."

"I hate to disappoint you, Bradford, but if you don't cooperate, this may prove to be the longest night you've ever known." Taking his coat, Carlton rummaged through the pockets and paused at finding a few guineas.

Carlton eyed him and tucked the coins into his own pocket before handing the coat back. "I've decided to collect my winnings early."

"Carlton," Radcliff growled out.

He pointed at the lacquered shoes set directly before Radcliff's stockinged feet on the floor. "Hand them up."

Shit. The bastard had lost the last of his mind. Knowing everyone was watching and would no doubt question his lack of cooperation, Radcliff grudgingly leaned forward and snatched them up.

Coming back up to his full height again, which was taller than Carlton's own, he shoved them at his brother and impatiently watched Carlton probe them. Finding nothing, Carlton threw them down onto the floor, barely missing Radcliff's feet.

Radcliff stared him down. Waiting.

His brother eyed him, as if convinced Bradford was responsible for the disappearance of that pendant.

"Carlton," Radcliff impatiently growled out again. They weren't young bucks who could be easily excused for acting like idiots in front of the *ton.* He happened to be a married man now

and had his wife's reputation to fend for. Not just his own.

"I hear you had quite an extravagant wedding and that you may be in dire need of funds. Pull out those pockets, Bradford, will you?"

"Go frig yourself, Carlton."

Gasps escaped from men on both sides of the line. As if none of them had ever heard the word.

Carlton smirked, clearly pleased he was getting a reaction. "Why would you refuse to be searched? Hmm?" He pointed at Radcliff mockingly, then strode on to the next man in line.

Men farther down now whispered amongst themselves, whilst others leaned forward to get a better view of him.

Hell. All he needed was the *ton* thinking he was in need of funds. "Search me," he called out after Carlton.

His brother paused, his dark brows going up as he made his way back over to him, his boots clicking against the wood floor. He paused before him again, that cocky gaze dominating his. "Pull out your pockets."

"I'll do better than that." Radcliff savagely unbuttoned his trousers, ready to bring an end to this nonsense. He allowed his trousers to drop, then promptly removed one muscled leg after the other, ignoring the cool breeze now circling his undergarments.

Radcliff snatched them up and flopped them at his brother. "Search every last stitch."

A few men chortled.

Carlton shifted his jaw, then tossed his trousers back at him without bothering to search them. "I suggest you put them on, Bradford. Before everyone sees how little you were born with."

More chortles floated about the room.

"All that matters is that I was born first." Radcliff grabbed his trousers and yanked them on, buttoning everything back into place. He shoved his feet into his shoes, not breaking their gaze.

Carlton adjusted his evening coat and leaned toward him. "Matilda came back. Women. They're like dogs." He sneered, pulled out the two guineas he'd taken earlier and tucked them into Radcliff's outer coat pocket. "You win on account of removing your trousers. I didn't anticipate that."

Radcliff narrowed his gaze. The man thrived on making people unravel. But if the bastard thought Radcliff was going to become unnerved for a woman who was not even his, the man was out of his mind. He had his own wife to oversee, a task that was proving far more challenging than he'd ever anticipated.

The double doors at the other end of the ballroom, which had been shut earlier during the search, banged open, causing Radcliff and all the other men in the room to jerk toward the sound.

His brows rose as a young footman in blue livery dashed across the expanse of the ballroom, his thudding boots echoing. The footman skidded to a frantic halt beside Lord Winfield, leaned toward the man, and whispered something to him.

Radcliff craned in an attempt to hear what was being said.

Lord Winfield winced and signaled the footman away.

Lord Winfield eyed them all. Then narrowed his gaze. "It appears the pendant has been recovered, gentlemen. From a wineglass set on the staircase. We apparently have a jester amongst us. I despise jesters."

Radcliff shook his head as a wave of curses swept through the ballroom. Carlton was such an ass. He'd done the exact same thing to another man years ago. Only it was a pocket watch. And needless to say, it never worked again after sitting in wine half the night.

Men stormed off, yanking on their coats, while

others laughed openly, rather amused by the unexpected bit of entertainment.

Carlton strode past Radcliff again and waggled his dark brows, catching the tip of his tongue with his teeth before veering toward the crowd of men leaving.

Radcliff approached Lord Winfield, grabbed the man's hand and shook it firmly. For Justine's sake. "I am afraid my brother is a bit too fond of playing pirate and for it I can only apologize."

Lord Winfield pulled his hand from his and adjusted his evening coat. "I do not share his sense of humor."

"Neither do I. Which is why I don't invite him to any more functions. Good night, my lord." Radcliff put up a hand and was about to leave, when he paused, remembering something. "Oh, yes. There is one more thing."

Lord Winfield eyed him dubiously.

"Her Grace has dropped her emerald necklace in that new fountain of yours."

Lord Winfield rolled his eyes. "Damn these women and their trinkets." He heaved out an exhausted breath. "Give me a moment. I'll have one of my servants fetch it out."

Radcliff chuckled and tapped the man's arm. "No, no. You don't understand."

Lord Winfield turned. "What? What do I not understand?"

"Give it to your wife. I believe she has earned it for recognizing quality. Good night."

SCANDAL TWELVE

Men will always ardently seek to claim that which you must closely guard. And you'd best believe I am not referring to your little heart.

How to Avoid a Scandal, Author Unknown

The Bradford residence that same evening

RADCLIFF CLEARED HIS THROAT and tugged on the sleeves of his robe as he slowly made his way toward Justine's bedchamber. He paused at her door and lingered for a moment, questioning if he was physically prepared to bed her. Blowing out a breath, he knocked.

"You don't have to knock, Radcliff," Justine offered in divinely warm and honeyed tones.

He wet his lips, assuring himself he was more than ready, turned the knob and edged into the room.

Justine lounged in the middle of her bed with a red leather-bound book. Meeting his gaze, she raised a brow and tossed the book off to the side of the bed with a thud.

She stared him down. "I want a tiger, not a lamb."

More than encouraged by her erotic words, Radcliff slammed the door shut behind him and met her gaze as he untied the only thing left between them.

His robe.

He shrugged the robe from his shoulders, letting it slide off his naked body and pool around his bare feet. He stood there for a long moment, so she could get a good look. His cock grew heavy and thick at the thought of finally claiming her.

She gawked at him, her cheeks flushing to crimson. Her lips parted, as if she meant to say something, but not a single sound emerged.

With a few short strides he reached the bed. He settled down onto the mattress beside her, atop the coverlet she huddled beneath, and casually rolled toward her. He propped himself on his elbow and lifted a brow. "How does it feel to have your own statue of David?"

She giggled nervously, and gestured—though without looking—toward his exposed lower half which was pointing straight at her. "That appears to be three times the size of what David boasts."

He grinned. "I'm so thrilled you noticed."

Grabbing hold of her hand, he brought it down onto his cock, guiding her fingers to close around its soft tip. A woman's touch, *her* touch, had never felt so good or so satisfying. He had never genuinely wanted a woman this much for himself, in his heart or his loins.

She sucked in a breath. "By God. I never—"

He grabbed her waist and yanked her body flat onto the mattress beside him. He sat atop her thighs, pinning her firmly into place. "Is there anything you wanted to discuss before we begin?"

She gawked up at him. "Pardon?"

He leaned toward her, brushing the soft strands of long, undone hair from her smooth, flushed cheeks. "Do you have concerns?"

"I…" Her hazel eyes observed him with a tangle of adoration and uncertainty. "Is it me you really want in this moment, Radcliff?" she whispered up at him. "Or is it your obsession that wants me?"

"I want you." He lowered his head to her soft neck, which was scented with achingly sweet rose water. He touched his lips to the side of her warm throat, repeatedly kissing its length as tenderly as he knew how. Although he wanted to ravage her there and then, without pausing a moment longer, he had every intention of waiting patiently for her natural instincts to take over, and prove to her that he had mastered his own body enough for them both to enjoy their night.

A SHAKY BREATH ESCAPED Justine as she shuddered beneath the length and width of Radcliff's smooth muscled body. Her husband never ceased to astound her, and all she wanted was to revel in this tender moment he was offering. A moment before they plunged into the abyss of pleasure.

Radcliff slowly lifted his dark head from where it was buried against her neck and hovered above her, as if needing to look at her face.

She blinked back up at his rugged, scarred face which was already lightly dusted with evening stubble. His scar certainly suited him. For it spoke of his character and of his heart. One side perfect. And one side not.

The black tips of his hair feathered her forehead as he lingered closer, gently pressing a large hand to the side of her face. "I have a confession to make," he whispered, his hot breath brushing against her cheek. "I survived these past two weeks by pleasuring myself. Repeatedly. I didn't want to, but I had to."

Her cheeks burned at the admission, and she knew she needed to speak before all rational thoughts disappeared. She guided her fingers along his jaw. "I appreciate you telling me and am asking that from this night forth, there are no more amorous sessions with yourself. Not ever alone and most certainly not ever before a portrait or any object in this house."

"Matilda's portrait comes down tomorrow as soon as I wake." He paused. "But the same would apply for you. You haven't been pleasuring yourself these past two weeks without me, have you?"

She gurgled out a laugh. "I haven't."

"Good. Otherwise it wouldn't be in the least bit fair."

She swallowed. "So you promise?"

"Yes. I promise."

She poked his bare, muscled shoulder. "You'd best swear it upon your honor and your soul, Radcliff. For how are we to create a genuine intimacy between us if you're off with yourself and I'm off with myself?"

He chuckled. "I do believe I'm blushing."

"I mean it, Radcliff. Swear it upon your honor and your soul. Swear to me you won't ever pleasure yourself whilst you are alone. I am beginning to believe it's important to our relationship."

His features stilled and grew serious. "Then I

swear it." He leaned in closer. "Now kiss me and do not make me suffer a moment more."

"I am yours from this night forth, Radcliff. Always." She quickly lifted her head to close the distance between their lips. He instantly pressed his warm mouth against hers and slid his tongue between her lips, grazing her own tongue.

A groan escaped him as his hand left the side of her face and trailed the outside of her arms. Incredible shivers raced throughout her body as his hand traveled farther down to her waist, buried beneath the coverlet.

Her heartbeat throbbed in her ears as he tilted his body to one side, momentarily removing his weight from hers. Still kissing her, his thumb rubbed her midsection in a circular motion, moving its way down her belly. Down to where they both wanted him to be.

She sank into the pleasurable sensation of his hot touch, which burned straight through the thin muslin of her chemise.

The tip of his tongue slowly traced her upper lip, then her lower lip. His entire mouth was soon molded against hers, his tongue delving deeper, toward the back of her mouth, twining and flicking.

A moan escaped her as she gave in to him.

His lips pressed harder, forcing her tongue farther into the wetness of his mouth. She feverishly pushed her tongue against his.

His hands took hold of her wrists and dragged her arms above her head. He shifted against her. His thick arousal pushed into her lower thigh, causing her to arch toward him.

She was more than ready.

His hands pinned her tightly as he dug his hips hard into her. Rubbing. Then circling. The searing heat of his body became her own. She could no longer stay still. Her body writhed.

He released her wrists and her mouth. His fingers grabbed the fabric of her chemise and lifted. His broad muscled chest expanded with a deep tremble. The fabric pooled at her belly as his large hand gently trailed up her knee to the soft flesh of her thigh. Tickles mixed with an exploding waterfall of sensation possessed her entire body.

She panted, unable to fight the feelings. His fingers stopped between her thighs and he gently tapped her wet folds. Her legs widened, fully opening up her core to him. He slowly pushed one finger into her, rubbing his palm against her most sensitive place. She gasped and he slipped a second finger into her. Then a third. He stilled and rubbed his palm firmly against her mound, then pushed deeper.

Pressure welled within her. She was so full. So wide open for him. She moaned.

He pressed harder and an unexpected searing pain rippled through her flesh. Her eyes fluttered open in astonishment.

He hovered above her, watching her face as his fingers firmly rocked back and forth and from side to side. "I'm readying you to receive me," he whispered. "Nothing more."

She couldn't even nod.

He instantly withdrew his fingers, trailing her moisture down her thigh. All the pressure vanished, and he slid down the length of her, his hot mouth sucking and licking her folds.

She drew in a shaky breath and watched in disbelief as his broad shoulders shifted and his dark head bobbed between her thighs, his tongue urgently lapping at her wetness. His fingers dug into her thighs as he spread her legs farther apart to make room for him.

He flicked his tongue over and over in the area that affected her most, making pleasure rise in the pit of her stomach with each pulsing touch.

How was she going to ever deny him again, knowing what he was capable of? Her breath hitched in her throat as she grabbed hold of his thick, soft hair and held him firmly, almost savagely, against her.

He moaned and blindly reached down and gave his erection several quick jerks, causing it to stick further out.

Every moment she was brought closer and closer to a glittering haven of utter bliss.

Her fingers blindly found the soft texture of his scar on the side of his face. A scar she had always wanted to touch but was afraid to until now. She rubbed it intimately, up and down, up and down, just as he was doing to her with his tongue, and inwardly wished she could melt that scar away beneath her fingers. Along with whatever else brought him pain.

His tongue stopped and with it her promise of heaven. "You make a man want scars all over his body," he growled against her.

She smiled.

Radcliff rose, letting cool air bathe her hot folds. Grabbing hold of her chemise, he yanked her up for a moment, and then jerking the cloth over her head and arms, he whipped it aside, sending it floating off the bed.

Justine panicked for a brief moment, realizing that she was stark naked beneath him. But the warmth of his velvet body, which had lowered back onto hers, covered her panic with assurance.

He licked her lips hard, leaving a sweet saltiness behind. "Taste yourself," he said in a low, rumbling tone.

It was something she would have never thought to do, but coming from him, it was oddly erotic. She feverishly ran her hands up and down the length of his firm, muscled back and grabbed for his buttocks, squeezing them. Enjoying their solid mass.

He slid his mouth lower and sucked in the nipple of her left breast, spreading gooseflesh across her entire body.

She arched against him, wanting him to suckle more. "Harder."

He chuckled against her. "You didn't like that before."

"I do now." Her pulse soared as his body ground against hers, and he pulled more of her breast into his mouth. His hand pushed down between them, and his fingers flicked at that wildly sensitive spot yet again.

"I vow to be gentle," he softly promised.

"I know you will," she panted. She held on to him, waiting for him to claim her entire body, heart and soul once and for all.

RADCLIFF GUIDED HIS SOLID cock into her and moaned in disbelief as he edged inside her hot, tight wetness.

He pressed farther into her. Slowly. She tensed beneath him, her core clamping down on his hard shaft. Ripples of ecstasy shot to his buttocks, and he choked. With one swift, solid jerk, he pushed past the last resistance of her maidenhead and buried himself deep within her.

Although his body demanded he thrust deeper, he gritted his teeth and waited, trying to protect her from the pain. From himself.

He swallowed and brushed a hand over the top of her head, memorizing the feel of everything belonging to her. "How is the pain?" he managed.

Her body gradually relaxed beneath him. "It was short-lived."

He swallowed, his body urging him to keep thrusting. He fought against it. "I will wait," he insisted hoarsely.

She slipped her small hands beneath his arms and gripped his waist. Hard. "Do not wait. Take your pleasure. And give me mine."

As if he needed to be told twice.

He slid himself out, then slid his full length back into her tightness. He did it painfully slow, in and out, trying to control himself, even as the explosive downpour of sensations threatened to take away the last of his reason.

Her tightness against his throbbing shaft was unbearable. All he really wanted to do was pound against her. Like an animal. "Justine," he hissed out, forcing himself not to move, lest he lose control. "It has been far too long. Let me finish you and then I shall finish myself with my hand. We will try again tomorrow."

She held him tighter against herself, practically clinging to him. "No more self-pleasuring. Not ever again. Do what you will and be true to what you want from me. I wish it."

Oh, God. He had to. He had to fuck the way his body wanted to. He jerked out of her wetness and after an agonizing pause, slammed himself completely into her, sending all those much needed sensations throughout his entire body.

A gasping breath escaped her, as her nails dug into his skin.

Radcliff thrust into her again and again, faster and deeper, his hips ruthlessly digging into hers. He watched her beautiful face and those full round breasts bob before him in disbelief. That she was his. All his.

He gnashed his teeth and pounded harder, eliciting gasps, moans and breaths from her with each aggressive movement. Watching her full lips part with each moan made him want to release not only his seed but every single thought and emotion he had ever kept within himself.

But he refused to settle for anything in that moment other than her climax.

Throwing her head fitfully against the pillows that surrounded her, she pushed her hips against him and moaned, "I feel it. I feel it."

Adjusting his grip on her waist, he drove into her again, faster, making sure he was angled better to hit the very spot she needed.

He watched her eyes close and her head tilt farther back, exposing the entire length of her neck.

"Oh!" she cried out in pleasured anguish. Her velvet flesh clamped in waves against his hardness. "Yes! Yes!"

He eagerly pushed on, tucking her soft curves into the contours of his flaming body. He dug harder into her wet warmth, trying to get closer. Needing to get closer.

As his climax penetrated every inch of him, he groaned, low and deep. His muscles tightened and his entire body quaked as he freely spilled his seed into her warmth. He wanted the incredible intensity of this pleasure to last forever. His cock continued to pulse, pouring into her, until there was nothing left within him to give.

Exhausted, he collapsed onto her warm flesh.

Even long after his heart returned to its usual steady beat, he continued to cling to her, strangely wanting and needing this closeness between them to last much longer than any release ever could.

He rolled onto his side, bringing her with him, and cradled her head against his chest. "You are the most incredible woman I have ever known."

She let out a small, achingly wistful sigh. "And you are the most incredible man I have ever known."

He traced her smooth cheek with his thumb and continued to lay there silently. The soft intake of her breath caught his attention. He lifted his head to look down at her. Her eyes were closed and her lips slightly parted. She slept.

Ever so gently, he kissed the top of her head and settled back against the pillows. The few candles in the room providing dull, golden light flickered out one by one until Justine and the room vanished from sight. But instead of the vast emptiness that usually greeted him at night, Justine's soft warmth and steady intake of breath assured him for the first time in his life that he was not alone.

He slowly grinned. It was the strangest and most incredible feeling in the world. He only hoped to God it never ever went away.

SCANDAL THIRTEEN

There is only one reason as to why a lady should read this book. And that is to prevent her from becoming a flapping fish upon a hook.
How to Avoid a Scandal, Author Unknown

AFTER MAKING LOVE TO Justine four times throughout the night, she finally begged him to sleep. So he let her, and in turn, spent the rest of the long night shifting and unable to sleep. A raging mixture of physical need and wanting to pour his every emotion into her slowly choking him. He felt as if he were losing his ability to define what it was he truly wanted and needed from Justine.

He swallowed and tried to steady his breathing even though his chest ached and his core demanded her. He squeezed his eyes shut and suffered in silence for what seemed like an endless night and in some small way wished he had never engaged her. For it was obvious, his body was overtaking his ability to function.

No sooner had daybreak streaked the morning

sky beyond the heavy curtains than Radcliff shakily slipped out of Justine's arms and scooted off the bed.

Removing himself from those soft, naked arms was like removing himself from grace. Despite the fact that their night together had been beyond anything that could ever be bound to earth, reality was paying him a visit. His cock had nagged him all night, never once allowing him to sleep. Even now, his prick was harder than granite, demanding relief. And he knew it had nothing to do with it being morning.

He swallowed, refusing to force himself on Justine. The last thing he wanted was for her to despise his advances. Especially now that everything was going so well.

The sharp coolness of the room tightened his naked body as he crept toward his robe. Gathering it quietly, he tested each floorboard with his weight as he moved toward the door. He opened it and then glanced back at the curves hidden beneath the thick coverlet. Justine's naked arm was outstretched and her chestnut hair buried against one of the pillows.

Stealing out into the darkened corridor, he shut the door behind him. He lingered in the hallway, his chest heaving, and glanced toward the direction of Matilda's portrait.

No. He shouldn't. It needed to come down. Right now. He turned away from it, then paused, digging his robe against the erection he'd suffered from these past few hours. Though a part of him knew it was wrong and that he would be betraying his promise to Justine, he preferred to disappoint her in this way than give her cause to dread and loathe his advances. Advances which he knew he wouldn't be able to control without quickly wearing out his welcome.

WITH EYES STILL CLOSED, Justine rolled over and dreamily reached out for Radcliff, wanting to draw his velvet warmth closer. Only…there was no warmth. Opening her eyes, she yanked the coverlet around her naked body.

The red curtains draping the bed were open, as were the matching window curtains. A gray, cloudy morning replaced the glorious, clear, starry sky of yesternight.

There, seated in a chair beside the window, was her Radcliff. Already fully dressed in a dove-gray morning suit. He leaned forward, both elbows propped on his knees, his dark head bent and his brows set in deep thought.

She sat up quietly and blinked, realizing the man was actually engrossed with reading her etiquette book, *How To Avoid a Scandal*. The one she'd flung away the night before.

Tilting her head, she continued to watch Radcliff read and wondered whether he really found it that interesting.

She gathered the coverlet closer around herself and finally whispered, "Good morning."

He glanced up and quickly shut the little red book, clearing his throat. "It's long past morning. It's two in the afternoon."

She wrinkled her nose. "Is it? Why didn't you try to rouse me?"

"It was obvious you needed rest."

She eyed him. "Were you actually reading my etiquette book?"

He snorted. "Trying to. By God, what you poor women are subjected to. I know I would have never survived if I had been born a woman."

Justine paused, then blinked, wondering if her etiquette book might actually help him and his obsession. It had plenty of good advice, aside from its blatant disregard of bedside manners. Perhaps—

He held up the book and waved it at her. "Were you actually forced to read this? Or was this something you chose to read?"

She eyed him, wondering how to go about presenting this idea without completely castrating his pride. "A bit of both. I read it a total of eight times."

His brows rose. "*Eight times?* Whatever for? Wasn't once enough?"

"That book was my path to better understanding what was expected of me when I first arrived in London. Although I had a very civilized upbringing with a governess, tutors, daily lessons in history, music, dancing, French and Italian, it was still all done in canvas tents or huts that looked like inverted baskets. I didn't play with aristocratic, white children. I played with dark-skinned children who, for the most part, treated me as though I were some exotic fruit. When I arrived in London, I realized I was still a piece of fruit in the eyes of those around me, only I wasn't so exotic. That was when I knew my upbringing had put me at a disadvantage. Heavens, I didn't even walk like the rest of the debutantes. It was by reading and rereading that book that I came to better understand how I was expected to behave."

Justine moved off the bed, taking the coverlet with her, and stood, feeling as if her legs were made of plum pudding. "I have an idea as to how we are going to help you master your obsession better. Are you willing to humor me?"

He eyed her, slapping the book against his trouser-clad knee, and sat back against the chair. "I have no trouble humoring you. I need to learn better methods of control. But might I suggest you clothe that delectable body of yours and keep it clothed whenever in my presence? Otherwise you aren't going to be of much assistance to me. At all."

Justine adjusted the coverlet, a rapid heat creeping into her face, and realized he was right. She might as well be wagging a gazelle in front of a lion. "Uh…so true. Why don't you wait in the study whilst I dress? Be mindful it may take some time."

"Take however long you need."

"Oh, and while you are waiting," she added quickly, "I have an assignment for you."

"An assignment?"

"Yes. I want you to create a list of ten things you think I would want during our marriage, along with a brief explanation as to why you think I would want those things." Her father and her tutors always forced her to write lists of ten when they were testing her understanding of something.

"I'll be in the study. Writing said list." He stood

to his grand height of six feet and strode past the bed. With the flick of his wrist, he tossed the etiquette book onto the mattress, then opened the door and disappeared, closing the door behind him.

Justine scampered over to the braided bell pull and yanked on it. She was going to have Henri put some extra effort into her appearance.

She collapsed onto the bed and lovingly snatched up the etiquette book, brushing her fingers alongside the edges he had all but recently gripped. "Radcliff dearest," she whispered aloud, as if he could hear her. "Everything I do, I do for you."

SCANDAL FOURTEEN

Sadly, many have long forgotten the purpose behind why a lady should curtsy. Above all, a curtsy is a humble form of "courtesy" laced with dignity and grace. If done right, it will be remembered by the person you are being introduced to for a very, very long time.

How to Avoid a Scandal, Author Unknown

WITH A LIT CIGAR IN one hand and a quill in the other, Radcliff stared blankly at the unfinished list, trying to think of what else he could scribe. Surely he hadn't missed anything. Of course, knowing Justine, she was probably trying to prove a point. That he didn't know a goddamn thing about what she wanted. And most likely, she was right.

He quickly reread what he had so far:

Ten Things My Wife Might Want From Me And Why

1. Respect (Because she deserves it)
2. Money (Because she and her parents need it)
3. Clothing (Because she is not Eve)

4. Jewelry (Because she looks stunning in it)
5. Children (Because she would be a perfect mother)
6. Excursions and Holidays (Because she misses Africa)
7. Romance (Because every woman wants it)
8. Me (Because without me the above wouldn't be possible)

And…? What? What more could she possibly want from him? Assistance in world domination? Most likely. Would Justine approve of it being number nine or ten? Not likely.

He brought the cigar to his lips, took in a long, searing aromatic puff and slowly blew it out. The smoke descended upon the parchment and dissipated into the air around him. He continued to stare at his own words in complete exasperation.

Dash it. Maybe he should start anew.

He tossed his quill toward the direction of the inkwell and the burning candle whose wax was dripping down onto the silver holder. Shoving the cigar between his teeth, he crushed the parchment into a small ball and whipped it over his writing desk toward the scattered pile of a dozen or so other mutilated lists.

Perhaps he should give her that entire pile. For there was certainly enough in there for her to make sense of.

In the far distance, the calling bell rang.

Radcliff ignored it and drew in another breath of his cigar before yanking it out from between his teeth with his left hand. Ten things. With his right, he plucked up the quill, which had splattered droplets of ink across his polished desk.

Ten things. Hell. There couldn't *be* ten things. Unless he included servants, carriages and the house. But then that would be eleven things.

The doors to the study fanned open and Jefferson cleared his throat. "Are you at home, Your Grace?"

Radcliff tossed the quill yet again in the direction of the inkwell, splattering more ink across the desk. He tapped the building ash at the end of his cigar into the small pan beside him, leaned back into his chair and eyed his butler. "Who is it?"

"A Miss Matilda Thurlow."

Radcliff's lips parted as the cigar slipped from between his fingers and fell onto his lap. He jumped and frantically snatched the cigar, scrambling to his booted feet and brushing at the dark mark imprinted upon his gray trousers.

Shit. At least he hadn't set fire to himself and his cock. Though that probably would have resolved everything.

Radcliff shoved the cigar into the ash pan. There

was only one reason he could think of as to why Matilda Thurlow would visit him in his own home and in broad daylight. Something had forced her to.

"Your Grace," Jefferson insisted. "The lady appears to be in dire need."

Radcliff stiffly straightened and drew in a deep breath that was anything but calming. What the hell was he supposed to do? Turn her away? Damn her. Damn her for putting him in this situation. "I will receive her here in the study. Fetch my wife, will you? *At once.* I do not wish to be left alone." Radcliff plucked up his cigar from the pan.

Jefferson bowed and departed.

Knowing that he would have to dash out his cigar, as a gentleman was supposed to whilst in the presence of a woman, Radcliff took one last puff and let the smoke slowly fume out through his nostrils.

He closed his eyes, savoring the heated, soothing taste, and wondered how he was going to remain steady-minded without so much as a cigar to occupy his hands.

Reopening his eyes, he crushed the burning end of the cigar and pulled open the top right drawer of the desk. Shoving the ash pan and cigar inside, he slammed it shut and repositioned his chair so that it angled toward the open doorway.

The clicking of heeled slippers soon filled the corridor beyond, and within moments, Matilda appeared in a flower-patterned carriage attire, cashmere shawl and matching bonnet. She slowly and carefully crossed the room, as if she were having trouble walking with her oversize belly. Her eyes remained downcast as she continued to approach him. Her face was pale and devoid of emotion, with new bruises scattered upon the side of her face and a swollen lip encrusted with blood.

Despite that, her blond hair was perfectly pinned into place within the dome of her bonnet, and her gown looked pretty and tidy.

Radcliff quickly stood but refused to look at her further. Pity was a very dangerous emotion when one was not in a position to offer assistance. He kept his gaze firmly affixed on the door, waiting for Justine to appear, hoping to God that she would soon so that he wouldn't have to do this alone.

"Thank you for receiving me, Your Grace," Matilda brokenly whispered as if they had never been formally introduced. Her voice seemed so distant, so uncharacteristically faint.

He stiffly waved her toward the direction of a

chair. "Yes, yes. Sit. My wife will be joining us shortly and you may speak then."

Out of the corner of his eye, he watched her hobble carefully to an upholstered chair. She turned, holding on to the arms of the chair, and sat. She sucked in a harsh breath but said nothing more.

To his relief, there was a quick clicking of heels and then the rustling of fabric as Justine whisked into the study, then paused, one small hand gripping the side of her full silk skirt, while the other hand gripped the etiquette book he'd been browsing earlier. She noted Matilda's presence before allowing her beautiful gaze to collide with his.

Radcliff's breath hitched, realizing how absolutely stunning his wife really was despite the pinched concern twisting her features. Long, unbound chestnut curls spilled down the sides of her pretty oval face. A face that was beginning to flush, and in turn, emphasize the delicate curve of her exposed throat.

Random flashes of her warm, velvet body next to his, the feel of her skin against his hands as he slid them up the length of her smooth thighs, their mingled cries of ecstasy, her fingertips digging into his flesh, all of it seared and consumed his thoughts even in that moment.

He willed his gaze to remain on her and her alone, wishing to God he could somehow make her understand how trapped he felt in that moment.

He eventually gestured toward Matilda. "Might I introduce Miss Matilda Thurlow." He then gestured toward Justine. "Miss Thurlow, this is my wife, the Duchess of Bradford."

Matilda rose from her seat, and despite the fact that she winced with each step, she managed to make her way toward Justine. Matilda curtsied as deeply as her physical state would allow before slowly rising. As if the curtsy had not been enough, she bowed her head to Justine, causing the yellow lace ribbons and artificial blue flowers atop her bonnet to quiver. "Your Grace. It is an honor."

Justine's arched brows came together as she searched Matilda's face in what was obvious astonishment. "Miss Thurlow. Your face. Are you all right? What happened?"

Matilda kept her head bowed and said nothing. She eventually drew her shaky gloved hands together, placing them upon her protruding belly. Her shoulders quaked.

A wrenching sob escaped Matilda, followed by another one. "F-forgive me, Your Grace. I shouldn't be here."

"Nonsense," Justine insisted. "'Tis obvious you

require assistance. What is it that you need, Miss Thurlow? What is it that my husband and I can do for you? Ask and it is yours. I will not allow you to leave until you inform us of how we may assist."

Matilda let out another sob. "I—I came to ask for five pounds. My sister, Yvonne, will not house me unless I have it. Whilst Carlton has...has taken everything I have. Everything. I tried to return to the brothel where I once worked, hoping to earn some money there, but they...they'll not have me as I am." She sobbed again.

Justine snapped her gaze over to him, clearly bewildered, before returning her attention back to Matilda. She leaned in closer to Matilda. "Miss Thurlow," she offered softly, touching her arm. "All will be well, I assure you. Please. Do not cry."

Radcliff blew out a breath, preparing himself for words he knew he had to say. And it wasn't going to be in the least bit polite. "I suppose I might as well be plain, Justine, and admit here and now that the night of our wedding, I left the house and assisted Miss Thurlow with a similar situation. Absolutely nothing occurred between us that night. I was merely offering assistance. And yet, despite that time, and the money I gave her, she still chose to go back to Carlton. She isn't a child. She ought to realize that there are consequences for making foolish decisions."

A gasp escaped Justine. "Radcliff!"

Matilda's sob grew all the more pitched and hysterical. "No, no. He is right. I should have never gone back. I hate Carlton! And I will hate him until my last breath is taken!"

There were far too many damn women in the house. And for the first time in his life, he was anything but amorous about it. "Jefferson!" he boomed toward the direction of the entryway. "Give Miss Thurlow five pounds and see her to the door, will you?"

"Radcliff!" The rustling of Justine's skirts now followed in his direction. She paused only momentarily during her march to glare down at the large pile of crushed parchments scattered at her feet. "What—"

"Your damn list," he supplied with a grunt. "Nine and ten kept eluding me."

"'Tis obvious they aren't the only things eluding you." She kicked them all out of the way with the side of her blue-heeled slipper, making a path for herself. She then whisked toward his desk and alighted abruptly before him.

Slamming the etiquette book down, she gripped the desk, leaned toward him and seethed, "Give her five pounds and see her to the door. Indeed. How can you be so cruel? 'Tis obvious she requires more than that. She requires a place to stay."

"She can stay with her sister."

"A woman who demands money from her own flesh and blood is not what I would call a proper sister."

Radcliff set his hands behind his back, trying to remain indifferent. "How is it my business to care? I find it disturbingly presumptuous that Miss Thurlow thinks she can repeatedly contact me like this. And more so, call upon my home at any given hour and impose herself upon my very name before all of London."

"Forget all of London, Radcliff. She is pregnant and battered. *By your own brother!*"

"Tell me something I do not know." He eyed the door and yelled out, "Jefferson!"

"You will not toss her out!" Justine hit her hand soundly against the desk, as if she were hitting a war drum and he'd better heed it. "Do you hear me? You will *not*."

"Observe."

Jefferson appeared. "Yes, Your Grace?"

Radcliff gestured sweepingly toward Matilda. "Please escort Miss Thurlow to the door. And see to it she is given not five pounds, but fifty, as I am feeling unusually generous today."

"Generous, my toe. This is my home, too!" Justine whirled toward the burly butler. "Never you mind him, Jefferson. Miss Thurlow stays. And while you're at it, be certain to inform the chef as well as the housekeeper, Mr. Evans, that we will be having a guest staying with us these next few weeks. Until the birth of Miss Thurlow's child."

Radcliff sucked in an astonished breath and choked out, "Absolutely not. She is *not* staying in my home!"

Justine ignored him, and continued to stare the butler down. "I will see to it that fifty pounds goes into your pocket, Jefferson. You can collect it from the house steward today. What do you say?"

Jefferson hesitated, his beady blue eyes darting among all three of them. "I shall inform the housekeeper and the chef at once, Your Grace." He bowed and departed.

Radcliff flexed his hands into fists, feeling his ability to remain calm waning. Even his own butler had turned against him. For fifty pounds that was coming out of his own damn pocket!

Yes, well, this matter was far from over.

He averted his gaze to Matilda and tried to keep his voice as cool and refined as possible. "Miss

Thurlow. Seeing as my wife and I seem to be in disagreement, might we ask for a moment alone? You may retire into the parlor just down the corridor and should you require anything during that time, my butler will see to your needs."

Matilda looked at them with puffy, tear-streaked eyes, which only emphasized the terrible bruising upon her face. "I should leave. I should have never come."

"No." Justine pointed at her. "You will stay right where you are."

"No, she will retire to the parlor until this matter is resolved," Radcliff snapped. "Miss Thurlow? If you please."

"Uh…yes, Your Grace." Matilda bowed her head, gathered her skirts and hobbled toward the direction of the entryway. Though it took her some time, she eventually disappeared through the doors.

Justine hurried toward the open doors of the study, slammed them closed and whirled back toward him. "The poor woman can barely walk!"

"She is well over eight months pregnant. What do you expect?"

"Oh, no. *That* sort of severe limping isn't brought on by pregnancy. More than her face was beaten, I assure you." Justine marched her way back toward him and stopped before his desk again. "Does her appearance not move you to pity? What sort of man are you?"

"Pity is a very dangerous emotion, Justine. It causes a person to disregard reality. And the reality is I have a responsibility to you, to myself and to my name." He yanked open the top drawer of his desk and pulled out the ash pan and cigar he'd hidden earlier. Setting them onto the edge of the desk, he slammed the drawer shut and gestured toward his extinguished cigar. "You don't mind if I smoke during our little conversation, do you? I find that smoking allows me to remain calm. Which I confess, as of this moment, I am not."

She snorted. "Puff away."

"Good." He plucked up the cigar and leaned toward the burning candle set on the edge of his desk. The tobacco hissed softly as he brought it back to life. Keeping the cigar between his lips, he straightened and sucked in a mouthful of much-needed hot, earthy smoke.

Pulling the cigar back out, he turned his head, and blew the smoke out to the side, feeling decidedly calmer. He slowly took up the ash pan with his other hand and rounded the desk. He paused directly before her. "She cannot stay here."

His wife lifted her chin to better meet his gaze. "Why not?"

He settled himself on the edge of his writing desk and set the ash pan beside him. It was obvious Justine wanted to be treated with the equality of a man. And he intended on gifting her that by being as honest with her as possible. "I suppose I should tell you something. Before any more is said."

She eyed him. "And what is that?"

"Early this morning, I took down Miss Thurlow's portrait from the wall, carried it into my bedchamber and made use of it one last time before having it removed from the house by one of the servants. It wasn't quite as pleasurable as it used to be but I genuinely required a sense of release."

Her eyes widened as she scrambled away, distancing herself from him. "You did what?"

He cleared his throat and, for a moment, couldn't believe he'd actually said it. Had he done it because his guilt was too great? Or perhaps because he was trying to make her understand why he couldn't have Matilda around, pregnant or not. He was not to be trusted.

"How could you?" she asked with a broken softness that was more achingly sad than accusatory. "You promised. You promised me last night upon your honor and upon your soul you never would."

Radcliff tapped the ash off his cigar and leaned toward her. "You need to understand something,

Justine. You need to understand that this obsession of mine isn't something I can readily control with a promise. It was either the portrait or you." He stared her down. "And I didn't want the portrait, Justine. That I know."

She glared at him, hazel eyes ablaze, her cheeks flushing, making every single freckle disappear. "Am I to somehow feel honored by that admission? Is that what you think?"

Radcliff ran the tip of his tongue across the lower half of his lip, wishing to God he was a different man. Wishing to God he was a man capable of making her proud.

He shifted against the desk and rolled the thick cigar gently between his fingers. "I am truly sorry. It was not my intention to break the promise I had so genuinely made."

"And yet you did."

"And yet I did." Christ. He was such a bastard. He really was. He and his brother alike.

Shakily inhaling another mouthful of smoke, he quickly turned his head again and blew it out to the side. Lowering the cigar toward his knee, he finally said, "I wish to be frank. I like you, Justine. More than I have ever liked any woman in my life."

Clear astonishment touched her features, her

arched brows momentarily flickering. "Why are you telling me this?"

He leaned toward her again, shifting his weight against the edge of the desk, and boldly met her gaze. "Because I want you to understand something. I want you to understand that despite this obsession of mine, I have always wanted to be a good man. Even throughout all those misguided years, all I ever wanted was to lead a life with one woman. And now, with you, I have that chance. Do not complicate my life—a life that is already complicated enough—by involving another woman in it."

She rigidly pointed a finger at him. "*You* are the one complicating your own life, Radcliff. No one is complicating it for you. Not I. Not Miss Thurlow. *You.*"

He feigned a laugh and wagged his cigar at her, causing a few ashes to scatter from its tip. "No, no. You see, right now, you *are* complicating it. How? By inviting my brother's pregnant mistress to stay here. In my home. Never mind my obsession, or what I think. What do you suppose the rest of London will have to say about this? Or your parents, for God's sake? What is more, it is only a matter of time before Carlton comes hunting her down. And then what? *Then what?* I am not about to duel my own brother over his mistress. Over a…a whore."

Justine drew closer, her hazel eyes fixed steadily upon him. "The only whore I see standing before me, Radcliff, is you. You and you alone."

Radcliff snapped his mouth shut in complete astonishment, unable to move, yet alone breathe. It was the way she had said it, with such conviction, that made him feel as though he were bleeding internally. What was worse, he knew she was right. He *was* a whore. A whore to his own cock.

"Why do you continue to debauch yourself at the cost of your pride and your honor?" she persisted, drawing steadily closer. "Why do you continue to debauch yourself at the cost of a promise you made to your own wife?"

He straightened, realizing her body was far too close for his liking. He froze when she set herself and her full lilac skirts firmly against the length of his trouser-clad legs, blocking him against the desk with her own body.

Their gazes locked, and he was faintly aware of her hand drifting toward the cigar he held against his knee. She slipped it from his fingers, lowering her gaze for a moment, then leaned toward the ash pan and dashed it out, leaving it there.

"Justine," he whispered hoarsely, feeling as

though he was going to stop breathing. "Why must you torment me like this? I am doing the best I can."

Justine caught his gaze. "If you think I am tormenting you, Radcliff, then you do not know me all that well. And if *this* is the best you can do, then I genuinely fear for you *and* this marriage. I truly believe we've been going about this all wrong. Eliminating your desires from your path is not by any means beneficial. For how are you to learn to control an obsession if your environment is being controlled for you? Miss Thurlow aside, I have decided we are going to bring back female servants into this house. Henri is a very nice young man but enough is well enough. I want a proper lady's maid. Is that understood, Your Grace?"

He swallowed and half nodded, acknowledging her words. She was right. He had to face who he was. And he had to do it without abusing her trust and paying others to make things more convenient for him. But what if he failed her? What then? Would she leave him?

Justine searched his face. "When I was much younger, and incapable of truly understanding, my father told me that when a man overindulges in any one thing, it means he is trying to compensate for something that is missing in his life. So what is it that is missing from your life, Bradford? Can you tell me? Do you even know?"

Radcliff looked away from the heated intensity within those eyes, feeling as if she were stripping away the last of his sense and sensibility. For he knew the answer to her question all too well.

The strain of becoming duke at the age of fourteen had made him seek out a means of escape. And physical pleasure, he'd quickly learned, was a breathtaking method of release.

Eventually, however, he had wanted and needed more. Being young at the time, he had felt no need to control it. Being a rake was acceptable, given his status. Yet somehow, the more pleasure he'd sought out, the less he'd actually received in turn. And despite all the women who had willingly flocked to him, he'd always felt used and alone.

Justine sighed. "I suppose there is only one way for us to go about this."

She reached around him and plucked something off the desk. She held up the etiquette book, then firmly grabbed his hand and placed the book on the flat surface of his palm.

"And so the dockside whore must learn to become a respectable lady," she drawled, tapping at the surface of the book. "Read it and ask yourself how you can apply female etiquette into *your* daily life."

She took several steps back. "I am asking you to do right by this situation, Your Grace. I am asking that you allow Miss Thurlow to stay with us until the birth of her child. After which time, a more suitable arrangement will be made. I trust, should you agree to shelter her, that you will not further abuse me *or* Miss Thurlow. For if you do, I vow to board the next outgoing ship to Cape Town with my parents. And you will never see me again. Do you think I ever wanted to stay here in London? I never belonged here amongst all these snobs and expectations. I only returned because my parents wished for me to marry. Which I did."

She bowed her head, her long chestnut curls swaying, then turned and whisked toward the doors. She pushed them wide and disappeared, the clicking of her slippers continuing down the corridor and what felt like out of his life.

Radcliff lowered his gaze to the small, but weighty, red leather-bound book he still held. Though a part of him wanted to dash the book across the room out of anger, out of the absurdity of what she proposed, he realized that if he didn't make some sort of effort, Justine was not only going to hate him for the rest of her life but would most likely disappear onto a ship and sail out of his life forever.

And he was beginning to realize that he didn't want that. He wanted to learn to be the best man he could be, the sort of man she could be proud of. He'd never had a moral compass. But it was time he found one before he was lost at sea and left for dead.

Radcliff tightened his hold on the book, letting the binding bite into the skin of his palm, and rose from the edge of the desk. "Justine!" he yelled out, striding toward the open doors.

He stepped out into the corridor, turned and paused.

Justine, who already stood at the far end of the corridor, turned slowly toward him, her skirts rustling against the white marble floor in the drumming silence that spanned between them. The light from the windows beyond barely reached her face, making it almost impossible to see her eyes.

He didn't know why, but he needed to see those beautiful eyes. Perhaps because he wanted assurance in light of what he was about to do.

He held up the book, shaking it at her, as he made his way toward her. "I will read this. And I will read it again and again, until I have come to understand the lesson you wish me to learn."

She didn't move. Nor did she seem to want to reply.

As he drew steadily closer, her eyes eventually became visible. And to his astonishment, they were squeezed shut. As if she were unwilling to look at him or face the situation at hand.

Imagine that. She wasn't the bold tough she professed herself to be. Like him, there were cracks within the marble.

He paused before her. The soft scent of powder and oranges, which his cigar must have earlier covered, encased him, and the strange urge to hold her in a way that did not involve anything but a simple, mutual offering of understanding and companionship, overwhelmed him.

In that moment, he suddenly realized it was never lust he had wanted. It was a companion. That companion being Justine. He wanted her smile. He wanted her words. He wanted it all. Never in all his three and thirty years had he yearned to have *this* sort of genuine understanding and *this* sort of genuine companionship from a woman.

And it scared the bloody shit out of him. Because he'd never depended upon anyone but himself for anything. But it was obvious that when it came to something as simple as his own happiness, he couldn't depend on himself at all.

He swallowed and shakily tucked the small book into his waistcoat pocket, trying to understand what was happening to him. "I have made a decision with regard to Miss Thurlow."

Her eyes fluttered open, and she gawked up at him with those hauntingly beautiful hazel eyes. "What is it?" she whispered.

His Justine clearly had her generous heart set on helping him *and* Matilda Thurlow. And by God, if he didn't admire the hell out of her for it. For she was tossing all of London to the wind and doing what he knew himself was the right and only thing to do.

Although he didn't have to agree to anything, for he was duke, damn it, he also knew that by agreeing, he just might save his own marriage and redeem himself in her eyes. Which was all that mattered to him.

He set his hands behind his back, reminding himself that Waterloo had not been won overnight, and formally announced, "I have decided Miss Thurlow will stay until the birth of her child. After which time, you and I will arrange something more suitable for the two. Preferably it will be abroad. Far from Carlton."

A stifled sob floated toward him somewhere to his left. His brows rose as he glanced toward

Matilda Thurlow, who stood in the doorway of the parlor with her hands rubbing her large belly.

Matilda smiled tremulously, and despite her puffy face and the bruising and bloody lip, her blue eyes practically sparkled. "Your Grace. Thank you for your never-ending generosity."

He cleared his throat. "I am pleased to be of assistance. Now if you ladies will excuse me, I admit to having some important business to tend to." He offered Justine a curt nod, then rounded her and did not stop walking until he had turned the farthest corner and was out of sight.

He staggered to a halt and stood there in the corridor for a dazed moment, wondering how the hell his life had ever gotten so complicated.

There was the echoing of steady steps, and the butler's large polished boots and oversize wool trousers appeared in the spot he continued to vacantly stare at before him. "Your Grace?" A gloved hand touched his shoulder. "Do you require assistance?"

Radcliff glanced up. "As a matter of fact, I do. Bring me a cigar, an ash pan and a lit candle. And while you're at it, bring a decanter of brandy. No glass required."

Jefferson paused, then quickly departed, his hurried steps echoing down the corridor.

Radcliff blew out an exhausted breath, reached into the lining of his pocket and after a few tugs, pulled out the etiquette book. He stared at the gold lettering mocking him with the words *How To Avoid A Scandal,* then bent it open, letting the pages naturally fall into place.

He blinked and read:

It requires unprecedented skill and patience if one is to become the perfect lady. Mind you, it is a skill and patience of which not every woman is capable. Though you may think you understand what is expected of you by your father, by your mother, and by all of society, it may be best to set all that aside. For expectations will always change. It is up to you to keep up with those expectations. Indeed, being a lady is an art no man could ever master, because it requires playing the greatest and most difficult of instruments, one that few know how to use—the brain.

Radcliff slapped the book shut. Christ. And that was just one paragraph. If he didn't know any better, he'd say he was allowing Justine to guide him through his obsession because he was stupidly and madly in love with her.

He swallowed. Actually, no. He *knew* he was in love with her. And that was the damn problem.

SCANDAL FIFTEEN

It is never fashionable for a lady to become
inebriated.

How to Avoid a Scandal, Author Unknown

Evening

THE SILENCE AT THE dining table was positively unbearable. Radcliff had rudely slung his arm around
the upper back of his upholstered chair, leaning as
far back as was physically possible, and ignored
his food. His appetite appeared to be for port and
only port. Of which, he was already on his sixth
course.

And then there was Matilda, who sat opposite
from Justine. Although her face had been washed
and her bloody lip tended to, making her appearance more bearable, the poor woman sat there and
stared vacantly into her soup. As if it weren't deli-
cious White *à la Reine* but water scooped up from
the bottom of the Thames.

Everyone's misery was going to suffocate Justine.

She set her spoon beside her porcelain bowl and eyed Matilda, offering her a smile. "Is it not to your liking, Miss Thurlow? Perhaps the chef might be able to offer you something else? You should eat. For the sake of the baby."

Matilda's blue eyes lifted up from her bowl. She stared at Justine, her eyes intently searching Justine's own face. Matilda's cheeks flushed, adding further contrast to the bruises on her face as she shifted in her chair and looked away. "Forgive me, but I must admit to being more tired than hungry, Your Grace."

"I understand." Justine gathered up the cloth napkin from her lap, placing it beside her setting. She rose, pushing her chair back. "There is no need for you to suffer on our account."

Rounding the table toward Matilda, Justine held out her hand. "Come. A good night's rest will bring on a better appetite in the morning." Justine glanced toward Radcliff. "Your Grace, you do not mind if we retire early, do you?"

He eyed them, then brought his crystal glass to his lips, finishing the rest of his wine with one swallow. He cleared his throat and shifted in his upholstered chair. "No. Of course not. I wish you both a very good night." He waved over to the servant standing off to the side, pointing to his empty glass.

Justine assisted Matilda from her chair, gently securing an arm around her upper body.

Matilda glanced toward Justine. Though she hesitated, she slid her own arm around Justine's waist. "You are too kind, Your Grace."

"Please. I would rather you call me Justine."

Matilda stiffened and shook her head, causing her blond chignon and curls to sway. "No. I could never—"

"I would be offended if you didn't. This is my home. And in my home I do not wish to abide by superficial airs. We are friends until proven otherwise."

Matilda stared at her.

Justine smiled and tightened her hold on Matilda. "I realize the circumstances of your stay are more than awkward, but if you promise not to judge me by my standing, then I promise I will not judge you by yours."

Matilda's own hold tightened on Justine as a small smile edged onto her lips. "Then you will call me Matilda in turn?"

Justine grinned. "Yes. I will."

Matilda's smile widened, her blue eyes sparkling.

"Do uh…you ladies plan on holding each other all night like that?" Radcliff drawled from across the table. He smirked and gestured toward them with his now-filled glass, causing the wine within it to sway. "I cannot help but feel excluded."

Justine rolled her eyes as she steered Matilda out of the dining room. Yes, he *would* feel excluded. "Good night, Bradford," she called out over her shoulder. "Try not to drink too much more. It appears to be affecting your sense of humor."

"I didn't realize I even had a sense of humor," he teasingly called back. "Cheers and a very good night, dearest. Dream of me, will you? Only be sure it's something good. For I certainly deserve as much."

Justine bit back a smile. Dream of him, indeed. He really was full of himself.

With arms interwoven and their skirts rustling against each other's, she and Matilda made their way toward the east end of the house. Nothing more was said between them. Though Justine wanted to ask Matilda more about her situation and why she had chosen Radcliff for assistance, she knew that she needed to give the woman a bit more time to settle in.

When they reached the bedchamber, Justine pushed open the door, then guided Matilda toward the canopy bed covered with a plush coverlet and pillows. Once she eased Matilda upon the edge of the mattress, she took a step back and sighed. "There. How is that?"

Matilda drew in a slow, deep breath and let it out, patting the bed with a hand. "I confess it's been weeks since I've had a bed to myself."

Justine could not help but note the genuine satisfaction in that tone and pitied the woman knowing the sort of treatment she endured at the hands of men, given her occupation. It was a savage world Justine had first glimpsed at the age of twelve within some of the villages in the Kloof, when women from rivaling tribes were seized and treated worse than the oxen utilized for travel. Her father had reluctantly explained the ways of men after she had repeatedly demanded to know why women were being forced to sleep on dirt outside of huts, being roped and were only occasionally brought inside those huts only to emerge sobbing.

It was the only thing about the Bushmen and Hottentots she had despised whilst growing up and one of the many reasons why she had insisted on protecting Matilda. She hadn't been able to do anything for those brutalized women in the Kloof, except offer food when no one was looking and cut the grass ropes binding their hands and feet, only to discover they refused to leave out of fear. But Justine knew she could right this.

"Should you require anything, ring for the servants. Don't be all too startled when a French man comes to your door. Henri is very lovely. I myself will only be a few doors away."

"Thank you. For everything."

Justine smiled. "You are most welcome, Matilda. I will see you in the morning. Rest well." She turned and swept toward the door.

"Justine? Might I…say something?"

Justine paused and turned. "But of course. What is it?"

Matilda rubbed the coverlet with both hands back and forth, back and forth, and eyed her. "I hope that my presence does not lead you to believe that the duke and I are involved. Because we are not."

Justine couldn't help but feel touched by the assurance. "I would have never offered you a room if I were in any way concerned with your presence. Your respectful demeanor allows me to trust you."

Matilda shifted on the bed and wet her lips. "Trust is something to be earned. And I confess I have yet to earn it. To be sure, I am unworthy of the kindness you have shown me today. Whilst I did come for five pounds, I also came to beg your husband for any form of protection. Even that of mistress, if need be. It wasn't until my eyes met yours that I realized what a horrid person I am to think I could ever impose myself in such a manner."

Justine swallowed and whisked toward her, affected by the woman's honesty. She lowered herself onto the bed, took hold of Matilda's hand and brought it into her own lap. She squeezed it assuredly. "You are merely trying to survive. I may very well have done the same. One cannot judge another in these circumstances."

Matilda glanced down at the hand Justine continued to hold. She drew in a shaky breath and lifted her blue eyes to hers. Stroking Justine's fingers ever so softly and tenderly, she leaned in and whispered, "In moments like these, do you know what I wish for? More than anything?"

Feeling as though she were acquiring a new friend, Justine closed the remaining distance between them, almost making their noses touch. "What? What do you wish for?"

Matilda paused and searched her face for a long moment, then whispered in a choked tone, "I wish I were a man. I wish I could do the sort of things I really want to do. Without the burden of shame. Without the burden of regret. That is what I wish."

Justine raised a brow at her and leaned away. "You don't need to be a man to do the things you want to do. You simply have to be more creative. Which is why we women shall always be superior. Because we aren't given the sort of pathetic excuses they are."

Matilda let out a small laugh, sliding her hand from Justine's, and shook her head. "I do believe I have finally found a kindred soul."

"That is my hope."

Matilda gasped and grabbed hold of her belly.

Justine's heart jumped. "What? What is it? You aren't—"

Matilda laughed, shook her head and grabbed Justine's hand, placing it against the side of her large stomach. Something pushed playfully against the palm of her hand.

Justine's eyes widened as she stared down in wonder at the quick movements still nudging her hand.

"The baby says thank you," Matilda whispered softly.

Justine's eyes welled with tears at the very thought of the little life within that belly. A poor little life that had no idea how trying it was going to be once it found its way to the outside world.

Justine smiled tremulously, pulling back her hand. Rising, she quickly headed back toward the door, not wanting to cry in front of her guest. "Good night. May you both sleep well."

Matilda breathed out a soft sigh. "Fare thee well, Justine, and a very good night to you, too."

WHERE ON EARTH WAS Radcliff?

He was not in the dining room, nor the drawing room, nor his bedchamber, nor hers. So where had he gone? She didn't know why she desperately wanted and needed to see him before she went to sleep. Perhaps because she already missed him and wanted to tell him how proud she was of him. He'd endured a lot in a single day and had graciously taken it all, even though he clearly required copious quantities of port to do so.

Justine paused outside the open doors of the study and was disappointed to find that it, too, was dark. She surveyed the shadows of the room and blinked, remembering Radcliff's earlier lists which had been crumpled and left on the floor. Her heart skipped. She doubted they would still be there, but curiosity lured her all the same.

Reaching up toward one of the sconces, where

a half melted candle burned, she carefully wedged it out, turned and moved into the quiet study. She squinted as she made her way around the room, making out the shapes of furniture.

She eventually paused in the middle of the room and searched the Axminster carpet only to find the crumpled papers had already long been collected. Drat. She didn't even get a chance to see a single one of them.

"Are you lost?" a deep voice asked from one of the darkened corners.

Justine screeched, her heart skidding as the candle jumped from her hand and thudded onto the carpet. It rolled away, the flame flickering sideways, creating a smoldering, smoking path. Her heart pounded as she frantically yanked up the front of her skirts above her ankles and proceeded to stomp at the wick with her slippered foot, hoping the house wasn't about to go up in flames.

After a few more stomps, she eventually managed to extinguish the candle—thank goodness. She paused, realizing she had officially sentenced herself to complete and utter darkness.

With Radcliff.

He rumbled out a laugh from somewhere behind and clapped rather enthusiastically, causing the sound to echo all around them. "My carpet thanks you for your noble rescue."

Justine let out a laugh, too, and clutched her skirts as she whipped toward the direction of his voice. *"Radcliff?"*

"No. The devil. I've come for your soul. And from what I hear, it's a damn good one."

Justine laughed again and wandered toward the direction of his voice. She edged closer until she was finally able to make out the shadowy outline of his large frame which sat on the outer edge of his writing desk.

Imagine. He'd been sitting there all along, watching her in complete silence as she had wandered about the room making a dolt of herself. "Might I ask why you are sitting on your desk in the dark?"

"Good question. I don't know." He let out a throaty laugh. "Might I…ask you something?"

"Of course."

"Am I allowed to admit I was just thinking about you in bed? And how I *know* I could never be able to fuck another woman? Not ever? Because I'd only find myself comparing them all to you?"

Justine was more than grateful her burning face was hidden in the darkness. She'd certainly heard blunt language, having grown up with her father, but surely this was not appropriate, even between husband and wife. "Your uh…compliments know no bounds, Your Grace."

"With a body as luscious as yours, Justine, my compliments should never have any bounds."

She choked. "Are you…*inebriated?* Or have you lost the last of your mind?"

"Both, actually."

She rolled her eyes. "Lovely."

He cleared his throat. "I should apologize."

"Yes. You should."

"I humbly beg for your pardon. I won't do it again. My mind. It's muddled."

"Thank you. Now I suggest you retire before you have to apologize for anything else."

He was quiet for a moment, then blurted, "You know…page twenty-four states that it's never fashionable for a lady to become inebriated. I understand all that and why, but this is probably where I should admit that I was never really all that fashionable to begin with and that I can only follow so many rules."

Justine laughed, unable to hide her surprise. "Why, Radcliff. You've been reading."

"That is all I did today."

She grinned. "I'm very proud of you."

"At least one of us is."

She laughed again and eyed his shadow, which still sat on the edge of the desk barely a few feet away from her. "You may not consider yourself fashionable, Radcliff, but I have always considered you to be."

"Imagine that. So. Were you looking for me?"

Although she wanted to tell him that yes, she certainly was, she didn't want to excite the poor man and create another misunderstanding between them. "Not to disappoint you, Radcliff, but no. I was looking for your list."

"Oh." He sounded disappointed all the same.

He rose, the desk he'd been sitting on creaking, and made his way toward her. Although she couldn't readily see him, she could feel him drawing closer. Her hands grew sweaty, and she wondered whether she should flee. After all, with him being inebriated, she highly doubted he would exhibit much self-control. And yet…she couldn't move. It was as if her skirts had been stitched to the carpet she stood on.

He paused before her, bringing with him the tangy sweet scent of cigars. After a long moment, he finally said, "Children."

She blinked. "Pardon?"

"Children was number five on my list."

Well, that was certainly unexpected.

"Tell me I am right and that one of the things you want from me and this marriage is children." There was a huskiness to his tone that caused her stomach to flutter way too much. "Tell me it is my children you want."

She took a large step back. "Well, yes. Of course. Eventually. When you and I are prepared to make such a commitment."

He took back the step she had placed between them. "At three and thirty, you doubt I'm prepared for such a commitment?"

"Age is not what determines whether one is prepared."

He sighed. "Will I ever be able to earn your trust again after what I did?"

"It will take time. You must demonstrate that you are earnest and in control."

"I am demonstrating control right now," he whispered. "Do you think I want to stand here, in the dark, and merely discuss the many ways I should avoid scandal? Is that what you think?"

She bit back a laugh, despite herself. "I am proud of the efforts you are making, Radcliff. I am also proud of the generosity you have shown Miss Thurlow today."

"I want you to be proud of me. I need you to be." He paused. "Can I…hold you?"

Her heart beat faster. She shook her head. "No. Not whilst you are inebriated. Tomorrow. When you are more aware of what it is you are doing."

"Then let me kiss you. I want to kiss you."

"No. Not as you are." She held up her hands, readying to push away his chest and his arms. But surprisingly, and thankfully, they did not come.

"What *can* I do, then?" he growled from her right, circling close enough for her to hear the intake of his steady breath and smell the port. *"Tell me,"* he insisted from behind and then from her left. "Tell me. So that I may do it."

Justine let out a shaky breath, willing herself to say exactly what was in her heart. "You can profess your love for me."

He paused directly before her and leaned in. "And why would I do that?"

The man certainly knew how to make a woman swoon. "Because I want more than lust from you, Radcliff. We're going to be together for the rest of our lives. Has that not ever occurred to you? Do you think you could ever learn to love me? *Ever?*"

He snorted. "Justine. Love is a mere…myth. You know that, dearest, don't you? 'Tis nothing but a stupid myth perpetuated by society to make everyone think someone cares. When in fact *no one* cares." He paused. "So what about you?"

Her brows rose. "What about me?"

"Do you love me?"

She snorted. "You seem to be missing your own point."

He huffed out a breath. "I suppose I am. But…let us say if you could genuinely put true emotion into the word *love* without any deception whatsoever, *could* you love me?"

She clenched her fists. It was as if he expected her to give him everything even whilst he in turn offered nothing. "No, Radcliff. I could not."

"Why not? I am your husband. It is your duty to love me."

He really was hopeless. And even more so when he was foxed. "You haven't really given me anything to love. Have you?"

"Oh, well, now. Allow me to change that." He grabbed hold of her hands, snapping them down hard between them, and dipped toward her throat, sliding his hot tongue down the side of her exposed neck, causing her to choke with surprise. "Do you love me now? Or shall I offer you more of my tongue?"

A gasp of a breath escaped her as she struggled to break free from his pinching grasp. "Radcliff!"

He released her and let out a booming laugh, stumbling backward, his heavy steps echoing within the study, and caught himself on the desk, still laughing. "Imagine. I have two beautiful women staying in my house. *Two*. And I can't have either one!"

He kept right on guffawing.

As if it were, in fact, amusing.

Justine scrambled back, breathing heavily. For the sake of his life, not to mention hers, and for the sake of their marriage, she had to make him believe—and make herself believe—that he was worth saving. That he could conquer whatever was consuming his soul. "The fact that you do not realize how dire your situation is worries me to no end, Radcliff. I can only do so much. You do realize that?"

His laughter ended abruptly as his shadow shifted toward her. "My dearest Justine," he said hoarsely through the darkness. "You needn't worry about me. Hell, you needn't even care. I, Radcliff Edwin Morton, have been duke since the age of fourteen. I have been overseeing everyone's life, from servant to tenant to my own brother, never once—not once—depending upon anyone for anything. I know how to take care of myself." He nodded, his shadowed outline staggering against the desk. "What I need right now is time away from

you. I cannot function when I'm around you. I…
can't."

He staggered again, his boots echoing from his
movements, and suddenly his shadow slipped from
sight with a resounding thud that landed somewhere
on the darkened floor.

Justine stumbled toward him, her heart pounding
so fast she couldn't catch her breath. "Radcliff!"

She fell onto her knees beside him and fumbled
to find his head, blindly trailing her hands across
the length of his buttons and up toward his silk
cravat and shoulders which were still encased in his
evening coat. Her fingers grazed his warm, stub-
bled face and the wide, smooth welt of his scar. At
least he was still breathing. But dear God, he wasn't
moving. Nor was he responding to her touch.

A helpless sob escaped her, but she somehow
willed strength into her voice. "Jefferson!" she
yelled over her shoulder back toward the dimly lit
entryway. *"Jefferson!"*

Hands jumped to her arms, and her heart skidded to a momentary halt. Radcliff's strong fingers
dug into the material of her gown. "No. I don't
need anyone. Not you. Not him. Leave. I need to
be alone. It is what I know."

"Oh, Radcliff," she whispered, feeling a tear
tracing its way down her heated cheek. Why did

she have to love him so much? And why did she want to believe that he could change? When he himself didn't even believe it?

She leaned closer toward him, cupping his face with her hands. "You are not alone anymore. You have me. You will always have me. You know that, don't you?"

His fingers relaxed, and he softly whispered up at her, "Yes. I do. And thank God you're incredibly good at fucking or I don't think I'd be able to survive."

Justine released his face with a solid push. Was that all she was to him? Was that all she would ever be? She smacked his chest. And smacked it again, even harder for good merit, wishing she could pound some sense into him. "I am worth more than a stupid *fuck,* Bradford!"

Running steps echoed from down the corridor. Jefferson skidded into the entryway of the study, his chest heaving, his large frame outlined by the faint candlelight beyond. "Your Grace?" he echoed, searching the darkness. "What—"

Radcliff grunted as he shifted and pushed himself to sit up on the floor. "I do not require anything, Jefferson. Go. Retire. Hell, leave the house for all I care."

Jefferson hesitated, then quietly turned and left the room.

The bastard. Justine fisted her hand and punched at Radcliff's shoulder as hard as she could.

"Ow, woman!" he roared. "What was that for?"

"For what you just said to Jefferson. That was completely uncalled for."

"What did I say?"

She choked back a sob she simply could not control. It was pointless trying to reason with him. Why fight so hard to save the soul of a man who didn't even care for his own soul?

Radcliff leaned toward her, his hand patting at her skirts. "Why are you crying? Justine, don't cry. Come. Come here."

Gritting her teeth, she shoved his hands away. Hard. "Do not touch me! You are not in a state to touch me!"

"Damn it all to hell. I can never seem to please you." He pushed himself up onto his feet and stumbled off to the side. He straightened and stalked toward the doorway. He paused, his broad back and tall frame outlined by shadows and faint light and said without turning, "I still like you." He nodded, then disappeared.

Justine let out a breath and pushed herself up

onto her feet, wondering how she was going to survive much more of this. She blindly made her way through the room and hurried into the candlelit corridor, not wanting to be alone in the darkness.

Bringing shaky hands to her tear-streaked face, she swiped away the evidence of her emotions. She wanted to believe that what Radcliff had really meant to say to her before leaving was that he loved her. That he loved her a lot. But it was going to take far more than words to make her believe that he was even capable of it.

"What did he do?" a female voice demanded. "I heard you shouting for assistance."

Justine froze, dropping her hand to her sides.

Matilda hurried down the candlelit corridor as best she could, her hands firmly holding up her belly from beneath, still dressed in her morning gown.

Justine's heart skipped. The last thing she wanted was for Matilda to worry about her. Matilda needed peace and strength for the birth of her child. Shaking her head and waving a hand about, Justine feigned a laugh as she approached her. "Nothing happened. Nothing."

Matilda paused before her, searching her face. Her gaze narrowed. "You lie. Why are you crying?"

"I am emotional, is all."

Matilda grabbed hold of her shoulders and gripped them so hard those fingers pinched her skin beneath the material of her gown. Leaning toward her, she shook her and hoarsely whispered, "Do not give him excuses. For that is how it all begins. One excuse after another. I gave Carlton those very same excuses, and yet, did I earn his love? Did I earn anything? No. I did not. I only earned my own self-loathing. Justine. Do not think you can earn the love of a broken soul. For you will not. Do you wish your life to be like mine? Do you wish to live each moment regretting that you even breathe whilst in the presence of a man?"

Justine swallowed and shook her head. "Bradford is not like Carlton. He would never raise a hand to me. I know he wouldn't."

"I never thought Carlton would raise a hand to me, either. But he did. Repeatedly. And the fact that they are brothers worries me." Matilda hissed out a breath and slid her hands down the length of Justine's arms, rubbing them.

Releasing her, Matilda glanced behind them, into the darkness of the corridor that was not illuminated by candles. "You shouldn't sleep alone. Sleep with me tonight. And if need be, every night." Matilda turned back toward her and wrapped her arm around her waist and slowly pulled her toward the direction of the bedchambers. "Come."

Justine allowed herself to be pulled along. "I am supposed to be assisting you. Not you assisting me."

Matilda squeezed her tighter against her side and belly. "This is what friends do. And after what you have done for me today, you are and will always be my friend."

Justine squeezed her back. Although Radcliff—not to mention all of London—might not approve of her new and very pregnant friend, she approved of her. And that was all that mattered.

Indeed. From this moment forth, she would personally see that Matilda's stay here at the Bradford home was something worth remembering. Something Matilda would tell her own child about for years and years to come. And Radcliff would contribute to the cause, whether it pleased him or not.

SCANDAL SIXTEEN

It is true. Life is often half spent before we ever come to truly understand its purpose. It is my hope, however, that I can prevent you from wasting any more of that life than is really necessary.

How to Avoid a Scandal, Author Unknown

BRIGHT, GOLDEN LIGHT pressed against the closed lids of Radcliff's eyes. His limbs felt unbearably tight and raw. The smell of port clung to his nostrils, to his skin. Even worse, the taste of sour port clung to his mouth.

At least he could breathe. Though hardly, seeing his throat burned and every puff of air crinkled his dry lips.

He winced, a headache pinching his skull.

Someone nudged his shoulder. "Your Grace?"

Radcliff opened his eyes and squinted against the brightness blinding him. As his vision adjusted to the unexpected sunlight pouring in through the glass windows, Jefferson's full face and large shoulders came into view.

He blinked. Why was he on the floor? In the receiving room? With his butler kneeling beside him?

Jefferson grinned down at him, his round blue eyes clearly amused. "For a moment, I thought you were dead, Your Grace."

Radcliff grunted out a laugh, then winced, realizing more than his head hurt. His chest and the rest of his body ached as if he'd been trampled by a coach and full set of horses. "Forgive me for disappointing you, Jefferson. I am still very much alive."

"Ah, now, I wouldn't worry, Your Grace. I am quite used to people disappointing me." Jefferson wedged his gloved hands beneath Radcliff's arms and pulled him up into a sitting position. "Are you well enough to stand?"

Radcliff nodded and, pulling in a deep breath, scrambled up to his booted feet and stood. He blinked, and as the room swayed momentarily, his mind began searching for the memory of the night before. He swallowed down the nausea rolling through him, and though he recalled very little, the one thing he did remember, the one thing that echoed within his thoughts with a clarity he could not forget, were Justine's sobs.

Oh, God. What had he done?

He glanced down at his trousers and fumbled with them, but found they were intact and properly buttoned. Yet that didn't mean he hadn't—

He turned and grabbed hold of the lapels on Jefferson's dark livery, yanking the large butler toward him. "What did I do?" he demanded. "Did I hurt her? Did I hurt my wife?"

Jefferson stared at him. "Not that I know of, Your Grace. But all that port and brandy didn't make you in the least pleasant. That I do know."

This was not happening. This *could not* be happening. He was supposed to make Justine proud. Not make her cry. Radcliff released the butler and stumbled back, nausea clenching his throat and stomach. "Where is she?"

"The duchess and Miss Thurlow departed late this morning, Your Grace. Two hours ago."

He choked. She wasn't already leaving him, was she? "Departed? To where?"

"Miss Thurlow was in dire need of clothing, given her gentle state. As you may recall she did not bring a trunk and did not wish to retrieve her belongings from Lord Carlton."

"You mean my wife took Miss Thurlow shopping?" he echoed. "Out in broad daylight?"

Jefferson eyed him. "Yes. It is indeed daylight, Your Grace. And that is usually when the shops are open."

Oh, damn. This was all his fault. What the hell had he been thinking drinking so much last night? "Did she tell you where she was going?" he demanded.

"No, Your Grace." Jefferson dug into the inner vest pocket of his livery and withdrew a page of folded ivory stationery. "But the duchess did leave this for you."

Radcliff slipped it from those large gloved fingers. Dreading every word, he unfolded it and read:

> Your Grace,
> Miss Thurlow and I have decided to enjoy this bright, sunny day outside the home. I hope you do not mind my extending your credit at a few shops.
> Respectfully,
> The Duchess of Bradford

Respectfully? He didn't like the way she'd written that word. Unlike all the other words that were neatly and perfectly scribed, *respectfully* had been scrawled with obvious haste. As if she'd been forced to offer him something and could only think of *respectfully.*

He stared at the name he had given her, the name of *his* wife, his Justine, and slid his finger across its length, not caring Jefferson was there to see it.

Drawing in a deep breath, he let it out slowly. He had a feeling he knew where Justine had gone. And he hoped he was right. The *ton* was anything but forgiving in matters such as these. Nor could he have Carlton hearing about their outing, or the bastard would only end up showing up at his door.

Radcliff folded the letter and eyed his butler. "Have my coach ready to depart within twenty minutes."

"Yes, Your Grace." Jefferson bowed and departed.

From here on out, he was going to prove himself to Justine. Even if it bloody killed him.

SCANDAL SEVENTEEN

In this society, the clothing you wear defines the
soul you wear. Have a care for both.
   How to Avoid a Scandal, Author Unknown

The Nightingale, 28 Regent Street

Rows of gleaming plate-glass windows revealed
a stunning Paris-green salon decorated with potted
palms, Venetian glass chandeliers, and mahogany
counters topped with Italian white marble.

Justine stepped beneath the stone colonnade,
away from the crush of horses and lacquered carriages loitering the cobblestone street behind her
and Matilda.

Eyeing the well-dressed men and women who
strolled leisurely, Justine tightened her hold on Matilda's arm, and together, they wove through passing
individuals and whisked into the arched entryway
of the shop.

Matilda placed a hand on her belly and pulled
them both to a halt. "They will stare, despite the

veil covering my face and bonnet, and will ask questions."

Justine squeezed her arm and pulled her onward. "Let them, *Mrs. Porter.* Our only hope is that there isn't another poor Mrs. Porter in London whose name we are about to slander."

Matilda laughed and glanced over at her. Leaning toward her, she whispered, "This really is so exciting and lovely of you. I've always wanted to shop at *The Nightingale,* but it was too expensive. Though Carlton would never admit to it, his funds were rather limited. A yard of material from this shop alone is well worth several pounds. And even Carlton, dolt that he is, knows it takes more than a yard to make a gown."

Justine laughed in turn, and together they swept into the shop where various women in expensive bonnets, carriage shawls and morning gowns inspected rolled-out bolts of brocaded silks, muslin, crepe, and moiré.

A young dark-haired woman, who was new to the shop since Justine had last visited with Radcliff two weeks earlier, hurried out from behind the counter toward them. Thick, pinned sausage curls dangled from beneath the white silk flowers and embroidered yellow satin ribbons woven into her hair. The flowers and ribbons meticulously matched the shade of her full gown.

The young woman swept to a halt before them and smiled brightly, her left cheek dimpling. "Good afternoon. I am Miss Wyatt. How might I be of assistance?" She paused, her smile fading as she eyed Matilda's face through the lace veil.

Justine quickly released Matilda's arm and stepped toward the shop girl, leaning in unconventionally close so as to keep her words from spreading to the group of women choosing fabrics for their gowns. "Miss Wyatt. My dear friend, Mrs. Porter, has had an unfortunate experience at the hands of her husband for which I pray you will not judge her. I merely wish to gift her with a few gowns that would better suit her needs during her gentle state. I have no intention of sparing expense and it will benefit you to be as gracious toward her as possible."

Miss Wyatt eyed Matilda, then turned to Justine. "Poor soul, to be sure, and gracious I always strive to be, but how will this be paid for?"

Justine pried her beaded reticule open and yanked out a calling card from the small stack Radcliff had recently ordered for her. She held out the ivory, gold-lettered card between kid-gloved fingers. "It may be billed to this address."

Miss Wyatt slid the card from her hand, read the inscription and glanced up, smiling brightly. She quickly curtsied. "It would be an unprecedented honor to be of service to you, Your Grace. If it would at all please you, I can measure Mrs. Porter in her own fitting room to ensure both your privacy and hers."

Justine grinned, rather pleased that a name could evoke such instant cooperation.

"I CANNOT WAIT TO behold my gowns!" Matilda gushed, adjusting the white lace veil back over her bonnet. "Thank you, Justine."

"There is no need. His Grace is the one paying the bill." Justine reached out and squeezed her hand. It had been so long since she had thought of nothing but genuinely enjoying herself. "Remain here with Miss Wyatt. There is no need to make you walk more than you should. I will see to it the carriage pulls up to the door." Justine offered a nod toward the shop girl, Miss Wyatt. "Thank you, Miss Wyatt."

"It was a pleasure, Your Grace. Mrs. Porter's gowns will be delivered within the week. Any adjustments will be complimentary, as always."

"Thank you." Justine beamed and whisked toward the door of the shop. Closing it behind her, she turned to hurry toward the pavement, but stepped right smack into a broad, solid frame.

"Oh!" She desperately tried to snatch hold of the man's dark satin coat to keep herself from teetering backward.

The man grabbed her corseted waist and yanked her scandalously toward his large, muscled body, steadying her with swift, strong hands. The curved brim of his black top hat shadowed his handsome but scarred face.

She gasped as Radcliff's obsidian gaze captured hers.

"Justine," his voice broke with huskiness.

She froze against him, his tone laced with far more than she was willing to offer in that moment. Not without an apology from him. Her gloved hands, which appeared so small in comparison to the expanse of his solid chest, still shamelessly fisted both his morning coat and the front of his gold-threaded waistcoat.

Justine instantly released him and stepped back toward the door behind her. "Good afternoon, Your Grace," she managed in a cool tone that implied she was anything but pleased with him.

He intently observed her and leaned in. "Assure me you haven't been using Miss Thurlow's real name in public."

So much for him dashing across London to apologize and fawn over her. She glared up at him. "My head isn't made of cork. I've been using the name Mrs. Porter."

He shook his head. "You should have never left the house. Not with her."

"And what was I to do? She needed clothes. None of my gowns fit her, and I wasn't about to drape a set of curtains around her."

"No matter. Where is she?" He wedged around her toward the door.

"In the shop. Why?" Justine stepped aside to give him space, but his hand reached out and curved around her corseted waist as they passed one another.

She sucked in a breath and stumbled away from his touch, back toward the crowded pavement. Aside from not wanting him to touch her after the drunken encounter he had yet to apologize for, her heart shamelessly pounded at the intimacy he was blatantly demonstrating in public. On Regent Street.

He opened the door and leaned in casually toward Matilda, who was still inside with Miss Wyatt. "I do beg your pardon, fair ladies. Mrs. Porter? Might you join me and my wife? It is rather important you do. Thank you."

Justine eyed him as he pulled the door further open.

Matilda soon waddled through the open door, reached out and grabbed hold of Justine's arm, bringing Justine close as she hurried them onto the pavement.

"Do not allow yourself to be persuaded by anything he says or does," Matilda insisted quietly. "He is only looking to redeem himself. They always resort to this sort of behavior."

Justine squeezed her arm, silently assuring her that she was not that gullible.

Radcliff strode toward them and rounded Justine's side, now towering unnervingly close despite the bustling crowd around them.

His smoldering eyes met hers from below the rim of his top hat. "I hope you found my credit satisfactory."

Justine narrowed her gaze in an effort to demonstrate that she was not about to shrivel up in his presence. "Why are you here?" she quietly demanded, trying not to bring too much attention to herself. They were, after all, on Regent Street. "I doubt you came all this way to ask about your credit."

His dark brows rose. "You are putting far too

much faith in London by parading yourself like this."

She stared up at him, abashed. "As if I care what London thinks anymore."

He leaned in closer. "You'd best have a care, Justine. You'd best. For if Carlton hears of this and shows up on our doorstep, what then? A veil isn't going to hide who she is. Now, as I have no intention of making a scene on Regent Street, I ask that you follow me." He quickly touched the front rim of his hat and strode past them.

His tall, broad-muscled frame strode toward a waiting carriage just a few feet away. Its black-lacquered door was dutifully held open by a young footman dressed in dark livery.

Though her pride wanted to throw a slipper at his head and knock off that hat knowing he still hadn't apologized to her, she knew he was right. And grumble though she may, it was rather endearing he cared enough to come all this way to oversee their safety.

Justine tightened her hold on Matilda's arm and gathered her skirts from around her slippered feet, eyeing those around them. "Come. We must go."

Matilda leaned toward her. "I ought to take a separate carriage. I don't wish to impose any more than I already have."

"Nonsense," Justine insisted, pulling her forward. "Radcliff is right. We mustn't linger or put too much trust in those around us. Come."

They hurried after him, trying to maneuver past men and women who seemed to suddenly take interest in them.

Radcliff halted before the open door of the carriage and turned, holding out a gloved hand to assist.

Justine guided Matilda toward him.

He, in turn, assisted Matilda into the carriage with the footman. Once Matilda was settled onto the cushioned seat inside, Radcliff turned toward Justine and held out his hand again, his eyes meeting hers.

She set her hand in his and gathered up her skirts. His large hand tightened around hers as she stepped up and into the carriage. She pinched her lips, lingering on his strength and warmth.

Justine released his hand and settled beside Matilda, letting out a breath. Though she wanted to talk to him about what had happened last night, she had a feeling it was going to be a very awkward ride home without discussions.

RADCLIFF FIXED HIS GAZE on the passing buildings and bustling crowds outside the glass window. It was best not to say anything throughout the remainder of the ride. It wasn't as if his damn words were in any way wanted or needed.

Matilda and Justine giggled and prattled on to each other about the shop, about the various fabrics chosen, about the cuts, about the courtesy shown by everyone there. Yes. About everything a man had no need to listen to.

Every now and then Matilda affectionately squeezed Justine's gloved hand and patted her knee. And Justine, in turn, affectionately did the same.

He swallowed and achingly watched as Justine's full lips curved into a smile as she beamed at Matilda, her cheeks rounding. It was obvious his own wife seemed to be enjoying Matilda's company far more than she had ever enjoyed his. He only had himself to blame.

When they finally arrived, Radcliff silently helped both women out of the carriage. He watched them disappear into the house, arm in arm, still gaily chatting until their voices faded into the distance.

He stood there for a quiet moment.

The footman eyed him—as if politely refraining from pointing out that he'd been abandoned by all—then folded up the stairs and slammed the door shut.

Radcliff sighed. He supposed he should let Justine enjoy her time with her newfound friend, without him hovering over her and burdening her with his presence.

He turned to his driver and called up, "Take me to Brooks's. I feel like having a meal and playing cards."

"Yes, Your Grace."

The footman quickly reopened the door and unfolded the stairs.

Radcliff nodded to the man and stepped back into the carriage. He should have been used to being alone. Yet his heart and soul ached in a way it had never ached in all his three and thirty years. And he knew Justine had everything to do with it.

SCANDAL EIGHTEEN

Love always arrives in the most unexpected
forms. Once you are able to comprehend that, it
will allow you to better understand that love is
far from being perfect. It is what it is.

How to Avoid a Scandal, Author Unknown

That evening

JUSTINE REPEATEDLY GLANCED toward the empty
seat at the dining table and couldn't help but worry
as to why Radcliff hadn't joined her and Matilda for
supper. In truth, she hadn't seen him since he had
returned them to the house that afternoon.

"Justine?"

She snapped her gaze to Matilda, who quietly
sat across the table. "Yes?"

Matilda sighed, set down her fork and knife
beside her plate, and lowered her chin in a genteel
form of reprimand. "You don't actually miss him,
do you? He didn't even offer an apology for what
he did to you last night."

Justine looked away and shrugged. "I know. I… worry about him, is all. After last night, I realized he really has no one to look after him."

Matilda sighed again, threw down her napkin and rose from her chair. She rounded the table as deftly as she could in her state and paused beside Justine. Taking up her hand, she insisted, "You have me now. You know that, don't you?"

Justine smiled at the hand that firmly grasped hers. She squeezed it and rose from her seat to join Matilda who still hovered at her side. "Yes. I do."

Matilda released her hand and observed her with sad, blue eyes. "Do you love him?"

Justine swallowed, and even though she did, with all of her heart, she was afraid to admit it aloud. Because it would only make her feel more vulnerable than she already did.

"Do not love him." Matilda's hands slipped up the length of her arms and drew her closer. "He is not worthy of your love. No man is. There are other things that can bring a woman happiness."

"Such as?" she muttered.

"Such as this." Matilda leaned toward her and brushed her lips against hers. She pushed Justine's mouth open with a hot tongue and circled the inside of her mouth as her hands roamed into her hair and loosened the pins holding her curls in place.

Justine froze as her mind tilted off its axis to understand what was happening to her.

Matilda's mouth pressed harder against hers, as hair now tumbled down around her shoulders.

Justine blindly grabbed Matilda's hands from her hair and stumbled back, gasping. "What are you—"

The rush of cool air pulsed against her lips. For a few passing moments, Justine couldn't even bring herself to look at Matilda. Yet alone move.

Matilda had kissed her.

With the urgency of a man!

"Forgive me," Matilda finally admitted in a low, raspy voice. "I…I've always wanted to do that. From the moment I met you. And given your father's observations, I knew you would understand. I tolerate men, you see, and have tried to tolerate them all these years because that is what society expects me to do. But I don't want to tolerate it anymore. I can't. I am disgusted with myself for pretending to be something I never was. And this is what I am. *This*."

Justine swallowed and scrambled back, glancing toward the male servants who quietly stood in the corners of the room. Despite all the flushed shaven faces, they continued to stand there stoically, eyes set straight ahead, as was their duty.

It was more than obvious Matilda didn't care about what she was revealing before them. Had Justine in any way misled Matilda to think she could do this?

Matilda continued to stare her down with fiery blue eyes. "It doesn't matter to me that you are married and must share his bed. We can enjoy each other as we are. He doesn't need to know."

"I…oh, God…Matilda—" Justine shook her head. And simply kept on shaking it, unable to find the words to even answer. For her heart, her mind and soul belonged to Radcliff, would always belong to Radcliff, and she could never betray him. Not for a woman. Not for a man. Not for anyone.

Matilda half nodded, as if privy to Justine's thoughts, and slowly stepped back. "I did not mean to burden you with my own desires. It is loathsome to desire a woman. I know. But is it any more loathsome that I denied myself happiness because of society? I… Forgive me, Justine. I didn't mean to kiss you. I—" She turned, gathered up her skirts and bustled out of sight.

Justine lifted a trembling hand and covered her swollen mouth, which still burned from the heat of Matilda's lips. What was she going to do? She couldn't tell Radcliff. He'd be livid. He'd toss Matilda out. And then what would happen to her and her child?

Oh, God. She needed to find Radcliff. She didn't want to be left alone in this state of confusion as to what she should or shouldn't do. She needed him. So desperately. For in that moment she realized something. She realized that if nothing existed between them, not love, not even friendship, anything and anyone could come between them. And she couldn't have that. She couldn't. Because she loved her husband far too much.

Two hours later

RADCLIFF DIDN'T KNOW why he still sat in the darkness of his carriage outside his home or why he continued to stare at the empty, upholstered seat across from him.

He closed his eyes, challenging himself to go straight into the house and tell Justine that he was going to be the man she deserved. Even if he had to crawl every inch of the way to do it.

The clicking of heels against the pavement echoed in the distance, and suddenly, the carriage door swung open so vigorously, it shook the vehicle.

His eyes popped open.

"Radcliff!" Justine stumbled up and into the carriage, dragged in the rest of her skirts and slammed the side door behind herself, falling into the upholstered seat opposite him. "I am so happy you're finally home."

"You are?" he echoed.

"Yes."

He blinked as Justine shifted into the seat, noting that she had his evening coat draped over the top of her head and shoulders like a shawl.

Radcliff chuckled. "Perhaps you should have bought yourself a shawl whilst you were out this afternoon."

She shook her head. "It isn't that," she whispered. "I needed something of yours to comfort me whilst I waited for you to return. I waited by the window all this time. Where were you?"

The glow from the carriage lamp shone in barely enough to light the side of her face. For some reason, her chestnut hair had escaped its pins and lay in a lovely mass of disheveled curls past her shoulders and waist.

He veered his gaze back to her face. "I was at the club. What is it? What happened? Why is your hair—"

"All that matters is that you are here." She yanked the curtains shut on each side of the windows, then scrambled toward him and onto his lap, the evening coat sliding down from her shoulders and falling onto the carriage floor.

He sucked in a harsh breath as she grabbed his shaven face in the darkness with chilled hands and kissed his cheeks, repeatedly.

He choked, trying not to touch her, and blew out a breath to keep his body under control. "Justine, you shouldn't—"

"Yes. I should. We ought to demonstrate to one another how much we care. Because we do. Do we not? Tell me how much you care about me. Tell me. I need to hear you say it."

"Of course I care. Justine—"

"Do you?" she insisted. "Do you really care?"

"Yes, of course. Justine, what—"

She knocked off his hat, causing it to tumble onto the seat, and kept on kissing his forehead and raking her fingers through his hair. "Touch me, Radcliff. Show me how much you care for me."

Christ. May he never awake from this bliss.

His fingers and palms gently brushed the sides of her soft, muslin gown, hesitating at first. "Perhaps we ought to take this inside."

"No. I want you to myself. Alone. Here. Now. Tell the footmen and the driver to leave us as we are. Tell them."

He swallowed and slid his gloved hands toward her corseted waist, convincing himself that he'd be a fool not to. He inhaled the faint, playful fragrance of powder and citrus clinging to her skin as feathery soft locks of her long hair fell heavily onto his hands, arms and shoulders. He focused solely on breathing through his mouth to prevent himself from losing too much control too soon, even though his cock was already painfully rigid.

He knocked on the carriage roof with a gloved hand and yelled out toward the window, "Secure the horses and retire! All of you! And you'd best not bloody linger!"

"Yes, Your Grace!" two shouts responded.

The carriage bobbed to the movements of the footman and the driver jumping off. Soon their hurried, booted steps echoed into the distance and disappeared.

Using his teeth, Radcliff stripped his gloves from his hands and whipped them aside. Firmly pressing his bare hands to the sides of her warm, silken face, he drew in a breath and whispered, "If you do not want this, Justine, then you'd best leave this carriage."

He couldn't breathe as he awaited her reply. He was afraid that one breath would push her and this unearthly fantasy away.

"I want more than this, Radcliff. I want you."

The heat from her body and those tender words from her lips melted away each and every barrier that had ever been set between them. He pulled her mouth down to his before she could even think of taking back her words. He forced her mouth open, urgently searching for that hot, satin tongue.

His body turned into a blazing, tingling mess such as he'd never known. Loosening the arm that he had wrapped tightly around her shoulders, he traced her back, traveling down, down the coolness of the gown that draped her body.

He shoved up her skirts until they were both buried in them to their chins and pushed her exposed open thighs hard against his cock. A growl escaped him as he continued to devour her mouth and his tongue probed hers.

He wanted this. Her. Always.

A shiver escaped her as his fingertips grazed the thin chemise interrupting the sensual journey he intended to make toward her quim. He shoved the garment up and out of the way, exposing her lower half fully.

Her fingers dug into his hair, gripping it so tightly it stung his scalp in an intoxicating way.

His cock throbbed as he lowered his mouth to her throat. Using the tip of his tongue, he followed the graceful curve from her earlobe to her bust line. Her chest rose and fell against his tongue from the sharp intake of quivering breaths.

To have her in his carriage, and at his will, was maddening. He never wanted this moment to end.

She wrapped her arms around him, tighter, kissing his chin, his scar, his brow.

His hands trailed down and then back up her smooth silk-stockinged legs, splayed on each side of him. "Why are you allowing this? I thought—"

"If there is nothing between us, Radcliff, nothing at all, not even these tender moments between us, anything and anyone can come between us. And I refuse to allow that to happen."

He untied the satin bows holding her silk stockings in place and let them slip into the darkness at his booted feet. He rolled her stockings down to her ankles, sliding his hands against the bare, soft skin of her legs beneath. "Nothing will come between us," he whispered. "I have never, nor will I ever, share myself with anyone the way I am sharing myself with you."

"Tell me what it is between us, Radcliff. Please. I need to know."

"Above all, it is devotion. Unlike anything I have ever known for any woman." His skin burned and his arm muscles tightened as he reached to unbutton the flap on his trousers. He dug out his thick cock, pulling it free from his undergarments.

"Will your devotion ever lead to more?"

"Words mean nothing, Justine. Let me show you how I feel." He held on to her corseted waist with one hand and guided his length into the opening of her wet warmth with the other. He buried himself deep into her with a shuddering gasp that almost caused every ounce of his seed to spill.

She moaned and gripped his shoulders, her sweet, tight wetness slowly riding him.

"Justine." He threw back his head onto the upholstered seat and gave in to every moment of having her, pulling her down onto him again and again. Harder and harder. Trying to show her how much his body, his mind and his soul were completely and utterly devoted to her and her alone.

"Radcliff," she gasped, dragging her nails from his shoulders up to his hair. She shifted against him and gasped again, gathering his hair into tight fistfuls, tugging harder.

He gripped her thighs tighter and yanked her down again, harder and faster onto his full length, trying to heighten her climax.

He felt her core tightening as her warm wetness slathered his rigid cock. He winced from the unbearable pressure as his body demanded release. No. He couldn't. Not until she—

She cried out, her voice drifting into the darkness around them. Her body shook as she arched and writhed in his arms. He slammed into her faster, wanting her to feel her pleasure all the more. When her hips bucked against him and then stilled with a soft sigh, he knew she was done.

Between heavy, almost painful breaths, his mind blanked and there was nothing more he could do but give in to the pleasure he'd been so desperately needing. He held her savagely in place against the length of his cock as his body shook with an explosive rush.

He moaned as he pulsed deep within her tight, wet warmth. He moaned again, louder, realizing he was still spilling his seed into her. He'd never had it last so damn long. He'd never had it feel this damn good. Never.

His arms fell away from her corseted waist and onto the upholstered seat of the carriage. He closed his eyes, mentally and physically exhausted, and wondered what the hell had just happened. It was unlike anything he'd ever experienced.

Justine gently freed herself and quietly climbed onto the seat beside him. Laying her head against his chest, she sighed almost wistfully.

Still dazed, he wrapped his arms around her and tightened his hold. "I may never have a need for pleasure again," he blurted, scarcely aware of his own voice.

She laughed softly against his chest and traced a finger down the buttons of his waistcoat.

They sat quietly in the carriage for what seemed like a very, very long time.

"Radcliff?" she finally whispered.

"Yes?" he whispered back.

"I must tell you something before we go inside."

"What is it?"

"Promise me, no matter what I say, you will not toss Matilda out of the house."

Radcliff froze, his heart pounding. He tightened his hold on her. "What happened?"

"Promise me you'll not toss her."

"I cannot damn well promise you something when I don't even know what it is you intend to say."

"Promise me." She shook him. And then shook him again. "For my sake."

God save him, why did he have to be so damn soft when it came to her? He blew out a heavy breath. "I… Fine. For your sake. Now tell me. What is it? What happened?"

She hesitated, then moved away and pulled open both curtains, exposing the glass windows. Dull golden light from the carriage lanterns filtered in.

She sighed and settled back against the upholstered seat beside him, pushing at her disheveled hair. She flicked her gaze across the length of him, sighed again and leaned in and, tucking his cock into place, buttoned his trousers.

"What?" he demanded, not caring for the silence she continued to exhibit. "What the bloody hell happened whilst I was gone?"

She met his gaze. "Matilda kissed me. It appears she prefers women over men."

Radcliff sucked in a sharp breath, shock flying through his gut. "What? She...*kissed you?* You mean on the mouth? Using her tongue?"

She lowered her eyes and picked up his gloves which were hanging off the seat. "Yes. On the mouth. And yes, using her tongue."

Radcliff's gut tightened in disbelief. As of late, the only times he'd ever seen Justine happy was with Matilda. And now he knew why. "Is that why you fucked me just now? Because guilt compelled you to? Because you're involved with Matilda? Is that what you are saying?"

"Please don't use that tone or that language with

me. And no. I simply wanted to ensure nothing would come between us. I wanted to share something meaningful with you after last night."

"And do you plan on sharing this something with Matilda, too? Is that what you are informing me of?"

"Do be serious. I never once encouraged her."

"No? Like hell you didn't. Don't think I didn't see your hands touching that woman every two breaths and in turn, her hands touching you. You might as well have announced to the entire world you were lovers." He paused and stared her down. "Are you lovers?"

She glanced back up at him, surprise flitting across her face. "No. Of course not. I—" She winced and shook her head. "My touches were never meant in that way. We are friends. Nothing more."

He drew his brows together. "A friend does not take advantage of another friend like that."

"She was not trying to take advantage of me. She was merely… She was hoping I felt the same way is all, and wanted me to better understand her. Radcliff. I cannot help but pity her knowing she has lived her entire life being something she is not. Surely, you can understand. You yourself have supported my father's studies all these years.

Studies that have more than proven there is nothing wrong with a woman loving another woman. Or a man loving another man."

Radcliff opened his mouth and shut it. Despite knowing she was Lord Marwood's daughter, he couldn't help but be stunned about her matter-of-fact approach to all this.

"Radcliff?" she whispered, now placing a hand on his knee. "Let her stay. Please. She knows I do not feel the same. She knows I am devoted to you and you alone and that I would never allow another woman or man to touch me."

Those words and the pressure of her hand and its warmth pushed him over the cliff of uncertainty he'd been hanging from, wanting to not only trust her but throw his entire soul into hers. He grabbed up her hand with both of his and held it so tightly he could feel her pulse against his own.

He searched her face. "Do you mean it? You would never allow anyone, not man or woman, to touch you the way I did just now?"

She leaned toward him. "I would never. Not ever."

Those words gave him a sense of peace he'd never known, because he believed her and knew he could believe her. He grazed his fingers across her knuckles. "And how do you know she won't take advantage of you again?"

Justine didn't move. She didn't even seem to blink. "I don't."

His pulse hitched in his throat. He struggled to remain calm. "Then how can you insist she stay in our home?"

She squeezed his hands. "Because it is the right thing to do. Because she has no one. Please. Give her one last chance. If she oversteps her bounds, you may personally escort her out of the house."

Unable to fight the stabbing agony of it all, knowing all he ever wanted for her was to be happy with him and with her life, he brought her hands up to his lips and savagely kissed them. "It is done, then. Because you wish it."

She blinked, as if fighting her own emotions, and smiled through tight lips. "Do you know what I also wish for more than anything in this world?"

"You are going to be the death of me, Justine. You do realize that, don't you?"

She laughed quietly. "No, no. I…what I wanted to say is that…that I wish you could love me. I wish you could love me as much as I love you. Because I do."

He choked, his chest tightening. Though a part of him had longed to hear those words from her lips all this time, he knew he couldn't linger on them, nor make her think he was accepting of them. For they were nothing but words.

He slipped his hands from hers and shook his head. Violently. "Do not say such things. Even if you mean them."

She stared at him. "Whatever do you mean? Why not?"

"My mother told my father she loved him every day. Every single day throughout fifteen years of their marriage. Until he up and died from apoplexy. I always thought they had a perfect, loving marriage, but in the end, she never meant the words she so freely offered him. She had given herself to another in a moment of pleasure she was not willing to even confess until it was too late. She only ever said those words to him because she was expected to and because my father had always wanted her to. I am not expecting you to profess your love for me. And you cannot expect me to profess mine. Because such words mean nothing. Not to me."

"I am not saying the words because you want or expect them of me, but because they represent what is in my heart." Justine blinked rapidly, then looked away. "Does this mean you'll never be able to profess your love for me? Not ever? Not even if and when you were to *feel* love for me?"

He sighed and slowly shook his head. "I'll never be able to say the words. But I will gladly show you what I feel and I will gladly prove to you what I feel. Each and every day. Does that not mean more than three insignificant words?"

"I…suppose. Yes." She nodded. She paused and whispered, "I know I do love you. And I hope you do love me. Good night."

Flinging the carriage door open, she gathered up her skirts and jumped down. Her slippered steps echoed as they rushed back toward the house. The entrance door opened and slammed, resounding like a shot through his head and through his heart.

SCANDAL NINETEEN

A lady should never lose her temper, Wrath damages far more than one's fair complexion.
How to Avoid a Scandal, Author Unknown

Two days later, early morning,
while Radcliff still slept

JUSTINE PACED RADCLIFF'S STUDY, not knowing what else she was supposed to do. Since that night in the carriage, it was as if Radcliff had ceased to exist. And it was breaking her heart to think that she had caused all of this misery by merely professing her love. This was not how a man was supposed to react to words of love.

Justine paused in the middle of the study, her gaze lifting to the large portrait hanging above the marble mantelpiece of the hearth. The portrait of a rosy-cheeked, beautiful dark-haired woman in a flowing daffodil-colored gown whose gloved hand was playfully propped against a garden wall. Radcliff's mother.

Those same black eyes Radcliff shared stared down at her. They seemed to be mocking her predicament.

"You destroyed him," Justine whispered up at the woman. "And in turn, destroyed our chance of ever knowing the sort of happiness we both deserve."

The woman continued to stare down at her, offering nothing at all.

Tears burned Justine's eyes as fury choked her. She dashed toward the hearth, reached up and grabbed the bottom of the gilded wooden frame of the painting. She gritted her teeth and yanked on it. Hard. It swayed against her jerking movements but remained tightly affixed.

"You are not staying in this house," Justine seethed, pulling harder. "I have finally found my purpose…someone I can call my own…and I will *not* allow you to cast a shadow upon it."

The portrait jumped off the wall and crashed off to the side of the hearth with a huge clatter, causing a small side table to fall over with a bang and an old vase to shatter into tinkling shards, pieces that may as well have been her own heart.

Justine stumbled toward the portrait and dragged its cracked frame toward the entryway of the study. She was getting rid of it. It was not staying in *her* home. She couldn't understand why Radcliff even kept it.

"Justine!" Matilda stood in the doorway of the study, eyes wide, her hands holding the sides of her large belly. "What… Are you all right? What are you doing?"

Justine set her chin and continued to pull the portrait toward the entryway, toward Matilda. "I'm removing this portrait is all."

The hallway bell chimed in the distance, echoing through the corridor.

Justine kept right on dragging the painting out into the hallway, past Matilda, who stepped back.

"Justine," Matilda whispered, reaching out a hand toward her. "It pains me to see you like this. Please don't—"

"You needn't fret," Justine drawled. "She isn't *your* relative."

Jefferson's shout echoed in the far distance as the scuffling of feet against the tiled marble shook the walls. A low, anguished cry shattered the air.

Justine dropped the portrait with a clattering thud and stood there for a frozen moment, her heart pounding as determined steps thundered in their direction.

What—

A man with an ivory cane hurried into view

barely a few feet away, turning toward her and Matilda.

Justine scrambled around the portrait and grabbed hold of Matilda's waist and arm as a young man with sharp blue eyes, dressed in expensive morning attire and a horsehair top hat, made his way toward them in a predatory manner. It took Justine all but a single moment for her to realize that it was Radcliff's half brother, Carlton.

Justine yanked Matilda toward the study. "Come! We must—"

Matilda pushed Justine off and away with a solid strength that caused Justine to gasp as she skidded backward toward the wall.

"No. I refuse to run." Matilda set her chin and stepped onto the face of the portrait lying on the floor at her feet. The wood frame creaked beneath her weight as she swept past. She snatched up one of several small bronze statues off the side table in the corridor and waddled straight for Carlton.

"Matilda!" Justine scrambled after her. "No! Don't!"

Carlton removed his top hat, exposing wavy, dark hair beneath, and flung it aside. "I should have known you were here." He shook his head, glancing about, and hit the point of his cane hard into the tile. "You do nothing but disappoint me, Matilda."

"I shan't disappoint you ever again." Matilda rushed at him, raising the bronze bust high above her head.

Carlton yanked his cane up into the air and swept it toward Matilda. The sickening pop of flesh being smacked resounded within the corridor.

Justine gasped as the bust crashed to the floor and Matilda stumbled and fell to her knees with a piercing wail.

Carlton adjusted his coat over his broad shoulders. He shook his head, his features twisting as he leaned down toward Matilda who now shielded her belly and sobbed. "Why do you keep doing this to me?" he insisted in a choked tone. "*Why?* Don't you understand that I—"

"Get out of my house!" Justine could hardly breathe as she marched toward him, fisting both hands. *"Get out!"*

Carlton straightened and eyed her. "I regret that you have to witness any of this, Your Grace, but you have no right to interject in our affairs."

"This is my home and she is my friend and therefore it *is* my right to interject. It is also about to become your brother's right, as well." She sucked

in a breath and screamed, *"Radcliff! Radcliff!"*
She only hoped he still wasn't sleeping.

"Enough." Carlton pointed the silver head of the
cane in her direction and stared her down with blue
eyes that were sharp, demented and eerie. "I ought
to hurt you, Justine. I really ought to. It would make
my brother bleed to see you suffer. I hear you are
so damn happy together. Are you? Tell me you are.
I want to hear it."

The corridor seemed to blur and spin out of
focus. She could feel the veins in her throat swell
as her heart pumped faster. Her mind blanked and
all reason fled.

She turned, wishing Radcliff had pistols or
swords hanging on the walls. Finding nothing but
paintings, she snatched up one of the bronze statues
remaining on the side table and made a dash at
him.

"You wish to come at me?" he barked, rounding
toward her. "Is that what you wish?"

Justine closed the distance between them and
whipped her makeshift weapon at his head. He
ducked, and it thudded into the wall, sending a
painting crashing to the floor. Losing all sense of
reason, she jumped forward and snapped out her
open hand—sending it flying toward his face.

Carlton caught it before she could make contact,

causing her arm to pop back from the swift movement. He bared his teeth and squeezed her entire hand with strong fingers, crushing it. Her vision blurred from the searing pain shooting up the length of her wrist and arm.

She gasped as he forced not only her arm but her entire body straight down toward the marble floor. Although she exerted every ounce of her strength to remain standing against the weight of his heavy body, it was no use.

Her knees cracked against the floor. She gasped again, only this time in disbelief.

Carlton released her hand with a satisfactory grunt by flinging it away and stepped back toward Matilda. He held out a gloved hand. "Come, Matilda."

Matilda sobbed, shook her head and did not move, her arms still cradling her belly.

"Matilda," he growled out. "Get up."

Justine tried to push herself up and onto her feet, only to find Carlton now towering over her. His gaze penetrated her soul. "Stay on the floor."

"I am not a dog, you bastard," she seethed up at him, setting her palms on the floor and pushing herself up.

The first blow of his cane bounced off Justine's back as quickly as it had descended, causing her to gasp as she stumbled forward. Though its deliverance was brutally hard and burned her backside like the touch of fire, she somehow managed to not only straighten, but lunge at him.

The cane descended again, cracking her shoulder before she could reach him. Her knees weakened as pain blinded her, and she fell past his frame, stumbling to the floor.

"What the fuck are you doing?!" someone boomed.

Justine gasped for air and sobbed in disbelief. She tried to push herself up but her arms shook.

Angry shouts and crashing ensued around her.

"I will murder you!" Radcliff's shouts echoed as if she were in a dream. "I will murder you and gladly hang for it!"

Though she could see Radcliff smashing his fist repeatedly into Carlton's head and violently throwing Carlton up against the wall, causing more paintings to crash to the floor, her mind could only veer toward Matilda who was panting and sobbing beside her.

"Justine!" Radcliff skidded into view on his knees at Justine's side, clothed only in a pair of trousers. He hovered over her, his hands shakily roaming over her face and shoulders as his bare, muscled chest heaved.

He gathered her gently against his warmth and searched her face frantically, his disheveled dark hair hanging in his eyes. "Justine," he choked, tears clinging to his eyes. "Jesus Christ. Are you all right?"

"Radcliff," Justine managed through her own sobs and delirium. "All is well."

"Your Grace!" Jefferson, along with a swarm of servants, rushed down the length of the corridor toward them. "Your Grace! He forced his way in!"

Jefferson, whose face was gashed, grabbed hold of Carlton, who staggered up from the floor, and dragged him toward the other servants who proceeded to bind him with their own cravats. It was the first time Justine was thankful all their servants were male.

"Bradford," Matilda panted as she scooted toward them, holding her belly. "Justine." She let out an anguished cry and rocked momentarily back and forth. "I...I am soaked. The baby. It comes!"

Justine blinked several times and pushed herself out of Radcliff's arms with shaky hands, her gown cushioning her movements on the floor. Scrambling to her feet, she swayed for a moment, her vision blurring. "Radcliff! The baby. We need a doctor. We need a bed."

"Justine, please." Radcliff gently guided her back down to the floor and cupped her face. "Stay here. For God's sake, don't move. I will see to her and have the servants call for a doctor. Stay here. I will be right back."

Justine nodded, then drew in several deep, steady breaths, trying not to allow the core of her pain to overtake the rest of her weakened senses.

Matilda let out another anguished cry as Radcliff approached her and swept her off the floor, rolling her into his bare arms.

Despite Radcliff wanting her to stay where she was, she pushed herself up off the floor and staggered after them. Nothing, not even her own body, was going to keep her from the birth of Matilda's baby.

SCANDAL TWENTY

The birth of a child always marks a joyous occasion, unless of course that child happens to be born out of wedlock…

How to Avoid a Scandal, Author Unknown

A LONG, ANGUISHED scream pierced the silence and shook the very walls of the corridor. Radcliff swiped a hand over his face and stood from the chair he'd set outside of Justine's bedchamber, unable to remain still.

This was not how he had envisioned Justine living her life as a duchess. Being beaten by his own brother. And now, assisting Matilda as she gave birth.

God save him from the images that continued to assault his heart and mind. His beautiful Justine…*his* Justine on the floor being caned. Like an animal. This was not how he had envisioned their life together.

Radcliff leaned against the wall and squeezed

his eyes shut as Matilda shrieked with an intensity that rattled his own bones.

"Forgive me, Justine," he whispered hoarsely. "Forgive me for not better protecting you."

That evening

"YOUR GRACE," DR. LUDLOW insisted. "Please. I am asking that you leave the room."

Justine stepped toward Matilda, who continued to writhe on the bed, refusing to obey the doctor. Matilda needed her. Now more than ever.

Sweat-soaked blond hair clung to the sides of Matilda's flushed face. She gasped, and another high-pitched scream escaped her parched lips, piercing the room.

Justine could take no more. She turned to Dr. Ludlow and demanded, "Do something! She cannot continue to suffer like this!"

The balding man grunted, shook his head and headed toward the wooden side table laden with various medical instruments.

Justine grabbed Matilda's moist hand and squeezed it comfortingly. "Have faith."

Matilda squeezed shut her eyes, half nodded and whispered, "I do. I do."

"The pain will pass. Soon. It will." Justine

leaned in and kissed Matilda's damp forehead.
Her lips stung from the heat of Matilda's skin; her
temperature was rising.

Justine glanced back at the doctor impatiently.

He wiped his hands on his apron and grabbed a
surgical knife from one of the trays scattered across
the table. He approached the foot of the bed and
stripped off the only form of modesty left to Matilda, exposing her oversized belly and her white,
bare legs.

Justine's heart nearly stopped as she scrambled
around the bed. She lunged at the man and grabbed
hold of his wrist. "What is it you intend to do?"

Dr. Ludlow stilled as his beady eyes met hers.
He narrowed his gaze. "The babe will die."

Justine tightened her grip on the man's wrist.
"As will the mother if you slice her open!"

Another scream echoed around them.

Dr. Ludlow slowly reacted to his hand. "We must
make a decision, Your Grace."

"No," Justine snapped over the loud, ragged
breaths of her friend. "Not this. Tribes in Africa,
sir, do not require the use of blades during birthing.
Find another way."

Dr. Ludlow sighed, turned and made his way
back to the oak table. He dropped the knife onto

one of the trays. "She has been struggling for too long. There is nothing more I can do."

"Dr. Ludlow," Justine breathed. "If you save her and the babe, I will see to it you receive a hundred pounds. One hundred pounds."

The doctor stared at her. Then nodded.

He rounded her and approached the bed where Matilda continued to pant loudly.

With marked determination, Dr. Ludlow gathered the linen he had earlier removed from Matilda's body and assembled it over her belly and bent knees like a tent. "Let us try this again, Miss Thurlow," he insisted, sticking his hands beneath the sheets. "There is no other way. You must force the babe out by using whatever strength you have left within you."

Justine jogged to Matilda's side. She scrambled onto the bed, grabbed hold of that moist, shaky hand and whispered into Matilda's ear, "You can do this. I know you can. I will help you. Use all your strength. All of it now."

"No. No. I can't." Matilda released an exhausted sob and squeezed her eyes shut. "Justine," she panted. "If the baby survives, promise me you'll raise it. Promise me. If it is a boy, name it Radcliff. And if it is a girl, name it Justine."

Tears clouded Justine's vision, and though she

struggled to remain strong, she felt herself inwardly crumbling. "You are not dying. And as such, I will not make those promises."

"Do not deny me!" Matilda half sobbed, half screamed.

Tears streamed down Justine's face as she blindly tightened her grip on Matilda's hand. How could it end like this? How?

"Justine!" Matilda screamed.

"I promise," Justine whispered, squeezing her eyes shut. "I promise."

As IT TURNED OUT, there was absolutely no need to promise anything. Matilda and her beautiful, dark-haired baby girl survived. Matilda was very weak, and had drifted into a deep sleep, but the doctor assured Justine all was well and that there were no signs of complications.

The doctor kept saying it was a miracle.

Though the servants had tried to coax Justine to leave on several occasions, she had decided to stay long enough to help bathe Matilda's newborn.

She'd never seen fingers and toes so small. Not on a human anyway. She'd never felt skin so soft. Justine smiled as she finished carefully wrapping the freshly bathed child in linen and gently gathered the soft weight up into her arms. She cradled its tiny head in the crook of arms that still ached from the blows she'd endured and smiled past tears, ignoring the pain. She couldn't wait to have a baby of her own.

Henri tsked as he brushed the curling ends of his blond hair out of his eyes and hurried forward, his slender arms outstretched. "Allow me, Your Grace. I have held many, many babes in my life and you require rest."

Justine kissed the softness of that small head several times, then carefully transferred the baby to Henri. She sighed. "Where is His Grace?"

Henri arched a brow as he gently swayed back and forth with the baby in his arms. "Outside the door. Where he has been all along."

"Thank you." Justine made her way to the door of the bedchamber. Before leaving, she cast a glance back. Henri cradled the baby in his slim arms, grinning down at her as if she were his own child. "*Enchanté,* Mademoiselle," he cooed, adjusting the wrapped linens around the baby's sleeping face. "Crying is permitted, but not at this particular moment. Your mama sleeps. And it is wise you sleep, too."

Justine bit back an exhausted laugh and left the room, closing the door behind her. Perhaps it was best Henri stay on, even once the female servants returned to the house. He was everything she could want in a lady's maid.

Justine wandered over to Radcliff, who slept on the floor beside the door, and collapsed onto the floor next to him in the candlelit corridor. "It is amazing what a hundred pounds can buy these days," she drawled.

Radcliff woke and tried to scramble up, but Justine dragged him down toward herself and wrapped her arms around his broad shoulders. She leaned into him, wincing from the effort. "All is well. Matilda and her baby are perfectly fine. That is all that matters."

"Come. Now that the babe is here, you must be tended to. We'll call for a bath and let you soak." Radcliff shifted into a crouching position and slid his hands beneath her, sweeping her up off the floor.

She flinched as his fingers grazed the welts beneath but managed to wrap her arms around him as he stood and carried her to his bedchamber. If *this* was not love, if he did not love her, then she knew for a fact that she knew nothing of love at all.

SCANDAL TWENTY-ONE

Always respect the wishes of others, even if those
wishes do not necessarily respect you.
        How to Avoid a Scandal, Author Unknown

Ten days later, morning

RADCLIFF ROTATED A THICK, RAW SHARD of deep
purple amethyst, the edges of the large stone
pressing into the pads of his fingers. He shifted in
the leather chair and held the amethyst up higher
toward the French window before him. Sunlight
peered through the sheer crystal, reflecting thin
purple-and-white prisms across the length of his
sable coat, striped waistcoat and gray trousers.

Leaning farther back in his chair, he stretched
his legs beneath the mahogany desk and knew
without a doubt that it was perfect for the necklace
he intended to have made for Justine.

A knock made him glance up. His heart pounded
at the thought of it being Justine. He'd hardly
glimpsed her these past few days, considering

all the time she spent at Matilda's side and with the babe.

"Justine?" he called out. "Is that you?"

The doors fanned open and Jefferson appeared. He cleared his throat. "Forgive me. Are you at home, Your Grace? Lord and Lady Marwood wish to apologize for calling at such an early hour, but are here to see you and ask that you not disturb the Duchess into joining your conversation."

Radcliff fisted the crystal hard. Though Justine's parents had been surprisingly silent these past ten days in response to the detailed letter he had insisted Justine write to them explaining what gossip never would, Radcliff had a feeling that their silence had merely been building to a storm that was about to rage and thunder. "I am indeed at home. I shall receive them here."

"Yes, Your Grace."

Radcliff leaned toward the desk cluttered with several gem trays which his jeweler had delivered the day before for inspection. He tossed the amethyst into a tray lined with red velvet padding and shoved his chair back, rising.

Circling the desk, he strode toward the middle of his study. He glanced toward the massive empty space above the hearth and couldn't help but smile, knowing that Justine didn't like his mother any more than he did. A new duchess now reigned.

Hurried steps soon echoed in the corridor, drawing steadily closer. Radcliff interlocked his wrists behind his back and turned to face the double doors, readying himself for high winds.

Lord and Lady Marwood strode in, arm in arm, both dressed in what appeared to be traveling clothes.

They paused side by side, forming a wall directly across from where Radcliff stood, and stared him down, as if they intended to gut him there and then.

Jefferson lingered within the doorway. "Will you require any further assistance, Your Grace?"

Not unless the man intended to help him duel with his in-laws. Radcliff cleared his throat at the thought. "No, thank you. You may close the doors behind you."

Jefferson nodded and folded the doors into each other.

The room hummed with lethal silence.

Lady Marwood lifted her chin slightly, reminding Radcliff of Justine's own mannerisms. "My daughter has informed us that the rumors circulating London are, in fact, true. That she was indeed brutalized by your brother. As if that weren't enough cause for concern, there are other claims Justine will not admit to. Claims that you are both housing a less than reputable woman who recently gave birth to your own brother's child. Is that true?"

Justine was going to have his neck for admitting it. "It is true," he managed. "Miss Thurlow was in dire need of assistance and I decided to offer her a form of charity."

"Charity?" Lady Marwood echoed. "Is that what you call housing your brother's mistress beneath the nose of your own wife? *Charity?* Yes, well, I am here to announce, Your Grace, that we are not at all pleased with you or this marriage."

Radcliff widened his stance and drew in a calming breath before letting it out. "I understand, Lady Marwood, and can only apologize for myself and for my brother's monstrous behavior. I vow never to allow anything of this nature to occur again. Carlton is being stripped of his yearly annuity and will find himself at the mercy of debt. As for Miss Thurlow and her child, they will both be departing on the morrow to Scotland to start life anew."

Lord Marwood sucked in a harsh breath and let it out through his nostrils. "That is all good and well, but my wife and I have decided it would be best to take Justine with us. Away from this quagmire and the horrid things London is spewing about our daughter. Rest assured, Your Grace, we will cover any and all expenses."

Radcliff narrowed his gaze. "What is it that you are informing me of, my lord?"

Lord Marwood nervously glanced toward Lady Marwood.

Radcliff stared them down. "There is no need for further pleasantries. I assure you I'll not take offence."

Lord Marwood drew in a breath and announced, "We wish to take Justine with us to Cape Town. We are moving there permanently and ask that our daughter be allowed to join us."

Radcliff clenched his jaw, refusing to believe they would take his Justine away. They had no right. She was his. Not theirs. Not anymore. "Cape Town is rather far from me and London."

"That is the point." Lady Marwood's sharp hazel eyes pierced the short distance between them. "Exposing Justine to a place she has always loved will set her mind and soul straight. Time to her own thoughts, not governed by you or London, should allow for her to make a better decision. Whilst we appreciate all that you have done for our family, it is obvious that which is most important to us has become neglected. If you ever cared about her well-being, Your Grace, we ask you permit Justine to join us in Cape Town for a year."

"A year?" Radcliff stepped toward them, trying to keep his anger strapped in place. "No. I will not allow for any of this. How dare you? How dare you come into this home and try to separate us? She is *my* wife. And she will remain at *my* side until death itself decides that we should part."

"She is indeed your wife, Your Grace," Lady Marwood tossed back at him. "Yet what sort of respect and happiness have you given her thus far? Have you heard what people are saying about you and about her? *Have you?* Do you expect me and my husband to quietly stand aside whilst her happiness is blown to dust? Perhaps you are choosing to deny Justine this opportunity of freedom because you know she would never return. Deep inside, you know that her happiness does not belong with you. How could it after everything you have put her through?"

Radcliff shifted his jaw. Despite what Lady Marwood thought, he knew without any doubt whatsoever Justine *would* return to him. That her happiness *did* lie with him. And that the moment Justine discovered she'd been hoodwinked by her parents, she would shake her fist and demand that he join her in Africa. That would certainly put to rest these ridiculous doubts her parents had about Justine's happiness and the state of their marriage.

Radcliff angled himself toward them with a renewed determination to prove them wrong. "I will cover any and all expenses, including your own, for two months. After two months, I will expect a letter written in her own hand informing me as to where her happiness truly lies. Will that suffice?"

"Yes." Lady Marwood curtsied and reclaimed her husband's arm. "I realize this may be difficult, Your Grace, but sometimes we must make sacrifices that are best suited to the needs of others. Please have her and her trunks ready to leave within the hour. My husband and I will be waiting outside in our carriage."

"You intend to depart in an hour?" he echoed. Christ. That would hardly give him any time to even hold her, let alone explain all of this in a rational manner.

Lady Marwood stared him down. "The arrangements to depart were made shortly after I received Justine's letter. We ask you not disclose our conversation. She is fiercely proud and would not take to our meddling."

That much was true. He smirked. "I shan't breathe a word."

Lady Marwood's gaze narrowed. "It is obvious you find this situation amusing. I assure you it is not." She spun away and whisked toward the doors, Lord Marwood striding after her.

"I shan't breathe a word," Radcliff muttered. "But I most certainly will scribe it."

SCANDAL TWENTY-TWO

Without truth, there is no substance. And without substance, there is no soul. If you tell lies, it will eventually take its toll.

How to Avoid a Scandal, Author Unknown

Forty minutes later

JUSTINE PEERED INTO THE STUDY Jefferson had insisted she go to straight away and spied Radcliff sitting behind his writing desk. She quietly watched from the doorway as he leaned forward and placed a small stub of red wax into the flame of a candle.

His dark hair fell into his eyes as he pressed the end of the melted wax onto the folded parchment. He cast aside the wax, letting it clatter onto the desk, then snatched up the glass handle containing his seal and pressed it firmly into the soft wax holding together the parchment.

He set the seal aside and glanced up, meeting her gaze from across the room. Though there was an unwavering intensity within those handsome dark eyes, after a few breathtaking moments, a grin slowly spread across his lips, crinkling that jagged scar. "Come, dearest. I must speak to you at once. We have very little time."

She quirked a brow and hurried toward him. Rounding the desk, she settled beside his chair. "What is it?"

He stood, his sable morning coat shifting around his muscled shoulders and arms. He held out the letter he had just sealed, his eyes never once leaving hers. "This is for you. All I ask is that you not open it until a week after you arrive in Cape Town."

She blinked down at the sealed parchment he held out and glanced back up at him. "Cape Town?" she echoed. "Whatever do you mean? Is that why Henri and the other servants are scurrying about packing trunks?"

He cleared his throat and smoothed the front of his cravat several times. "It was supposed to be a surprise but I…" He cleared his throat again, dropping his hand from his cravat, and met her gaze. After a long, quiet moment, he smiled. "I am afraid I am not very good at these things." He nodded and snapped the parchment toward her again. "Take this. Your parents are waiting for you in a carriage outside to take you to Africa."

"What? Why? I don't—"

"Don't ask any questions, Justine. Simply trust your husband in this and enjoy your unexpected holiday. Henri will assist you in preparing for the journey ahead. You have only twenty minutes, so make use of every one of them."

"Twenty minutes?" Justine yanked the parchment from his hand and gawked up at him as she tightened her hold on the letter. "I can't even put on my bonnet in that period of time, let alone prepare for a trip to South Africa. What is more, Matilda departs for Edinburgh tomorrow. I have to see her and little Justine off."

He reached out both hands and rubbed the sides of her upper arms, rustling the puffed sleeves of her morning gown. "I will see Matilda off myself," he said in a low, reassuring voice. "After everything you have done for her, I am quite certain she will understand. I hope you can trust me not to overstep my bounds with her or anyone whilst you are away. I belong to you, Justine, and you alone. Even my obsession cannot battle that."

Her brows came together, and she couldn't help but feel muddled about what it was that was happening or what he was saying. "I don't understand. Why am I leaving? And why aren't you—"

"I planned this trip weeks ago," he quickly said.

"I wanted to surprise you. But then this entire mess with Matilda and Carlton occurred and it all fell aside. But I refuse to cancel it. You deserve a good holiday with your parents. Now go. They're waiting for you outside. I will join you soon. That I promise."

Her heart raced at the thought of returning to Cape Town. Returning to that simple life so far away from the eyes of the *ton*. Returning to a life of heat and paradise with endless blue skies in which the only rule was breathing and living. A life she desperately missed. And it was going to be hers again. In fifteen minutes!

But the thought of leaving Radcliff behind for even a day didn't suit her at all. "This is wonderful, Radcliff. And I cannot thank you enough. But might I suggest we go about this a bit differently? Why not allow my parents to travel ahead first, so that I can see Matilda and little Justine off. I hope you do not mind but I intend to give Matilda a hundred pounds to see her through whatever lies ahead."

She leaned toward him and nudged him. "Once she is gone, you'll finally have me all to yourself. And *then* once you are ready to leave, we can both depart to Cape Town. Together."

A heavy breath escaped him as his thumb

brushed the side of her face. "As much as your little plan tempts me, understand that I have matters to oversee here in London. I am in the process of stripping Carlton of all funds. It's a mess I ought to tend to before I can depart and I prefer you not be around for it. I will join you as soon as I am able. I promise here and now, Matilda will receive the hundred pounds you wish her to. But what I want, Justine, more than anything, is for you to take some time to yourself and enjoy being with your parents. Do it. For me. For us."

She blinked. Then blinked again, realizing of what he was offering. He was offering Cape Town. In fifteen minutes! He was offering time alone with her parents. In fifteen minutes! London and all of its stupid snobs and gossip be damned. She was going home.

A grin ruffled her mouth as she excitedly searched his handsome face. "Oh, Radcliff. A more generous gift I've never known. Not ever. You'll join us as soon as you are able? You promise?"

He half nodded, his thumb now tracing her lips as his hand pressed more firmly against her cheek. "As soon as you wish it, dearest," he murmured.

A bubble of laughter escaped her as she grabbed his face with both hands, crumbling the parchment he'd given her against his cheek. "I adore you! I absolutely adore you! Thank you!" She kissed him soundly on the lips. And then kissed him again.

Radcliff grabbed hold of her waist and pulled her close, pressing her firmly against the warmth of his large body. He tore his mouth away from her lips and buried his face into the curve of her neck, tightening his arms around her.

"Justine," he murmured against her shoulder. "The parchment in your hand is a token of my affection. Open it a week after you arrive in Cape Town. Not a day sooner. My hope is that it will keep you company whilst we are apart."

Justine closed her eyes and savored having him and his words so close. "Thank you," she whispered back. "I love you, Radcliff. I love you so very much."

The room grew quiet, and all she could hear was her own breath mingling with his. And though she knew he would never say the words in turn, in that moment, it didn't really matter. Because in her heart she knew he felt the same. She could feel it in the way he continued to hold her so tightly against himself. His embrace bespoke emotion. Not lust.

Radcliff eventually drew away, releasing her. Stepping back, he rounded his chair and waved her off. "Hurry now. And whatever you do, don't fall fancy to the charms of some Hottentot whilst we are apart."

She laughed. "Never. You are my one and only Hottentot." She grinned and pointed to the parchment in her hand. "I promise not to open this until I reach Cape Town. No matter how tempted I may be."

His hands gripped the chair and he smiled. "Good. Have a safe journey, my dearest Justine."

"I will." She blew him a kiss, drew in a breath, then dashed off to tell Matilda and little Justine.

The following morning

RADCLIFF PACED THE TILE FLOOR of the foyer, willing himself to focus. The all-too-brief kiss Justine had so ardently offered him before she left still lingered like sweet, burning brandy. It had barely been a day, and it already felt like a year. He was beginning to believe he'd bloody muffed everything up with his blind determination to prove her parents wrong.

The echoing of steps and the rustling of skirts caught his attention. He turned.

Matilda made her way toward him, dressed in a pretty cornflower silk gown and a matching oval bonnet, carrying her bundled babe in her arms.

A babe she had named after his Justine. Matilda paused before him and met his gaze.

Radcliff did his best to smile, even though it required quite the effort. "Your trunks have been strapped atop the carriage, Miss Thurlow."

"Thank you, Your Grace," she replied coolly.

He wasn't going to miss her. Not at all. Carlton aside, Justine's parents aside, the woman had tried to bed his own wife. Right under his nose.

He shoved his hand into his inner coat pocket and pulled out a bundle of crisp notes he had counted out earlier. He held it out. "A hundred pounds to see you through your journey and the next year. If you are wise with it, it will last longer."

Matilda's gaze softened. She glanced down at the peaceful, sleeping babe in her arms and shook her head. "I cannot."

He sighed. "It is not I who offers this, but Justine. She insisted upon it, and as such, I ask that you show your gratitude by taking it."

Matilda glanced up and blinked rapidly, a lone tear spilling down the length of her pale, smooth cheek. She quietly reached out a gloved hand and took the money, fisting it in her hand before tucking it beneath the babe she held.

"I know what you did, Bradford. Don't think I don't. Do you not realize she kissed that letter of yours during my achingly brief farewell with her? She foolishly insisted that in it she would finally find the words of love she's been waiting to hear all this time. But you and I know better, don't we? There are no words of love in that letter, are there?"

He lowered his chin but said nothing.

She narrowed her gaze. "I swear upon whatever is left of this soul that if you ever injure her heart, I'll not only find my way back to London, but I will see to it *your* heart never beats again. I would have never let Justine leave my sight. Not even if hell were riding my skirts. And therein is the difference between a man's love and a woman's love. A woman fights for love. Whilst a man runs from it." She set her chin and swept past, carrying herself and little Justine toward the carriage.

Radcliff stepped back, snorted and slammed the door so hard that the crystal chandelier in the foyer above him chimed. One thing was for sure. Matilda didn't know a damn thing about men. Or women, for that matter…

SCANDAL TWENTY-THREE

Shedding tears over anything, especially a man,
is terribly bad form.
How to Avoid a Scandal, Author Unknown

Cape Town, South Africa
Two and a half weeks later

JUSTINE BROUGHT HER HANDS TOGETHER and deeply
bowed in greeting to Aloysius, causing the large
satchel around her waist to sway. Aloysius was her
father's dearest friend from years past who had
guided them from station to station throughout
most of South Africa, brilliantly distinguishing
not only locations but also the tracks and paths of
every animal they had sought to study.

Although Aloysius's coarse, curling hair had
completely whitened and his round face had
thinned, the man still wore his usual leather attire,
which most Hottentots and Bushmen wore. The
long leather kaross covered his broad shoulders and
backside, whilst the fore-kaross covered everything

below his hips, leaving his throat, narrow chest, ankles and feet bare and exposed for the world to see.

Aloysius waved her toward the sun-burnt grass beneath the shade of an old, gnarled tree. He and her parents had already laid straw mats and spread a feast of wooden bowls bearing ostrich eggs and oxen blood boiled to the consistency of liver. "Joosteen," he insisted, gesturing a dark hand toward an empty mat beside her parents. "Seet."

Justine bit back a laugh and shook her head. The man never did get her name right, even after all these years. Nor did he seem to offer better food. But what did any of that matter now that she was back home?

She pushed her bonnet back from her moist forehead and swiped at the sweat trickling down the sides of her face. Gathering her cotton skirts from around her booted feet, she quickly made her way toward him and her parents, needing to escape the pulsing heat of the sun.

Whilst it was divine to finally be back in Cape Town, without Radcliff at her side it all seemed pointless. But today, at long last, was an extraordinary day. Not merely because she and her parents had reunited with Aloysius after two years of being away, but also because today marked the week after her arrival into Cape Town. It meant she could open her letter from Radcliff, the letter she'd been carrying within her satchel every day.

Justine kneeled onto the straw mat and ceremonially arranged her skirts around herself. "How have you been, Aloysius?"

Inquisitive dark eyes met Justine's as he lowered himself onto the mat beside her. He grinned crookedly and nodded about his wellness. He then clasped his thin, brown hands, shook them and then pointed at her, signaling how pleased he was to see her again.

Justine clasped her hands, in turn, then pointed at him and grinned, showing how pleased she was to see him. "And how is your wife? How is Cokkie?"

"Cokkie?" He clucked his tongue and rolled his eyes. "Nag. Always. Eck."

Justine burst into laughter. It was so good to know he still remembered their conversations. Even after all this time.

Lady Marwood leaned toward them. "Wherever did he learn the word *nag?*" she drawled in astonishment. "I don't believe I've ever heard him use that word before. Not in all the years I've known him."

Justine winced as she cleared her throat. "His

memory is impeccable. One of our last conversations before we left Africa involved me complaining about you. And how you are forever nagging me and father."

Lord Marwood chuckled, his cheeks rounding. "Yes. Your mother most certainly does nag, doesn't she?"

"Charles!" Lady Marwood exclaimed, smacking him soundly on the shoulder with the end of her closed parasol. "I do not nag."

Lord Marwood snorted. "Yes, you do."

"I do not. Nagging refers to someone being incessant."

Lord Marwood snorted again. "My point exactly."

Justine smirked at Aloysius. "Do you see what you started, you naughty man, you?"

Aloysius grinned. Though his dialect was, for the most part, Dutch, she had always chosen to speak to him in English and found him to be very attentive and quick to learn.

He grabbed up a small wooden bowl filled with thickened, dark brown oxen blood—or blood pudding as she referred to it—and promptly held it out toward her.

Justine smiled and shook her head. "No. Thank you."

Aloysius sighed and shifted from his squatting position, sticking out the bowl toward her father, brows raised.

"Ah, yes. Thank you, Aloysius." Lord Marwood leaned toward the bowl and scooped up a small amount of the dark brown paste with his bare fingers. "This is what I call South African caviar, Justine. You really should try it. 'Tis very, very good."

Justine wrinkled her nose. "I don't like caviar any more than I like boiled oxen blood. You, of all people, should remember that the last time I ate oxen blood, I spent two days heaving it up, not only through my mouth, but my nostrils."

Lord Marwood shrugged and sucked the brown paste from his fingers. "Even the French cannot compete with such cuisine. Is that not so, Aloysius?"

Aloysius nodded in agreement and gallantly passed the bowl toward her mother, who also scooped up a small amount onto her fingers.

Whilst the others ate, signaled and chatted amongst themselves, Justine drew in a deep, steadying breath and opened the leather flap of the satchel hanging around her waist.

She pulled out the folded, sealed parchment she had carried with her these past many weeks and smoothed out its crinkled edges affectionately. Finally.

"Justine." Her mother scooted toward her, her thin brows coming together as she eyed the letter. "Must you read that here and now? We are visiting."

"Nonsense. Today is officially a week since I've been in Cape Town and I have absolutely no intention of waiting another moment to read it. I am quite certain Aloysius won't mind. I'll even show him the letter when I'm done. If it isn't too naughty, that is." She waggled her brows, her fingers sliding toward the red seal which was already detaching from the heat. The wax bent away, instead of cracking, as she separated the seal and unfolded the letter.

She held her breath and quickly read:

My dearest Justine,
First, I must apologize for betraying your confidence and not fully disclosing the truth behind your journey. Your parents were genuinely concerned about the state of our marriage and asked that we spend time apart to allow you to better decide whether your happiness does, in fact, belong with me. Whatever you decide, dearest, I can only thank you for forcing me to make a personal inventory of my life. You have done far more for me than I could have ever done for myself. After reading that damn etiquette

book of yours, I realized something. Men are in many ways at a disadvantage and lack the sort of guidance women are given. Though I suppose too much guidance, as if often imposed on women, can be quite the burden, as well. A lack of guidance and a lack of understanding of my own needs is what ultimately pushed me toward my obsession. I have no doubt it had commenced with the strain of being duke at an age when most boys were barely out of the nursery. Constant responsibility brought on by the demands of those around me, including my mother and brother, who cared only for their own needs, always made me want to escape the world around me. In having this open and rare understanding of myself, I know I will be able to overcome this obsession, and I wish to thank you for making this broken man feel whole again. I look forward to your response and know we will not be apart long.

Gratefully and forever yours,

Radcliff

Justine's breath hitched in her throat, and despite the incessant heat of the day throbbing around her, she felt as if ice were spreading across every inch of her skin. Her hands trembled as she fumbled to fold the parchment, refusing to look at Radcliff's words anymore. Refusing to believe he would allow her own parents to separate them like this. To prove what?

Shoving the parchment into the satchel, she

settled her gaze on her parents who were enthusiastically discussing their travels.

Her mother paused, sensing Justine was watching them, and met her gaze from across the straw
mat. After a long, quiet moment, Lady Marwood
blurted, "He told you."

Justine swallowed and half nodded. Her mother
and father had both known. They had known all
along. And yet never once did they say a word.
They had cruelly tried to separate her and Radcliff.
Her own parents, who she thought loved her.

Lady Marwood leaned forward and reached out
a pleading hand. "Justine. It needed to be done. He
was destroying you and your very name before all
of London."

Unexpected tears blurred Justine's vision as she
pushed herself up and stumbled to her feet. "How
could you?" she choked out. "How could you even
propose separating us? He is my husband and I love
him."

Lady Marwood scrambled to her feet, as well,
but did not attempt to approach. "How can you
claim to love a man who allowed you to endure
so much? He is anything but perfect. Can you not
see that? You need time away from him to better
understand your situation."

Tears trickled down the sides of Justine's cheeks

as she stepped out of the shade and back into the searing heat of the sun, a sun she wished could melt away the inner torment chilling her soul. "What little you know. Radcliff taught me something invaluable. Something I never truly learned to appreciate until now." More tears trickled down her cheeks. "Self-respect is far more important than the respect given by others. He also taught me that love isn't something that can be put into words, and that love is indeed far from perfect. It has many flaws. But everything in this world has flaws. Even you have flaws, Mother. And yet…I still love you. Don't I? I still love you despite the fact that you ripped apart my very soul and tossed it to the wind as if it were yours to toss!"

Lady Marwood stared at her wordlessly, then stumbled toward her, past Lord Marwood, who stared down at his hands. "Justine. I was only trying to protect you. I didn't realize—"

"No, you didn't realize. Because you didn't ask." Justine spun away and stalked in the direction of her canvas tent pitched on the other side of the field. How could her parents and Radcliff betray her like this?

SCANDAL TWENTY-FOUR

If it weren't for wretched grief and wretched suffering brought on by the rigors of life, the wondrous joy of finding love would seem rather insignificant and meaningless. Would it not? As the French always say, "Mis en place." Or as we English say, "Everything in its place."

How to Avoid a Scandal, Author Unknown

Ten weeks later, late morning

RADCLIFF LOOSENED THE CRAVAT that had been choking him all morning and pulled back his stiff collar, stripping it entirely from his neck. He tossed it onto the writing desk and leaned back in his chair, staring at the large pile of financial ledgers he had yet to touch. They were piled beside Justine's red, leather-bound book, *How To Avoid A Scandal.* He had already read it eighteen times and toted it around everywhere. Hell, he even slept with it, tucking it beneath his pillow, as if it could in any way replace what was truly missing from his life—Justine.

He huffed out a breath. Ten weeks. Ten weeks and not a word. Not a single goddamn word. What did her silence mean? That their marriage was over? That she had found happiness elsewhere?

Though he tried to convince himself day after day after day he could do without seeing her again, he could do without talking to her again, he could do without making love to her again, it was no use.

He couldn't do.

And for the first time in all his three and thirty years, he had no taste for *any* physical pleasure. The thought of pleasuring himself or taking any other woman into his bed but Justine only brought the taste of bile to his lips.

Steps echoed in the distance and drew steadily closer. Jefferson walked into the room. He came to a halt and stoically held up a sizable, brown-clothed package along with a stack of letters piled in a pyramid fashion. "Today's post, Your Grace."

Radcliff tightened his jaw and violently shoved Justine's etiquette book off the desk, sending it flying. He snatched up one of the thick ledgers beside him and flipped it open. Slamming it before him, he stared down at the numbers lining the columns and muttered, "Set it somewhere. Anywhere. I don't have time for the post. I have to finish tallying these damn financials. One of the joys of being responsible."

Though his financials didn't need to be tallied for another week, he didn't want to think about the post. Didn't want to go through the same crushing disappointment he went through every single day when it arrived.

Jefferson cleared his throat. Twice. "Your Grace, this package is from the duchess."

Radcliff's stomach flipped as he glanced back up at Jefferson. "Is it? She sent word?"

His butler smiled. "That she has, Your Grace."

His chest tightened as he eyed the parcel Jefferson held up, along with the rest of the post. Although a part of him wanted to believe his Justine was sending him a gift to tell him how much she missed him and how much she loved him, a much larger part of him feared that it was in fact quite the opposite. For all he knew it could be a human skull with his name on it.

Jefferson lifted a thick brow and strode toward him. "I never doubted she would send word. Not for a moment."

Radcliff awkwardly cleared his throat and pushed back his chair. He slowly stood, trying to appear calm and indifferent. What he really wanted to do was make a dash for that parcel like a child about to play its first game of Snapdragon at Christmas.

Rounding the desk, he headed toward Jefferson, attempting to keep the thundering beat of his heart at a steady pace. He wanted to believe Justine could not breathe another moment without him.

Radcliff adjusted the sleeves of his coat as if he had all the time in the world and paused before Jefferson. He plucked the correspondence from atop the bundle without deigning it a single glance, shoved the letters into the pocket of his morning coat, and swept up the bundle.

He was pleasantly surprised by its hefty weight straining his arms. "Thank you, Jefferson."

Jefferson nodded. Then lingered and eyed the parcel.

Radcliff protectively drew the package closer to his chest, then lowered his chin and stared the man down. "You do realize, Jefferson, that this is between *me* and the duchess? Not *you,* me *and* the duchess?"

Jefferson sighed and stalked out of the room.

Radcliff shook his head. He wasn't the only one missing Justine. All the servants, especially Henri, didn't know what the hell to do with themselves.

Blowing out an exhausted breath, he wandered over to the hearth, turning the hefty cloth package over in his hands, feeling the misshapen contents within shifting and clacking.

He seated himself on the floor before the hearth and set the package on the Axminster rug. Swiping his moist hands against the sides of his wool trousers, he leaned forward and dug his fingers beneath the loosest part of twine he could find. With a violent, sharp tug, he snapped apart a section of it from the side of the package, then attempted to unravel the twine holding the wool cloth in place.

"Christ, Justine." He rumbled out a laugh and continued to unravel more and more of the twine from around the package. "You never did make anything easy for me."

The never-ending twine finally found its end, and the cloth unfolded. Rocks of various sizes, texture and color tumbled out, scattering onto the rug before him.

Radcliff blinked. He leaned forward and sifted through the array of stones, trying to make sense of her gift as grit and dirt dusted his fingers. Hell. There was nothing but rocks and more rocks. About two dozen or so of them. With no letter of explanation.

He swallowed and gathered them all, piling them

back onto the wool cloth. What the blazes was she telling him? That she wasn't in any way pleased with him? That it was over? That he might as well tie all these damn rocks around his waist and throw himself into the Thames?

Damn her. He'd waited ten weeks to hear from her. Ten whole weeks. Merely to receive a pile of rocks?

"Fuck." Radcliff yanked up the bundle and jumped to his feet. Using every ounce of bitterness and frustration he'd harbored within him all these weeks, he flung it across the room toward his desk, toward the desk she had sat on so many times. The cloth burst open in midair. Rocks clattered and tumbled toward the hearth as the wool wrapping floated down and settled on the wood floor.

He drew in several harsh breaths, trying to calm himself, and strode toward the hearth. There had better be word or he was taking the next ship out to Cape Town and hunting her down for an explanation.

Yanking out the correspondences tucked in his coat, he riffled through them one by one, looking for a letter from Justine.

Invitation.

Invitation.

Invitation.

The season was over and yet the invitations never ceased. He shook his head and discarded each invitation into the burning coals of the fire, not caring about replying to any of them. He burned each and every one and was about to toss in the very last one, when he recognized Justine's neat, elegant writing.

He flipped it over and cracked apart the large yellow wax seal bearing the earl's crest. Turning it, he frantically unfolded the parchment and drew in a breath.

My beloved Radcliff,

He let out the breath he was holding. An intimate opening. Good. Exactly what he'd been hoping for. He wet his lips and read on.

Forgive my silence. It has taken me some time to decide what it is I should say. I suppose I should commence by being as civil as possible.

His fingers pinched the edges of the parchment, crinkling it, as the muscles in his forearms tightened. He forced himself to read on.

I wanted to send you a gift from my travels, something that wouldn't wilt or die. Hence the rocks. Ever since I was a girl, I've collected them from various places to which I traveled. Every stone reminded me where I had been and what I had done. Seeing you are not here with me, I am sending them along in the hopes that you can envision the various places I have already been. That said, I am done being civil. I am sorely disappointed in you. I feel betrayed, and with each passing day, I am beginning to believe that you do not love me, that you never loved me, or you would have had no need to prove anything to my parents. If I am in any way wrong about your feelings, I hope you will seek to amend the way I feel as quickly as possible. I do not want a letter. I do not want words or empty promises, for you are right. Words mean nothing. And they most certainly mean nothing when there is so much distance between us. I have learned that showing each other how we feel is far more important to me than the words we share. I will be residing in The Kloof over the next four months visiting with an old family friend. It is a small Hottentot village located near the Asbestos Mountains. By wagon and oxen, it should take you three weeks from Cape Town to reach me. If you love me, Radcliff, make this long journey and never leave my side again. Whether we stay here in Africa or return to London matters not to me. All that matters is that we are together. If, however, you do not love me, I ask that you remain in London and grant me a divorce. For I cannot live like this. Nor do I wish to bear the name of a man who does not love me. I never expected you to be the perfect man. I only ever expected you to be a good man. And that, my dearest Radcliff,

I already know you are. I ardently await your
arrival.
Yours forever and always,
Justine

Even after all this time, even after all these
weeks apart, she still wanted him. She still needed
him. As much as he still wanted and needed and
loved her.

"Justine," he whispered.

He raised the letter to his lips and kissed her
name, then gently refolded the parchment, tucking
it into the inner pocket of his waistcoat.

He drew in a deep, satisfying breath and let it
out. Feeling as if he could conquer all of Africa
with the swing of an arm, he spun toward the open
door and boomed, "Jefferson! Pack all of the goddamn trunks! You and I are leaving for Cape Town
on the next ship out!"

The Kloof, South Africa
Six weeks later

THE SUN STILL SEEMED to pierce straight through
Justine's bonnet and the many layers of her cotton
traveling gown, which clung to her sweat-moistened
skin. Now and then, a hot breeze danced past her,

cooling her skin and providing her the momentary relief she needed from a long day spent in the heat.

She knelt and plucked up a small cleaved asbestos rock from the coarse, dry ground. With a sigh, she stood, fingering the rough edges of the rock and walked back toward the direction of the hut she and her parents had been residing in these past nine weeks with Aloysius. She paused outside the opening of the hut and turned toward the wicker basket set off to the side. She tossed the rock she held into it, causing it to clack against all the other asbestos rocks piled within it.

"Fifty-seven," she murmured.

Fifty-seven days since she had sent Bradford the ultimatum. Fifty-seven. She only hoped the post out of Africa was as reliable as the post was in London. But then, she'd sooner blame the post for his absence than face the reality that Bradford simply did not love her.

She sighed and eyed the blue cloudless sky, which was already tinged with hues of orange and pink as the sun began to make its descent. She stepped toward the opening of the hut. Her father sat cross-legged on the straw mat in the far corner, busily sketching his latest observations of lizards, like a little boy lost in his own world. Her mother sat next to him, her head propped against his shoulder, quietly watching him.

Justine tried not to let her thoughts linger on what it would have been like sitting in that same hut with Bradford, her head propped against his shoulder. She forced the image away, knowing she'd only start blubbering.

Her mother suddenly lifted her head. "Justine!" A huge smile flitted across her lips as she rearranged her skirts around her legs and sat up. "Where have you been? We've been waiting all this time for your return."

Justine shrugged. "I've been about. Why?"

"I suggest you run off to the river at once, before it gets too dark. You really need to tidy yourself up. Aloysius is preparing a special feast and has invited all the men from the village."

"Again?" Justine drawled.

Her father snorted, lifting his gaze from his sketching. "He enjoys watching all of the men fawn over you. You know that."

Justine rolled her eyes. "I wasn't nearly this popular in London," she muttered, untying the small bow from the lace ribbon holding her bonnet in place. "I suppose I should go to the river. There is more dust than skin on me."

She stripped the bonnet from her head and tossed

it into the hut. She removed all of the pins holding up her hair, causing it to cascade down her back, and tossed them into the hut, as well. "I promise to return before nightfall."

Her mother was quiet for a moment, then called out, "I love you, Justine."

Justine half nodded, but otherwise did not acknowledge her. It was so difficult to hear such words. They reminded her so much of Radcliff.

Turning, she hurried toward the river just beyond the hill, wanting to escape her parents as well as her own thoughts. Eventually, the rush of water in the distance met her ears. As she neared the river, Justine unhooked the entire front of her beige cotton gown, exposing her chemise beneath. Stripping her boots, stockings, garters and her gown until she stood only in a thin chemise, she draped them on a boulder.

She was so thankful to be without a corset. Even her mother had insisted it was too hot and rather pointless to wear one.

Looping her long, loose hair behind her ears to keep it from getting in her eyes, she carefully made her way around the rocks as they pinched the soles of her feet. She then dashed straight into the cold, rushing water, her chemise billowing around her legs. She sucked in a breath and waded farther in, balancing herself against the strong current.

She lowered herself into the water, drenching her hair, the refreshing sensation of the day's sweat sweeping off in a single dip. Justine stood and gazed out across the valley beyond. She stood there listening to the water rushing around her and the chatter of birds.

She didn't know how long she stood there, gazing out into the valley whilst standing in the river, but the sun was beginning to fade into the horizon, darkening parts of the sky. She turned to make her way back to her clothes on the river bank, then froze, her heart skipping as it came to a halt.

For there, with one brown leather boot propped against a boulder and a billowy, white-sleeved arm set on the knee of form-fitting beige trousers, was none other than Radcliff himself.

Her husband.

His dark gaze met hers across the short distance remaining between them. He grinned as the wind tousled and feathered his dark hair around his scarred face. He scanned her breasts, which she knew were very visible through her sheer, wet chemise, and waggled his brows. "I have to say, Africa has the most impressive wild animals I've ever seen."

She burst into laughter and stumbled through the rushing water toward him, unwilling to believe it. "Radcliff! You came. You actually came!"

"I would have arrived sooner but the oxen leading our damn wagons refused to move any faster. And then when I did arrive, you were bloody nowhere to be found. So your parents insisted I come to the river and wait for you here." He jumped over the rock before him and landed with a huge splash in the water. He waded toward her, meeting her halfway, the water rushing up against his muscled thighs.

She paused directly before him. Tears overwhelmed her, blurring her vision. Though she wanted to throw herself into his arms and drag him down into the water, she was afraid this was merely a glorious dream. One that would disappear the moment she tried to touch it.

Radcliff grinned, crinkling the scar on the side of his face as he spread his arms wide open. "Are you just going to stand there, Duchess? Or are you going to give your husband the greeting he damn well deserves?"

Justine let out a choked sob, grabbed him and pressed against the solid heat of his hard chest. "I thought you wouldn't come. I thought—"

"Shh. None of that." He grabbed hold of her face

with both of his large, warm hands. His dark eyes searched hers for a long moment. His gaze was so fiery, yet so heartrending, everything inside of Justine melted and screamed at the same time.

"I love you," he said hoarsely above the rushing of the water.

She took in a sharp breath of utter astonishment, searching his face. "Bradford—"

He quickly lowered his dark head and brought his mouth down onto hers. Her pulse thundered as she melted into the moment she'd been dreaming of for so many, many long weeks.

His hot tongue playfully nudged her mouth farther open, sensually sliding against her own, circling, pushing, ever so slowly and ever so tenderly kissing her.

Although Radcliff was clearly trying to slow this moment between them, she wasn't up for a slow and prim reunion. Not after all the months she'd been without him.

This was Africa. And the *ton* was nowhere in sight.

Tearing away from their kiss, Justine fisted his shirt and yanked the tucked ends savagely up and out of his trousers.

He sucked in a breath as she swept it up past his

smooth, broad shoulders, off his arms and over his head, leaving his chest bare.

She whipped his shirt aside, letting it land atop the water. It quickly floated, down the river and eventually out of sight. "I hope you brought more than one shirt, Bradford."

"As if I have a need for shirts anymore." He dug his hands into the water, fisted her chemise, pulled the wet, clinging material up over her head and tossed it. It, too, quickly floated down the river and out of sight.

He grinned, his hands skimming across the expanse of her exposed, wet breasts. "I hope you don't mind, but I took the liberty of burning your etiquette book. I am done being a lady. With your permission, dearest, I want to go back to being a whore. Your whore, mind you. But a whore all the same."

Justine laughed and yanked him closer against her naked body. "How about you go back to being a man instead? *My man?*"

"Hell, Duchess, that's even better."

* * * * *

  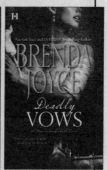

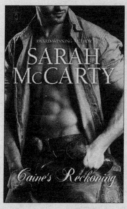

REQUEST YOUR
FREE BOOKS!

2 FREE NOVELS
FROM THE ROMANCE COLLECTION
PLUS 2 FREE GIFTS!

YES! Please send me 2 FREE novels from the Romance Collection and my 2 FREE gifts (gifts are worth about $10). After receiving them, if I don't wish to receive any more books, I can return the shipping statement marked "cancel." If I don't cancel, I will receive 4 brand-new novels every month and be billed just $5.74 per book in the U.S. or $6.24 per book in Canada. That's a saving of at least 28% off the cover price. It's quite a bargain! Shipping and handling is just 50¢ per book.* I understand that accepting the 2 free books and gifts places me under no obligation to buy anything. I can always return a shipment and cancel at any time. Even if I never buy another book, the two free books and gifts are mine to keep forever.

194/394 MDN E7NZ

Name _____ (PLEASE PRINT) _____

Address _____ Apt. #

City _____ State/Prov. _____ Zip/Postal Code

Signature (if under 18, a parent or guardian must sign)

Mail to **The Reader Service:**
IN U.S.A.: P.O. Box 1867, Buffalo, NY 14240-1867
IN CANADA: P.O. Box 609, Fort Erie, Ontario L2A 5X3

Not valid for current subscribers to the Romance Collection or the Romance/Suspense Collection.

Want to try two free books from another line?
Call 1-800-873-8635 or visit www.morefreebooks.com.

* Terms and prices subject to change without notice. Prices do not include applicable taxes. N.Y. residents add applicable sales tax. Canadian residents will be charged applicable provincial taxes and GST. Offer not valid in Quebec. This offer is limited to one order per household. All orders subject to approval. Credit or debit balances in a customer's account(s) may be offset by any other outstanding balance owed by or to the customer. Please allow 4 to 6 weeks for delivery. Offer available while quantities last.

Your Privacy: Harlequin Books is committed to protecting your privacy. Our Privacy Policy is available online at www.eHarlequin.com or upon request from the Reader Service. From time to time we make our lists of customers available to reputable third parties who may have a product or service of interest to you. If you would prefer we not share your name and address, please check here. ☐

Help us get it right—We strive for accurate, respectful and relevant communications. To clarify or modify your communication preferences, visit us at www.ReaderService.com/consumerschoice.

MROM10R

Try these Healthy and Delicious Spring Rolls!

INGREDIENTS

2 packages rice-paper
spring roll wrappers
(20 wrappers)

1 cup grated carrot

¼ cup bean sprouts

1 cucumber, julienned

1 red bell pepper, without
stem and seeds, julienned

4 green onions
finely chopped—
use only the green part

DIRECTIONS

1. Soak one rice-paper wrapper
   in a large bowl of hot water
   until softened.

2. Place a pinch each of carrots,
   sprouts, cucumber, bell
   pepper and green onion on the
   wrapper toward the bottom
   third of the rice paper.

3. Fold ends in and roll tightly
   to enclose filling.

4. Repeat with remaining
   wrappers. Chill before
   serving.

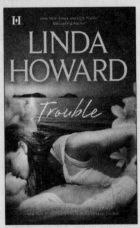